"Please sit down,

cufflink clicked on the desk as he folded his hands in front of him, interlocking his fingers.

She sat. He was motionless. Only staring at Lainey. His gaze bore into her soul, unearthing every thought about him. She blushed.

"Mademoiselle," he said. "Why did you choose to intern for Alpine Foods?"

The question caught her off guard. Weren't they talking about pet food product reviews? And hadn't she answered the question in the interview?

Under the weight of his deep, penetrating gaze, Lainey stammered. She wanted to glance away, but she couldn't. When other people asked her, *Why Alpine Foods in Switzerland? Why not stay in the States?* she had said, "The Swiss eat two pounds of chocolate a month. Where else would I want to go?" Which was the truth. But she had a feeling he didn't want a flippant answer about the Swiss diet. Lainey would never please M. Claremont enough for him to recommend her to Chocolate.

Praise for Amey Zeigler

"From the start, *THE SWISS MISHAP* grabbed my attention. The well-developed characters, the scenery, the typical Swiss mentality all drew me into the story; so much so that I burst out laughing at the hilarious mishaps. Amey Zeigler skillfully crafted a romantic tale with a touch of intrigue."

~Didi Lawson, author

~*~

"*THE SWISS MISHAP* is a sweet and satisfying romance that will capture your heart. Lainey and Yves's story left me with the desire to hop on a plane to Switzerland, eat pounds of chocolate, and fall in love!"

~Laurie Winter, award-winning author of Winner Takes All

~*~

"*THE SWISS MISHAP* is delightfully entertaining and deliciously funny."

~Renee Durfee

~*~

Amey Zeigler is also the author of
BAKER'S DOZEN,
a romantic suspense,
published by The Wild Rose Press, Inc.

The Swiss Mishap

by

Amey Zeigler

The Swiss Mishap

Contact Information: info@thewildrosepress.com

Cover Art by *Tina Lynn Stout*

The Wild Rose Press, Inc.
PO Box 708
Adams Basin, NY 14410-0708
Visit us at www.thewildrosepress.com

Publishing History
First Sweetheart Rose Edition, 2019
Print ISBN 978-1-5092-2634-4
Digital ISBN 978-1-5092-2635-1

Published in the United States of America

Dedication

For Regina—for all the great memories in Vevey
and the continuing friendship

Acknowledgements

Writing a book is a group effort. Though I am the one typing out the words, I could not have done it without some valuable people in my life. A huge thank you to my Beta readers: Christine Deppong, my longest and first Beta, Sara Regan, Klixi Cannon and Lindsay Neeley for their valuable input. And much gratitude to my critique partner Andrea Watts for her helpful insights and her suggestions. *Muchas gracias* to Christina Bailey for her extensive chocolate knowledge. Thank you to my editor, Kinan Werdski, who was excited as I was about this project; to Tina Lynn Stout for the beautiful cover design, and to Rhonda Penders at The Wild Rose Press.

Blowing thankful kisses to my ANWA writers group for their unending support and love. Also, the Wacky, Wild Women Writers group: Alyana, Ali, and Hailey, from whom I learned a good deal, thank you!

Thank you, of course, to my mother, who encouraged me and never tires of my stories. To my father, who laughed out loud when I read this to him. A shout out to my sister, who had to grow up with a storyteller sister and still finds my stories entertaining. To my brothers, who are funnier than I am. And the biggest debt of gratitude to my children, who might have—ahem—eaten cold cereal for dinner on occasion and who remind me when I need to "mom." Thank you to Robert, my husband, who has been with me every step of this writing journey. He has inspired me, let me neglect him and the housework, encouraged me, and supported me through it all and never once thought I was crazy. He is my first reader, and my best critic.

Chapter One

The security guard at Alpine Foods said they were not expecting Elaine Peterson for her internship in the Chocolate Department. Gripping her luggage, she crossed the lobby of the Alpine Foods corporate building.

The *thub-thub-thub* from her bag's broken wheel echoed off the wooden panels behind a mahogany reception desk. Well-heeled employees scurried past her, staring at her from the corners of their eyes as if she were dragging in a carcass.

Lainey held up her head, hoping the guard was mistaken. She'd spent the last four years at Stanford, beaten out two hundred other applicants, and flown twelve hundred miles across the Atlantic. At the receptionist's desk, she parked her luggage upright and threw her carry-on over the valise.

"*Pourais-je vous aider, mademoiselle*?" the male receptionist asked in yaw-yawing Swiss French, eying her over the top of the tall desk. "Can I help you?"

"*Je…*" she began. She fumbled for the right words. Out of the corner of her eye, she saw her carry-on slide. With a jerk, she caught the bag, but the jostle sent several chocolate wrappers to the ground. Without glancing up, she *knew* the receptionist thought she couldn't keep it together. Not a great first impression. She had to apologize. "*Desolée*."

Exasperated, she picked up the wrappers, stuffing them one by one into her pockets. The first chocolate bar she ate as a pre-boarding snack. The second she devoured when they delayed her first flight at Sky Harbor Airport. The third slipped down her gullet when she missed her connection at the Glasgow airport. And, of course, the fourth. The fourth she snarfed while she waited for the promised driver to pick her up at the airport in Geneva. When no one showed, she boarded the train to Vevey.

She thought she was only late. Now she was freaked out.

After picking up the wrappers, she faced the receptionist with the best smile she could manage after a nearly thirty-hour transit and very little sleep. He asked her again if she needed help. She understood, but it was as if a plastic bag was suffocating her brain. She deserved a fuzzy head after staying up late with Nadine the night before a six a.m. flight, rehashing every detail. What went wrong?

Her head throbbed, and she explained in halting French, "My name is Elaine Peterson. I'm here for an internship in the Chocolate Department with Madame Grocher." Her four years of university French broke through the fog. From her carry-on, she removed a folder. "I have correspondence from Marie Claire Remonter in Human Resources. It says right here, I was supposed to report this morning for orientation."

The receptionist arched his brow and clicked a few strokes on the keyboard, then faced her. "There must be some misunderstanding." His condescension sucked more wind from Lainey's deflated spirits. "Madame Grocher isn't expecting you. She isn't even in today."

"What?"

"I will call Marie Claire." He directed her to the seating at his side. "Wait there, please."

Leaving her bag by the desk, she slinked to the high-backed black seats to stare out the glass walls at the lacy snow draping the Alps reflected in Lake Geneva. But even the beautiful scenery couldn't distract her for long.

Did Madame Grocher nix her position because she was late? You know Swiss punctuality—fifteen minutes early was five minutes late. Imagine being four hours late. No, no. She wasn't even in. Something else was amiss.

Maybe Lainey mixed up the dates. Europeans write day/month/year, not month/day/year like Americans. Or she misread the date when she made her flight plans. She breathed in, relieved.

Somewhat.

She'd triple-checked the date. And besides, there was no twenty-sixth month.

What else could it be?

A woman entered the lobby from the paneled doors, clacking in impossibly high stiletto boots. "Elaine Peterson!"

So this was Marie Claire. Different than the glossy brochure they sent Lainey. She wore an exaggerated gypsy style rather than office casual. With a slight hand, she brushed a long, crimped strand of dark hair behind her triple-pierced ear. She would be able to straighten this out. "What are you doing here?" she asked in English.

Not a good sign.

Lainey's stomach dropped. She struggled to

respond. Her throat was so dry, it was as if she'd eaten straight cocoa powder. "I'm supposed to report for my internship in the Chocolate Department today, right?"

Marie Claire responded in English.

Mostly.

"*Desolée.* Did they not you contact?" she asked, wide-eyed.

Lainey shook her throbbing head, unsure who "they" were.

"*Oh, là, là.*" She faced the receptionist and spoke rapidly. Judging by the speed and accent of her French, Lainey guessed she wasn't Swiss. Probably French. Marie Claire gesticulated and glanced at Lainey. Dread grew in her stomach, leaving a foul taste across her unbrushed teeth.

Finally, Marie Claire broke from the receptionist to face Lainey. "There was a telephone call, the eighteenth?"

"The eighteenth? Last week." What was she doing the eighteenth? It was the day before Nadine threw her a going-away party.

Marie Claire consulted her notes. "We left a message with Nadine Hart."

"What?" Her best friend received a phone call canceling her internship and didn't tell her? Why?

Nadine was so not getting any souvenir chocolate.

"*C'est dommage. Le département de chocolat* cannot you take."

Marie Claire's bluntness quickened Lainey's heartbeat. Heat radiated from her face, her heartbeat pulsed into her head. Her brow lifted off her skull. Please, don't pass out, she silently prayed. She didn't want to know how hard the granite floor was. "Why not?"

"Bad economy, *vous voyez*," she said. "Their budget was cut *dernière minute*. There is no money. You have to return home."

"But I've come so far." She couldn't return home, not when she was in the lobby. Not when she could almost smell the chocolate. She closed her eyes, breathing deeply, hoping to stop the train wreck inside her head. All she envisioned was the image of her beaming parents waving goodbye as she bustled through security. What would their expressions be if she returned home tomorrow? "What am I going to do?" she asked.

Marie Claire shrugged with a pained expression on her face.

Chocolate! Lainey needed chocolate!

Her tongue lolled in her mouth, craving a molten blob of chocolatey goodness to soothe her spirits and calm her heart, but the delayed flights depleted her choco-stash. There was nothing left—zilch, nada, *rien du tout*.

"Is there somewhere else I can work? Some other department? Some other job?" She would mop floors, empty trash cans, anything at Alpine Foods. She didn't say this aloud. It wasn't the best bargaining chip to appear too needy. Maybe she could wander the lobby with a sign around her neck, "Will work for chocolate." Her nose tingled. She sneezed. She always sneezed right before she cried. "Please. I'm willing to do anything."

Marie Claire handed her a scented tissue, biting her lip, her eyebrows peaked with sympathy. She patted Lainey's hand. "Wait. I see what I can do. Maybe one of the other departments can you take." She lifted the phone at the reception desk, dialed a number, and spoke in such rapid French Lainey couldn't keep up.

Lainey bit her lip. *Cheer up, Lainey.* Lots of things went wrong in foreign travel. At least she had her luggage. She hugged her carry-on to her chest. And she didn't die during the flight. A bit of turbulence maybe. Okay, she might've wet herself in the bathroom as the plane rocked. But over all, it was an uneventful trip across the Atlantic. And Marie Claire was going to see what she could do. There were many things to be grateful for.

Her tummy rumbled, reminding her for the umpteenth time she hadn't eaten much but chocolate in over twenty-four hours. And did she hear a whistling sound or were her ears ringing?

She swooped her shoulder-length hair behind her ear and rubbed her thighs. They were not rail thin. More rounded and well fed.

Marie Claire hung up, a huge grin on her face. "I sent your CV to Eve Claremont. Eve agrees to you give interview. Her English communication is *trés bien*...better than mine."

Madame Claremont will interview her? A nervous shiver filled her horribly stressed body. Just then, the door opened again.

Out came a pencil-thin woman in a pencil-line skirt, with pencil-lined eyebrows. Behind her trailed a gorgeous man in a suit—if one could say a man was gorgeous—with dark, serious eyes and angular features. He consulted his phone. Lainey was glad he didn't glance at her. He was the type of guy who would make her blush if he caught her staring at him.

Just then, his gaze met hers, an intense, meaningful stare. Blushing, she ignored him giving her a once-over and focused instead on the woman. Legs shaking, gratitude swelling her heart, Lainey stood and held out her hand. "Thank you for taking the time to interview me, Madame Claremont."

The woman's too-big eyes widened in disdain. Lainey might wither right on the granite. Should she have said it in French, not English? Was it rude of her to greet someone in English in a foreign country?

The ringing in Lainey's ears grew louder. Voices sounded strangely far away. She was just about to repeat herself in French when the woman eyed the man behind her. In fact, everyone stared at him. Their gazes met. His eyes were even darker than her own chocolate brown, and his eyebrows raised in surprise.

"I am Yves Claremont," he said in English.

In French, "Yves" sounded like "Eve."

Heat flashed Lainey's face. The ringing in her ears increased into deafening numbness. M. Claremont's gorgeous features disappeared into darkness.

When the blackness faded, she was lying on the cold granite floor. She had a great view of it. Very clean. And, as predicted, hard.

Someone held her hand, and everyone was speaking French. Throbbing pain nearly overtook her when she tilted her head toward Marie Claire, who patted Lainey's fingers.

Her long, crimped hair tickled Lainey, her flowing shirt draped across her midsection. Up this close, a tiny hole was visible in Marie Claire's thin nose. "Oh, *ma pauvre*," she said. "*Ça va*?"

"I'm sorry." Lainey's voice shook. "I haven't

really eaten much. I must've passed out."

And Yves, uh, it sounded like a girl's name, no, *Monsieur* Claremont—she would only call him Monsieur Claremont—was on the phone, his jaw flexing, his dark eyebrows gathered.

She laid her head back down on the granite.

At her side, M. Claremont knelt. The scent of his cologne weakened her. In a good way.

"I am so sorry." She stared up into his concerned face. "Marie Claire used the feminine pronoun 'her' before 'communication' in English. I thought she was referring to a woman." She chuckled uncomfortably.

His heavily-lashed eyes were penetrating, dark, and serious. He leaned in and whispered to Lainey, his voice low and soft. "I am very much a man." A hint of intensity flashed in his eyes. But then it fled, and he was as cold and clipped as ice chips. "Sabine will bring you something to eat while we talk," he said louder in English. He placed his hand under her shoulder to help her up. His gentle yet firm touch sent electricity through her body. "You must be famished." His clipped French accent was incredibly sexy.

She stopped herself. He might be her new boss.

The sugar and caffeine had finally run out. She nodded feebly.

M. Claremont directed her to the chair near the wall of windows. "Wait here." He crossed the lobby to direct Sabine in French.

He was not overly tall or short. About six feet, she would guess. But lean. He moved with the grace of one who purposefully, consistently worked out. And, Lainey guessed, paid for an expensive barber, judging from the perfect way his dark hair settled in the back.

He returned, arranging a chair across from her, occupied with something on his phone. “We’ll wait until you’ve eaten.”

His English was hot chocolate to her soul. His voice soothed her and warmed her inside. Within a few moments, Sabine entered the paneled doors with a tray and set it in an empty chair near her with an unmistakable cold stare in Lainey’s direction.

Wait, a tray?

Apparently, the Swiss did not go half-measures on anything. On this tray sat two buttery croissants, sliced pears and peaches in a ceramic cup, a sandwich of thin-sliced ham and cheese on a crusty chunk of French bread, and two silver-blue wrapped pieces of chocolate, all over a lace doily—a four-star spread.

Shaking loose the real fork, spoon, and butter knife, she spread the cloth napkin on her lap. After sugary slurps of fruit, she started on the sandwich. While chewing, she peeked at M. Claremont. He glanced up from his phone. His eyes slid purposefully to hers. His eyebrows peaked at just the right moment, asking if she was okay.

She returned with a half-smile.

So scrumptious.

The sandwich. She was thinking about the sandwich.

Another bite. Was it hot?

He held out his phone, exposing a designer watch encircling his wrist. “Now you’ve eaten a little, we can start. I have reviewed your CV. I am ready to see what you can do for our department.” He broke to glance at his phone. “You earned an English degree at Stanford. French minor. You worked full-time to support yourself at university. Tell me about Homemade Meals."

She swiped her mouth to stall, folding the napkin across her lap once more. When she glanced up, his gaze penetrated hers, interested and attentive. For a heart-stopping moment, she was calm. What she learned from Homemade Meals wasn't something easily explained on a CV. It needed to be shared.

She cleared her throat to eject the rising tremors. "Homemade Meals is a non-profit specializing in bringing healthy meals to housebound elderly people in the Bay Area."

He raised an eyebrow. "And how did those experiences prepare you for this internship?"

Her throat strangled her breath. Everything was riding on this. She struggled to tailor her responses without knowing which department she was applying to. She decided to keep it honest and general. "The awesome people at Homemade Meals helped me realize food is a meaningful way of communicating care. Nourishing not just the body but the soul. I learned baking brings me joy, and this was a way to share my talents."

M. Claremont smiled curtly then glanced down at his phone again for reference. "Ah, yes. I'm sure it's a lovely story, and no doubt you've told it many times." He lifted his gaze to challenge hers. "And the people you served, can you tell me something about them? Something aside from being elderly."

The edge in his voice expressed doubt in her sincerity. He thought she'd padded her resume for appearances. But this was a question she had no trouble answering.

She sat up straighter. His eyes widened at her

confidence. Good. She enjoyed surprising people. "First on my route was Lavina. She enjoyed my chocolate cream puffs almost as much as an Oakland A's game. Her son played baseball years ago in high school, and it was all she ever talked about. Then Susan, crushed on some soap opera star from the eighties. Nobody I knew. But after searching for the reruns online, we discovered they weren't available anywhere. She loved my hazelnut-chocolate cookies-and-cream sandwich cookies. Dipped them in cola." Lainey wrinkled her nose. "And Esther still crochets. Ninety years old and still crocheting. Made me a scarf and mittens despite her partial blindness. Said she crocheted by touch. She ate three helpings of my chocolate chocolate-chip bread because she said she wanted to die happy. Should I continue?"

"No, thank you." He almost smiled, but cut it short. "You were scheduled for the Department of Chocolate. Tell me why?"

"My uncle traveled to Switzerland and, for my ninth birthday, brought me back an Alpine Foods Extra Milk chocolate bar, the most delicious thing I had ever tasted." She didn't mention her parents' rocky marriage while her dad's business tanked, or her tweenage strife. Chocolate continued to act as a warm, fuzzy comfort blanket. "I want to bring joy to many people."

"I see." His expression changed to almost a scowl. "If I am pleased with your work, I'll give you a recommendation for a full-time position to Madame Grocher."

"So, you'll take me?"

He stood and returned his chair, his eyes never leaving hers. "I think you are just what we are looking for."

Marie Claire, who had waited at the desk, crossed to them. She asked something in rapid French.

He switched over to French flawlessly when he consulted with her. Thankfully, the food regulated her blood sugar, and his French became more clear. "Yes, we'd love to have her in our department. Now if you will make the arrangements."

"There's the matter of her stipend."

"What matter?"

"During your interview, I checked and you have no money in your budget."

M. Claremont did not even miss a beat before answering. "Take it out of my salary." He nodded curtly and stalked to the door out of the lobby.

Marie Claire glanced at him in exasperation when he slid his card through the security reader.

M. Claremont paused before the open door, then faced Lainey. "I forgot. Do you have any questions?"

Lainey answered without hesitation. "Which department do I report to?"

M. Claremont raised his eyebrows. "Pet Care." Then, before slipping through the door, he said, "See you at seven forty a.m. Sharp."

Pet Care? Pet Care. A hint of terror weakened her knees. She swallowed hard.

"You are lucky to work with M. Claremont." Marie Claire held paperwork in her hands. "Everyone wants to intern with him."

With her heart still beating and dread growing in her throat, Lainey switched to French, too. "How come?" She would have to think about Pet Care later.

"Because he is the best department chair. He

aspires to be the youngest Vice President in Alpine Foods history. He is hardworking and ambitious, but also fair and cares as much for the success of his subordinates as his own. Sadly, he gives everything to his ambition and is not much fun." Bracelets jangled when Marie Claire squatted next to Lainey to hand her the paperwork. She frowned. "Now, Sabine will find you a temporary apartment. Housing is limited here and very expensive. You don't have a phone?"

"Mine died right before I came."

"Ah, and we promised one on arrival." Marie Claire stood. "As well as reimbursements for any travel costs. I will get you the necessary forms."

After a few moments, Sabine returned with printed instructions to a temporary, furnished apartment. She handed Lainey a clamshell cell phone. "This only makes calls within Switzerland, and there is no Internet access."

Pet Care and no Internet access? Lainey gulped. "No social media?" Panic rose in her throat.

"No. The Swiss have this thing about productivity," Marie Claire muttered before retreating.

When Sabine removed the tray, Lainey swiped the two wrapped chocolates. "Thank you. The meal tasted great." She motioned to the remnants. "Was it your lunch?"

"No." Her eyebrows were still furrowed. "It was Yves' lunch." She spun without further explanation.

Weighing the chocolates in her hand, Lainey pocketed them for later. She stared at the door where they all left. She wished she had thanked him.

****

Yves stalked toward his office. He didn't really

need a new intern. What about her made him hire her? He bit his fingernail. Then he remembered he was trying to quit the habit and dropped his hand. Perhaps her sincerity. And her situation. He couldn't very well send her back to the States.

While Yves was distracted, Luc Pessereaux cornered him in the hall. His large forehead gleamed in the overhead fluorescent lights. "Enjoying your new office, Department Head?" he asked, using formal French to mock Yves and his position.

Slipping past him, Yves responded cordially. "Yes, thank you, I am. But I'm not planning on being there long." He continued down the hall.

But Luc stopped him again by stepping in front of him. "Already looking for another place to work?" Luc smirked and shoved his hands into his pockets. "Or climbing up the ladder? You just received a promotion last year."

Facing him, Yves arched an eyebrow but said nothing. Abruptly side-stepping him, he continued down the hall. He had no time for Luc. There were people you assist, and there were people who assisted you. Luc was neither of those. His arrogance made him beyond help. And his incompetence made him useless.

Luc parted the silence, behind Yves. "At some point, you won't succeed on your name alone. Someday you'll misstep, and you'll fail, just like your old man."

But Yves ignored him, instead biting his nail to keep him from saying something he'd regret later.

Entering his office, he didn't notice his gorgeous view of Lake Geneva sparkling in the sun's touch. Instead, he opened his computer at his desk. What could the new intern do? What was her name? Elaine

Peterson.

She majored in English, right? He glanced through several unfinished tasks. Gui Moucher had neglected to write up several brochures. Perfect for someone schooled in writing. But she required training.

His schedule prevented him this week. Tomorrow was positively packed, including several phone calls first thing in the morning. He needed someone else.

Sabine's large eyeballs beamed on him before he acknowledged her. She haunted his doorway.

Perfect. Just the person he wanted to see. "Will you train Mademoiselle Peterson tomorrow in some of our programs? The American intern can input data for analysis and then write advertising pamphlets and marketing campaigns."

Sabine cocked her hip and crossed her thin arms. "Gui was supposed to write those."

"Yes, but since he's not doing his job, someone has to." He handed her a stack of folders. "Please give her these." He glanced up. "And be sure to train her on the STS so she will be able to translate when finished."

"Of course."

"And remind the new intern of the strike tomorrow. I will pick her up on the way into town." As one of the few employees who owned a car, it was his duty to be courteous.

She stood at the door, facing him. Again, her gaze trained on him.

He raised his eyes to her. "Did you need anything else?"

"I wanted to invite you to dinner Friday. At my house."

"Are you having a dinner party?" he asked,

distracted. He was answering an email from Marie Claire asking how much she should withdraw to pay for the new American intern.

"No. A friendly dinner. Just the two of us."

After sending the email, Yves blinked a few times with the realization of what the offer intended. He had gathered her not-so-subtle hints indicating her interest before, but he always discouraged her. He hoped her overtures would never become overt. He sighed, clasping his hands in front of him, choosing his words carefully. "Company policy strictly forbids fraternizing. Remember Jean-Claude and Marielle."

"They were sloppy."

"They were breaking the rules."

"We can be subtle."

"Someone always finds out."

"Rules are meant to be broken."

"Even so, I cannot jeopardize my career—both our careers—for *supplementing* our relationship." Besides, subtlety was not one of her strengths.

"I would take any risk."

"Thank you. You are highly complimentary. However, as a diligent employee, it would be a shame for you to throw away years of hard work." He cracked a smile. "I'm not worth it."

"But you are."

"I only care about one thing."

Her eyes narrowed. "Work will always come first for you, Yves Claremont. One day, you will look back on your life and wish you had not wasted it chasing your ambition."

She took his rejection better than he expected. Still she waited. "You know what you need? You need a heart."

Yves raised an eyebrow at her suggestion.

Sabine licked her lips. "And as a friend, I am warning you to watch Luc. I heard he's threatened to come after you."

"I'm not worried."

"He has powerful friends in executive positions."

Yves focused on flipping through the market research before him. "How can he win? He can't even organize a decent market analysis report."

Chapter Two

On the stuttering bus, Lainey moved through a living postcard. Vegetation grew anyplace there was dirt. Trees shaded lush grass. Between faded green limestone buildings, she caught glimpses of the towering mountains on the far side of the lake. She distracted herself with the scenery so she didn't have to think about the next four months of Pet Care. But it was an internship. And a foot in the door.

At the Montreux bus stop, she descended to a cobblestone street in an older part of town. Densely packed houses, with clay tile roofs and textured limestone walls, darkened by soot and time, crowded the sky.

At her building, exoskeleton pipes hung on the exterior walls. Dank smells of many feet and years of wear were trapped in the matted carpet on the inside stairs.

In her apartment, a mattress sat on the wood floor. No other furnishings. A small kitchenette hid under a window on the far side. She grinned at the thought of a shower in her own bathroom after her transit. At least she had her own private space.

First order: wash up. She unzipped the big suitcase. Her thousand-dollar wardrobe, specially purchased for this internship, would ensure she would be professionally dressed.

For a second, she stared, not recognizing the contents.

"Oh no!" She seized a man's checked flannel shirt and aftershave. An unfamiliar smell wafted up. "Oh, no, oh, no. This isn't my bag."

There was no claim check. A small tag read, Hector Ghetty. Great. *Sorry, Hector*. She wasn't sure how the mix-up happened. It was the only black suitcase on the carousel. At least she could shower. And perhaps borrow a flannel shirt for tomorrow. Except nobody looked good in flannel. Okay, maybe some fashion models. And hot guys in winter catalogs with broad shoulders, boots, and steamy mugs. And most Canadians.

But without her other luggage, she didn't have—*gulp*—clean underwear. Dripping wet from her shower, she rummaged around in her carry-on to find her emergency pair of underwear.

A word about these panties. They were her least attractive pair. The pair she wore on her dates with her ex-boyfriend, Aaron, to make sure they wouldn't go all the way. The baby pink granny-pants covered all her cheeks except for a hole in the unraveled seam in the bum-side of the crotch. Just wearing them was degrading. But a fresh pair would feel so good and a must after a shower.

She slid them on. No one was going to see her underwear anyway.

It was only for a day. After a small nap, she would search for fresh underwear.

****

After catching a late bus to the *gare*, she discovered nearly everything closed before eight at night. She bought a dinner of Alpine Foods Orange Almond chocolate at Albertos, a twenty-four-hour convenience store at the entrance to the train station, and a phone card to call home.

First, she needed to call the airline to exchange her bag. She found the customer service number from her ticket and called with her cell phone to arrange a swap at her work. Apparently, Hector had taken the wrong bag. Next, she needed to call Nadine. She had a lot of explaining to do.

A large, blue, space-agey phone booth lit up the sidewalk. With shaking fingers and a chocolate bar hanging from her mouth, she slid in the pre-paid card and dialed Nadine, hoping she would answer a foreign number.

"Nadine, I'm so glad you picked up," she said as soon as Nadine answered the phone.

"Lainey, what's wrong?"

She didn't know what to say. She pressed her head on the keypad, making it beep. "Everything. Everything is going wrong."

"Things often go wrong in foreign travel."

"Why didn't you tell me Alpine Foods cancelled my internship?"

Pause. "Are you in Sweden?"

"I'm in Switzerland, Nadine."

"Oh, yeah. Sweden. Switzerland. Same thing." She giggled. "I just couldn't tell you. You'd worked so hard to get this internship. You've wanted this since we were nine years old. I hoped if you just showed up, they'd give you the internship."

How could one be mad at a best friend when she was so well-intentioned? One must forgive. Someday.

But today was not the day.

"Did you get the internship?"

"Not *the* internship. An internship." Lainey explained M. Claremont's impromptu interview and surprising offer to hire her.

Nadine's voice brightened. "See, I told you it would all work out."

"It's not in Chocolate."

"What department is it in?"

"Pet Care."

Alpine Foods had a finger in every foodstuff imaginable—water, crackers, soda, baby food, confectionary, chocolates, dog food, cat food, canned goods, dry goods, frozen and refrigerated meals manufactured and sold on nearly every continent inhabited by man. And fate dealt her Pet Care.

"With your history and all, working in Pet Care will be awful."

"No, it was awful not to tell me. Anyway, it's really stressful living in a country where I don't really speak the language."

"I told you they speak Swedish, not French."

Lainey sighed.

Nadine continued. "Martin says—"

She was always quoting Martin, her cool but nerdy Star Trek-loving boyfriend, majoring in Computer Science at Stanford. He said he wrote some linguistic program utilizing a highly optimized recurrent neural network. He said it was the "new hotness" in speech processing for Machine Learning. Whatever that meant.

"Sorry to interrupt. But I only have twenty francs left. How do I get a stellar recommendation for Chocolate?"

"Lainey, you're smart and resourceful, prepared for everything. You'll get it."

Lainey didn't feel prepared for this. Ten francs left. "I'm making so many mistakes."

"You've always kept your notebook of things to improve. Write the unexpected things and how to fix it. You've always learned from your mistakes."

"Okay." She had bought a notebook at Albertos. "But I'll need another one. Or a bigger one. With lots of pages." Four francs left on the phone. "I have to go."

"Before you go," Nadine shouted into the phone. "I have to tell you, we're engaged! Martin asked me, and we're getting married."

Engaged? She was engaged? Lainey was about to congratulate her, but the line was cut.

A soothing French female voice asked her to deposit more money or be cut off. When she didn't respond, the voice thanked Lainey for using the Swiss phone company. She held the red receiver, reading the amount of change left on her card. Seventy-two *centimes*. A sinking pit formed in her stomach when she slid the card from the slot.

She leaned against the edge of the glass, a lump lodged in her throat. The weight of a thousand plaques of chocolate pressed on her. Her breath halted in her chest.

Perhaps she should stand in the phone booth until the oxygen gave out, then suffocate and die. Her nose tingled, and she sneezed. Full-blown tears fell from her eyes.

On the way back to her room, she checked the morning bus schedule sandwiched in the plexiglass at the bus stop. Once home, she listed in her mini notebook what had gone wrong since she arrived. In no particular order:

1. Internship canceled. Probably should've quadruple checked.

2. Forgot my French. All four years of it. Should have bought the language program and practiced on my flight instead of watching TV.

3. Spent all my Swiss francs. I'll at least get reimbursed.

4. Flight delayed. Not sure how I could've prevented a delayed flight. New goal: make enough money to own a private jet. (She crossed it out—that was the chocolate talking.)

5. Pet Care…

****

Jet lag plagued Lainey when the alarm went off the next morning. The sun hadn't crested the mountains, and Lake Geneva was a calm sheet of reflective glass when Lainey stumbled down the cobblestone road between the limestone buildings toward the bus stop.

Foggy haze surrounded her. Moisture saturated the air. It clouded the light. She had three minutes until the bus arrived. Thank goodness for Swiss punctuality.

At 7:38, she glanced down the street, biting her lip. She didn't see a lumbering bus parting the fog. 7:40 came.

She glanced again at the chart posted between the plexi.

For the first time she noticed a paper taped near the time tables, curled in the moisture. With a finger, she pinned it down to read.

A *grève*? Today? Dread grew in her stomach. A strike. There would be no buses today.

Parking the suitcase, she opened her phone to call, but before she dialed, a steel-gray sports car with a trident on the grill parked alongside her. Odd for this shoddy neighborhood. Must be lost. Then the power window sank into the door. Her stomach sank, too.

"Madmoiselle Peterson."

Her heart stopped. She ducked her head to see inside the luxury car.

M. Claremont.

****

Yves had little patience for the American this morning, no matter how impressive her interview was yesterday. Why was she wandering the street with her suitcase? "Get in," he said in English, unsure of her fluency in French. Americans rarely spoke another language well, even if learned at university. Perhaps they never had the opportunity to practice. "I've already been up to your apartment searching for you."

"*Je suis desolée*."

At least she knew how to apologize in French. It was a start. "Didn't Sabine tell you I was picking you up this morning?"

"No." She slid across the leather interior.

Yves stowed her bag in the back. Once she was in the car, he jerked the gear shift. He glanced at the clock. He had several phone calls to make. The tires ground across the cobblestone in a forced a U-turn.

He scrutinized her outfit. The oversized plaid shirt drowned her pleasing figure. "You cannot go to work in those clothes." Where did she think she was employed? A lumber mill? He bit back a smile.

"I don't have anything else," she said. "My suitcase. There was a mix-up. The airline is exchanging them at work."

That would explain the valise. Yves couldn't withhold an impatient sigh. The Swiss airlines were supposed to be the finest in the world.

They headed down the shaded streets to *centre-ville* until he plunged them into the darkness of a parking garage near a huge glass-sided department store. "You can pick up something here." He dialed his phone while they opened the car doors.

Heading toward the store, Yves locked the car with a beep, while conversing with Madame Dreyfuss, the plant manager in Fribourg. His tongue struggled with German.

Mlle Peterson entered and stopped, presumably stunned by the sumptuous displays of color and fabric, overwhelmed by decent fashion.

"Quickly," he urged her, through Mme Dreyfuss' direct questions and scintillating opinions of dog food management.

Mlle Peterson selected a skirt and a few shirts to try on. Still in conversation, Yves followed her into the fitting room to the bench opposite her cubicle, making use of this lapse of time. He glanced up as the fitting room curtains swallowed her.

She wasn't beautiful. Not by European standards. Not tall and thin. No showy features. But she had just enough curves in all the right places—

Mme Dreyfuss' German shook him from his thought. He said goodbye to her after resolving her concerns and called Hiroko about the new merger deal.

From Mlle Peterson's fitting room, something fell to the floor with a *clunk*. Yves glanced up to see if she needed help.

Instead of her face peering through the curtains, a bum, clothed in pink except for a small unraveled seam, split the panels. His eyebrows rose in surprise. Then Yves dropped his head, his face burning a bit. Did she see him? He didn't mean to see. Heavens knew he could never mention it. He faced away to bite his tongue. It was the first laugh he'd had in a long time.

****

Lainey shot upright, red-faced and embarrassed. She hugged her phone, which had fallen from her pocket, to her chest. Did he see? Mustering her courage, she peeked through the parted curtain, grasping both panels between her hands.

But M. Claremont bowed his head, speaking—a Far Eastern language?—on the phone, across from her, his face hidden from view. Did he see or didn't he? Disconcerted, she drew the curtains closed again. Was his head down the whole time, and she had nothing to worry about? She chewed her lip. She certainly couldn't ask him about it.

After trying on all the outfits, she found a flattering ensemble complementary to her reddish hair. She tucked her old clothes under her arm and parted the stall curtains.

"Much better." His eyes lingered a tad longer than necessary. His approval warmed her. "Your watch?"

"What about my watch?"

"It doesn't work." But then he returned to his phone, speaking now in Spanish.

She glanced at the watch. It kept perfect time. Lainey shrugged.

Occupied in conversation, M. Claremont followed her to the cashier where the clerk scanned the tags still hanging from her clothes, bagged her used articles with more than a bit of repulsion, and calculated the total.

M. Claremont, phone still at his ear, proffered a card from a sleek billfold. Lainey shook her head. With a short nod, he backed away from the cashier desk to continue his conversation.

From her bag, she removed her wallet and slid her bankcard through the reader. Declined. She tried again.

Nothing.

She handed it to the clerk to slide manually. She ran it through the machine. Again nothing.

Next, Lainey handed her a credit card. Rejected. She squinted her eyes shut in embarrassment, her nose tingling.

She'd called the bank to inform them she was in a foreign country. Did she give them the wrong dates? Or maybe they heard Sweden. Either way, Lainey's bank probably thought her card was stolen. She'd already used all the Swiss francs she exchanged on the expensive and unexpected train and bus fares yesterday and the chocolate the night before.

As the cashier asked her if she had any other way to pay, Lainey sneezed, closing her burning eyes.

When she opened them, M. Claremont was handing his bankcard to the cashier.

"Thank you. I'll pay you back," she whispered.

Without pausing his conversation, he shook his head.

"Take it out of my first paycheck, then."

Understanding passed between them. Then he nodded.

With the transaction completed, she crumpled the bag under her arm and popped off the tags, then followed him out to the car.

Once they were both in, he thrust the car into gear. They rode in relative silence out of the city. Lainey watched him shift the car. There was just something so incredible manly—sexy, but she didn't think those words—about watching a man shift a well-made machine. The gear shift became an extension of his hand. His whole body was in tune with his car, the body and the engine working together.

M. Claremont's jaw flexed a few times when he glanced at the time on the computer-filled dashboard, lit with all sorts of gadgets and electronic…things.

The phone rang. A light blinked on his dash, and a sultry women's voice announced the name of the caller. Serge Biscinni.

"*Pronto*," M. Claremont said, speaking in fluid, uh, Italian? While listening to a conversation in Italian, she traced a finger over the silver *GranTurismo* embossed in the leather dash. He hung up.

"Maserati," he said.

She shot him a questioning glance. She didn't speak Italian.

A faint hint of a smile spread across his lips. Men. Whatever. She vowed to search the Internet for *GranTurismo* as soon as possible.

"We don't have to speak English," she said. "We can speak French if you want."

"I've heard you speak French." He peeked over his designer shades. The corners of his mouth twitched in a smile. Or she imagined it. "English is fine."

"But I should practice."

"*Comme vous voulez*." As you wish. A concession. But in formal French.

An aura of suave sophistication surrounded him. A drive underneath his cool facade. Very different from Aaron, who expressed, loudly, every thought. Every grievance aired. M. Claremont seemed focused. Controlled. Emotions penned inside a cool facade.

She shouldn't compare M. Claremont to her ex.

****

For the first time, Lainey would witness what hid behind those great gray doors. M. Claremont excused himself for other important errands when Sabine retrieved her from the lobby and escorted her through the barrier to the unknown. On the other side of the door, the office bustled with compact excitement. Lainey caught snatches of French as people passed by in twos or threes, discussing charts and graphs.

Up the elevator to the fourth floor, Sabine led her to a large room filled with a labyrinth of gray flannel-lined cubicles. A general buzz of productivity rose from the invisible faces tucked in the four sets of squares.

At a corner where two breezeways intersected, Sabine stopped at an L-shaped notch cut from a cubicle to make way for a pillar. Next to the pillar sat a two-foot by three-foot desk nearly spilling out into the perpendicular breezeway. A laptop sat on the desk.

"This is your place." She gestured toward the desk.

In the middle of the cubical hall? Certainly not the glorious spot she had envisioned. But it was only until she earned a position in Chocolate, she reminded herself. Keep an eye on Chocolate. "M. Claremont said I have an assignment."

"It's on your desktop," she said. "Department meeting will be in one hour in the conference room."

"Where's the conference room?"

But instead of answering, she swiveled, leaving in a cloud of perfume.

Clearly, someone needed to eat more chocolate.

Lainey seated herself at the desk and opened the laptop lid. She should at least search for the assignment. Or email Sabine or M. Claremont for more details.

Browser, browser. Her eyes flitted to each icon. No browser. She found a LAN email client with a staff email list embedded in an address book. That was it. No outside Internet access. At all. How would she contact her family? She cleared her throat. This would be more difficult than she thought.

She emailed Sabine asking about the assignment and the location of the conference room, then waited for a response. A few minutes passed. She resumed searching for an assignment. She clicked on each icon. Everything was in French except a few trade names of programs. After clicking around, she decided it must be hidden somewhere and threw up her hands in exasperation. A whole hour wasted. Without anything to do in the few minutes before the meeting, she ran to the bathroom.

When she returned to her desk, a small red box with a bow sat in the center. She glanced around to see if the giver was nearby.

Maybe it was a welcome gift from Alpine Foods. But since she worked in a nook, not even a real cubicle, it seemed improbable. But who knew what kind of company policies they had?

She tugged the ribbon and cracked open the red velvet box with a creak, searching for clues of the giver. Inside, a wristwatch circled around a form. She cocked her head and glanced at the watch she bought at

ShopCo, with a green faux leather band. Ugly, but extremely functional. She gazed at the new one. An all stainless-steel face etched with flowers and set ten minutes early. She flipped it over for the price tag.

250 CHF

Who would send such a gift? She already had a watch. Besides, the new one was too expensive to wear. She clamped the case closed with a snap and moved it to a corner on her desk. Only a few more minutes until the meeting.

A door opened at the far side of the room. Over the top of the cubicles, she spied a group of men threading their way through the room. M. Claremont's dark hair stood out among the white-haired men. There was an unmistakable power about him, confidence. His gaze met Lainey's. He tapped his watch, raising a questioning eyebrow.

She shook her head. She hadn't forgotten about the meeting. It was in ten minutes. Maybe everybody here arrived early. He frowned and stalked out the door. Maybe he expected her to follow them.

She hesitated, then headed for the doors, following the direction of the pack of men. Once through the doorway, she searched for the group. At the end of the hall, the trailing pack rounded the corner. She followed them into a double-doored room with soft leather chairs around a long, sleek, dark, giant chocolate-bar table. She entered the room.

Every man, and the two women, craned their necks to stare at her.

"*Je suis desolée que je suis en retard.*" She apologized for being late, casting her eyes around for an empty seat.

"Who is this girl, and why is she here?" A voice boomed from a large man seated at the head of the table. Several men reassured him. "I want her out of here."

One of the women nodded obsequiously. M. Claremont swiveled in his chair, and raised his eyebrows in surprise.

Scowling, he jumped up from his seat and with haste, tugged her out of the room. His impetuous move disoriented Lainey. Her face burned with comprehension. Not the conference room. Not her meeting.

Heat emanated from her shirt. Once alone in the hall, M. Claremont dropped her arm, but her eyes couldn't meet his.

"*Je suis—*" she wanted to say an idiot, but he cut her off in English.

"It's okay."

"*J'allais…à la salle de conférence.*" Giving up, she continued in English, dropping her gaze to the floor. "Sabine said I had a department meeting in some conference room. But she didn't say which conference room. I emailed her, but she never responded."

"Ah." The hard lines of his face softened with understanding. "Follow me." He swiveled, heading down the hall, outpacing her. She caught up with him. He gave her a sideways glance. "You are not wearing the watch I sent you."

"You?" For some reason, her face flamed again. "But I already have a watch." She raised a wrist to show him.

"You need a Swiss time-piece. Yours"—he nodded at her ShopCo special—"was probably made in China.

Here we are."

He stopped at a door labeled Department of Pet Care. Dread filled her heart as she entered the room. With a few last words of departure, M. Claremont closed the heavy wooden door behind him, with finality. She wanted to cling to him, to beg him to take her to the Chocolate Department.

But instead, she summoned her strength and faced the gathered crowd. Sabine sat at the head of the table, her Ping-Pong-ball-sized eyes glaring at Lainey. Two men and a blonde woman faced each other at a U-shaped table.

Sabine introduced them. The tall blonde, Britta, with a last name only a German could pronounce, was the Production Manager. She nodded her head slightly in acknowledgement as if her angled body might shatter with any further movement. Opposite her, the two men, Luc Pessereaux, with a large forehead, was Stats and Cost Analysis. The thicker Gui Moucher, director of Marketing and Advertising, sat on his right.

Luc spoke flawless sing-song French as he presented material with graphs and charts. His hair was slicked back exposing his full forehead, '50s hoodlum-style. "Reviewing the detailed graphs, I can't help but wonder, is this strategy the best one? Wouldn't it make more sense to produce products similar to our competitors rather than experimental innovations which may not work?"

Sabine deferred. "Yves makes those decisions."

The hoodlum asked several questions during his presentation of the statistics.

The clock ticked. Lainey fought the jet lag weighing on her eyelids.

"When M. Claremont comes—" Sabine said at last. As if on cue, and precisely one hour from the time he left, Yves Claremont burst through the doors.

"*Bonjour, bonjour*!" The whole atmosphere in the room changed. His incredible energy infused everyone. Britta and Sabine sat up straighter.

Lainey recognized the sound before it came into view. A shudder filtered through her heart as if pricked with shards of glass.

A dog.

With a leash, M. Claremont led a playful, mid-sized dog with a short, dark coat into the room.

Lainey jumped up, spilling her chair behind her. She swallowed. Closing her eyes, she focused on her breathing and remembered her eight years of therapy with jovial cat-lover Elsie Bly. She had sat and stroked a cat sculpture on her desk as they talked. Lainey imagined Elsie's voice in her head: "Dogs aren't out to get you, Lainey. Most of them just want to play."

She needed to get over it. But not today.

With a shaking hand, Lainey righted her chair, worried the rest of the team had viewed her panic. Instead, they focused on the dog at the front of the room. Lainey sat, drawing her legs up to her chest. She needed chocolate.

"This is Futé," M. Claremont announced, parading the prancing dog around. Maybe in Pet Care, people brought their dogs to work. Lainey gauged the others' reactions. But they were equally astonished. Gui and Luc exchanged glances.

Futé, the black dog with a tuxedo patch of white on its chest, captured everyone's attention. It pranced around biting at the leash. It barked. Lainey jumped in her seat, heart pounding.

Unleashing the dog, M. Claremont and Futé danced a *pas de deux*, as he enticed the dog by letting it chase him in a circle after a treat he held in his hand. Then M. Claremont crouched to hug its neck, scratching behind its ears, and rewarded Futé with a treat. His enjoyment and affection for the dog were strangely attractive. Lainey almost wanted to join him, if he wasn't so close to mandibles of death.

The blonde, Britta, finally smiled. "He's cute."

M. Claremont continued to talk while playing with the dog. "I borrowed him for today." From his pocket, he extracted another treat, asked Futé to sit, then rewarded the dog when it complied. "Good boy." He patted its head.

From another pocket, he retrieved a bone and set it in front of Futé, who held it between his forepaws to gnaw.

Lainey held her breath.

Teeth scraping bone.

If she ever needed chocolate, now was the time.

M. Claremont faced them for a few seconds, waiting expectantly. Nobody moved. They all watched.

Finally, he spoke again. "Isn't somebody going to come up and pet the dog? Ask me questions about my friend here?"

His subordinates shifted awkwardly in their seats. Lainey was frozen, staring wide-eyed at the dog.

M. Claremont squatted near the dog, stroking his coat. "Can anyone tell me what breed of dog Futé is?"

No answer.

His brow creased. "He's a greater Swiss mountain dog." He paused. "What kind of food would you recommend for a one-year-old dog?"

Again silence.

M. Claremont grew impatient. "How many of you are pet owners?"

No hands.

"None of you?" He shook his head.

"I have a bird," Gui said, but M. Claremont ignored him.

"How can we sell pet food if none of you have any understanding?"

Britta nervously clicked her pen, then realized it made noise and stopped.

"I want you all to come out of your seats and introduce yourself to Futé. Don't worry. He's a friendly dog."

Britta complied first. Then Sabine hesitantly. Britta folded herself in half, then her knees popped as she squatted to be level with the dog. Futé raised his head at the approach and relished the scratches behind the ears. Next, Sabine awkwardly bent and patted the dog.

Then the two guys rose in slow motion, as if it pained them to leave their chairs, pushed in their seats, and strolled up to the dog with hands in their pockets. The larger of the two, Gui, waved from about a foot away. "Hello, doggie."

Luc, with the slicked hair, gave a short pat to the head then stuck his hands back in his pockets. They formed an uncomfortable circle around the dog.

Then M. Claremont stared at Lainey. "Mademoiselle Peterson?"

She returned his stare.

"Are you coming to greet Futé?"

She shook her head, not wanting to explain to all

her new co-workers her history.

"Is there something wrong?"

At M. Claremont's question, they all stared at her.

She chewed her lip, her face burning. "I hate dogs," she whispered.

M. Claremont scrutinized her through slitted eyes, as if he had allowed a wolf in among his sheep.

Lainey needed chocolate, and she needed it now.

"Go ahead and sit down," he said at last. They dispersed. M. Claremont led Futé to the door where someone escorted him out into the hall. Lainey breathed when the dog left, relaxing.

Chocolate. She needed chocolate.

Thoroughly embarrassed, Lainey glanced to where M. Claremont stood at the front of the room, staring intently at her. "Everyone has met our new intern, Elaine Peterson, *n'est-ce pas*?" M. Claremont clapped his hands together. "*Bon*. I think we are out of touch with our customers. I will think about how to solve this problem."

"But we have surveys and statistics," Luc protested.

"They tell us what we think to ask. But we don't even know what to ask. I want to know what they really want. We need to probe deeper. How can we find out more about their needs?"

No one said anything. Lainey raised her hand. "Why don't we just ask them?" Gui sniggered and Luc rolled his eyes. Maybe her suggestion was too obvious. Her face warmed in embarrassment.

"Excellent idea, Mademoiselle Peterson." M. Claremont clapped his hands. "*Bon!* I will think more on this. Until next week."

He adjourned the meeting. On her way out the door, Sabine detained her by loading her with a pile of folders and directions to enter the data. When the beam of her too-big eyes finally glanced away, Lainey darted through the door.

Returning to her desk, Lainey passed a wall of windows facing the front walk and gardens. M. Claremont stood on the grass, his suit flapping in the wind off the lake. He was pointing out different bushes and flowers to the groundskeeper next to a garden cart loaded with tools. Nothing was below his notice. He directed everything. Even the gardening.

At her desk, Lainey juggled the paperwork, finding room for it all on her desk, and reanalyzed the French.

Then she saw it.

A pair of three-foot-long, hooked bypass loppers came through the gray maze, held above some unseen head. It attracted the attention of several cubicle dwellers, who popped up their heads like gophers. Some even followed the pair of loppers as the tool danced in the air through the maze, drawing closer and finally stopping.

At Lainey's desk.

M. Claremont peeked from behind the loppers. "Your watch, *mademoiselle*." His eyes flashed with seriousness, his lips in a straight line.

Lainey stuck out her hand in utter amazement. He slipped one curved tine under her faux leather straps and with a snip, cut it in two. It fell to her desk with a clank. On the back it said, Made in China.

The crowd whispered among themselves.

He held out his hand to the red velvet box. "Please oblige me by wearing the Swiss watch."

With her eyes rooted to him, she released the watch from the box. When she fumbled with the latch, she glanced down. In a swift movement, he dropped the loppers, trapping them between his knees, and bent to help her. His soft touch warmed her skin.

"Now you have an appropriate and functioning watch." He held her wrist for a split second longer than necessary. Tucking the loppers under his arm, he pivoted, strode through the parting crowd and disappeared behind the doors.

****

At the end of the day, the airline brought her bag. Lainey lugged it to the bathroom to slip on fresh undies, but all her lacy underwear was missing.

Before investigating further, Lainey jumped when her phone buzzed with a text from M. Claremont. "Meet me in my office. ASAP"

Dread grew from her shoulders to the base of her neck.

Inside his office, Marie Claire from Human Resources sat in a chair while he stood behind the desk. "Have a seat," he said in French.

She sat next to Marie Claire. Lainey gulped.

"You need a place to stay, yes?" M. Claremont stood surveying the stunning view of the Dents du Midi over Lake Geneva. The sun peeked over the mountains, leaving beams of sunlight streaming through the clouds.

"Yes."

"Marie Claire has volunteered to let you room with her."

She stole a glance at Marie Claire, and swore an oath in her heart to be the best roommate. But then, when was rooming with a co-worker ever a smart idea?

"You can move in this weekend." Marie Claire gave Lainey a scrap of paper with her address. 57 Avenue du Général-Guisan. Almost across the street.

Before leaving the office, she glanced back at M. Claremont to thank him, but he had already gone back to working at his desk.

Chapter Three

Updated notebook (*carnet*) recording all these events:

13. Lost luggage. Switched it back

14. Found some kinky unmentionables in Hector's luggage. He stole my underwear!

15. Drain backed up in sink. Found a coat hanger and fixed it.

16. Displayed my granny panties in front of my uptight Swiss boss.

17. Department store wouldn't take my card. Called bank and corrected misunderstanding.

...

36. Confused decimals with commas in the European number system and upset my boss. Did research into numbers.

37. Tripped on cobblestone walking to the bus stop in the dark. Skinned knee.

38. Found a mouse in my apartment. I didn't squeal. Or kill him. He's lived there longer than I have.

****

Saturday morning, Marie Claire escorted Lainey across the street to the apartment and up to the fourth floor. The two-room apartment barely looked lived in. The galley kitchen had no dishwasher. Under the counter, a dorm-sized fridge hummed. A small table with two chairs sat near a window.

In the kitchen, Marie Claire listed rules for trash, pointing to small bins. "Compost goes in a compost bin in the alleyway. For recycling, all boxes must be tied together with string, and cans separated from glass. If not, they will fine us for any and every infraction. And you absolutely must not forget to apply for your Permit M."

To work in the *canton de Vaud*, Lainey needed to apply for a working permit. She made a mental checklist of things to do on Monday.

Lainey's window opened to a splendid view of a train track. However, beyond the tracks, rows of tiered golden grape vines sliced the side of a hill, contrasting with the cerulean blue sky.

On the opposite side of the apartment, Marie Claire's window faced the lake and the rugged Alps obscured by the clouds. The weak sun stained the floor.

"Sorry, you don't have more than a mattress. We'll find more furniture for you some Tuesday. I only live here on the weekdays. On most weekends, I am with Jean in Thoiry, across the border in France. You'll have the whole apartment to yourself on weekends. Help yourself to anything in the fridge," she said from her room, dialing her phone. "There's the key to the *cave*. You can store big stuff. We'll go shopping when you finish unpacking."

After unpacking, which meant leaving her suitcase near her bed, Lainey wandered past Marie Claire's room, where she was yelling into the phone, and headed to the kitchen to scavenge for something to eat.

Blackberries, yogurt, endives, persimmons, thick slices of bread, butter *biscuits*, *palmiers*, raspberry jam, mayo in a tube. This was an epicurean lifestyle.

She glanced suspiciously at a box of milk in the fridge. While she lived in Switzerland, Lainey decided to eat like a European. No American cold cereal for breakfast.

Then she spied it. On the counter. A pastry still fresh from that morning wrapped in a piece of bakery paper.

Pain au chocolat.

Marie Claire did say to help herself to anything in the kitchen, right? Which meant she wasn't saving the pastry for anything. And why interrupt her important and loud conversation to ask about a measly pastry? Surely she wouldn't mind.

Lainey picked up the pastry. It was light and fluffy. It hardly weighed anything. The puff enveloped the chocolate like a hot dog in a corn coat. She bit into it. Mmmmmmmm. Flaky-buttery, choco-goodness. In a few bites, the whole thing was gone.

More air than pastry, really. To an epicurean, it was the quality not quantity that counted. Well, that was breakfast. She smacked her lips, satisfied. She should get ready.

She was about to leave the kitchen when her stomach rumbled. The only thing Europeans ate for breakfast was one measly pastry?

It wasn't going to last her all day. She searched for something to top her off.

From the mini-fridge, she found a vanilla yogurt. The berries were so temptingly fresh. She grabbed those, too. So cute in their diminutive plastic crate. She sprinkled a few into the yogurt. Now it needed a bit of crunch. She creaked open the cupboard. There sat a bag of muesli. What was muesli anyway? A bowl of granola cereal was pictured on the front. Granola. Healthy, right? Feeling so healthy and European, Lainey sprinkled some into her hand, tossing it into her mouth. Tastes burst on her buds. Oh, heavenly angels. She uncrinkled the bag, searching for the name of this food from the gods.

Chocolate Crock. With morsels of chocolate. Why didn't this exist in America? She gobbled another handful, picking up the fallen morsels to eat them. Then she filled her cup of yogurt.

She ate spoonfuls of Chocolate Crock, barely skimming the surface of the yogurt. She could eat this stuff for every meal. She ate each grain out of the vanilla yogurt and refilled the cup.

Why would anyone settle for plain cereal when this existed? Maybe she could set up some sort of trade alliance to import some. It would be a hit in America. Lainey could see the commercials now: Gotta have my Crock. Genius. She still had some yogurt left over. She refilled her cup.

What was in it anyway? She examined the back of the bag after she set it down. The ingredients listed oats—healthy. Sugar, well, sugar was not, but something had to make it tasty. Palm oil was the healthy oil, right? Puffed rice. In rice cakes. A totally a good-for-you food. Chocolate—mostly healthy. Her eyes wandered to the nutritional information. She nearly choked on her third helping of Chocolate Crock.

Twenty grams of fat for every hundred grams.

How much of this stuff did she eat? She stared into the bottom of her twice-filled yogurt cup which held almost two hundred grams. Ugh.

Eighty grams of fat!

Not including the pastry.

Her stomach ached with heaviness. What had she done?

A rash of foul French tumbled from Marie Claire's lips as a box dropped from her overladen arms. Lainey met her in the hall. Marie Claire finally hung up her phone. Kicking the box down the hall with great drama, Marie Claire headed toward the front door. She spoke French so rapidly, Lainey couldn't understand.

"Everything okay?"

Marie Claire tossed an overnight bag on top of the box. "Jean refuses to come to the gala in November."

"Gala?"

"The big event to mark promotions and bonuses."

Lainey followed her back to her room. She leaned on the door frame as Marie Claire gathered a pair of stylish boots.

"Everyone must dress up and bring a date, usually. They do it once a quarter, but this one is the formal one. Jean says he's not coming."

"Why not?"

"He's not a black-tie-type of person. Doesn't jive with the conservative Swiss." From her bureau she brought Lainey a framed photo of the two of them. Jean, with a nose ring, draped an arm over the top of her shoulders. His sleeveless shirt showed off a tattoo on his shoulder, barely visible on his dark skin. Huge earrings overtaking his earlobe. His jeans were all ripped up.

Yeah, he might feel out of place.

"Is he French?"

"Algerian."

"Ah," Lainey said, handing back the picture, and

Marie Claire returned it to the bureau. "Do I get to go?"

"You work for Alpine Foods, *n'est-ce pas*?"

"Yes."

"Then you must go." She headed for the kitchen, pinning her unruly hair up in a clip she found on the dresser.

Lainey followed her. "But I won't have a date for the gala."

"Don't worry about it. It's not until November. Maybe you have a boyfriend back home. He can fly out?"

"Aaron and I broke up."

"Perhaps we both need to do some convincing." She gave Lainey an arched eyebrow then glanced around the kitchen. "Hey, where is my pastry?"

****

A fall breeze swept across the valley capturing moisture from the lake. Coming from the desert, any temperature below seventy degrees gave Lainey the chills.

The marketplace buzzed with action. A stand of flowers, assembled in buckets, made a wall of color. At another booth, Marie Claire circled the stands, plucking apples and pears off pyramids of carefully stacked fruit huddled under the shade of an awning. She exchanged coins with the aproned grocers who bagged and knotted the fruit together.

One of the men, seeing Lainey's hesitancy, handed her a pear to taste. At first bite, it gushed on her face. She wiped the juice from her chin with her sleeve. Never had she eaten anything so deliciously ripe.

But Marie Claire grabbed her and tugged her on to the store.

"Thank you for letting me stay with you." Lainey kept pace with her toward *centre-ville*. Cars zoomed by, dangerously close with the metallic smell of exhaust.

"Don't thank me. Thank Yves."

"Oh?"

"He asked me if you could stay with me."

Lainey chewed on the bit of information.

At a crosswalk, Marie Claire's scarf fluttered in the wind. She glanced around the intersection, not waiting for the light. She stepped out into the street. Lainey followed. Everyone else waited for the signal.

"Will he recommend me to Chocolate?"

Marie Claire was halfway across the road. "Don't be disappointed about Pet Care. You are lucky to be working for Yves. His department is one of the top producing at Alpine Foods. In fact, they are hoping to sign a deal with a Japanese distributer by the end of the year. If he succeeds, he'll be in line for another promotion. If so, he will be the youngest Vice President Alpine Foods has ever promoted."

"How old is he?"

"Twenty-eight."

Only five years older than Lainey. She'd love to be Vice President of Chocolate in five years.

They entered a grocery store with a giant M on it. "You know a lot about people."

"Know?" From her coin purse she grabbed a Swiss franc and slid it into a slider chaining two orange carts together, releasing a pin connecting them. She yanked them apart with a clash of metal. "I work in the Human Resource department. We know all the dirt on everyone."

Sounded juicy. "Oh, do tell."

She peered at Lainey from the corner of her eye. “I could get into trouble, you know.”

Lainey shrugged. It was the same in the US. The HR department had access to a lot of private information. Marie Claire probably signed a gag order of sorts.

“It’s only gossip. But you are my roommate. And an intern, not an official employee of Alpine Foods.”

Not yet, anyway. Someday in Chocolate, she hoped.

Marie Claire bit her lip. “But only if you promise not to tell a single soul. Or I terminate you. Like this.” She knifed her finger across her neck. Lainey wasn’t sure if she meant figuratively or literally.

Lainey nodded. Speaking might convince Marie Claire to change her mind. She was proving she could keep her mouth shut.

“Okay.” Marie Claire squinted out across the store, heading for produce. “In your department, one of the marketing directors who had come up for a promotion was found sleeping with an intern. Monsieur le President found out and fired them both. On the spot. Careers ruined. Both disgraced.”

Lainey gulped. “Got it. No workplace romances.”

“I didn’t say no romances.” She gave Lainey a meaningful stare as she maneuvered around the cookie aisle. “Just don’t get caught.”

Once in the produce department, Marie Claire stacked lettuce heads and carrots in the cart. No bag, just straight on the metal. “Most people date people outside of work. Luc’s girlfriend is a piece of work. I met her at the company picnic a few weeks ago. Artificial hair, teeth, nails, boobs. There wasn’t a limb or a feature not messed with." A shudder filtered through her shoulders as she snatched pots of *crème fraîche*, depositing them in the cart.

Lainey struggled to imagine anyone with Luc. He had sleaze written all over him.

Marie Claire grabbed a wheel of Camembert in a wooden crate. "As for the others, I've never seen Gui with anyone steady—a new girlfriend every six months or so. Britta, of course, has a sweetheart she sees in Berne, some stiff Swiss-German who only bends to sit down." Cups of pear and apple *compôt* went in the cart. "But—" she lowered her voice to a whisper—"her kids are really messed up. One daughter has several children, and they don't know where she is or who the father is. The poor children, two girls and a boy, live with her, and she supports them. Sad, really."

Lainey followed her to the cereal aisle. She was tempted to grab another bag of Chocolate Crock since theirs was almost empty. Instead, she grabbed some healthy-looking wheaty bricks.

"Then there's Yves."

For some reason, when she mentioned his name, Lainey's heart leapt. Too warm to be comfortable, she removed her sweater and draped it over the cart, listening intently.

"He brings different girls to things. He brought Hiroko Takeda to the company picnic."

"Who?"

"The daughter of Atatakai International's CEO. She is also their acquiring specialist. I think they are dating."

"Oh."

"It's hard to tell if Yves is courting her or her

company." There was a flash of metal when she stuck out her tongue—a stud she only wore on weekends. "But let me tell you this, *mon amie*: Never marry a Swiss man." She pressed forward to the juice aisle, stacking a box each of pear, nectarine, and apricot juices in the cart.

Lainey hurried to keep up. "What?" She didn't catch what Marie Claire said.

"Never marry a Swiss man. Look around."

Lainey glanced around the store, then realized Marie Claire didn't mean literally.

"You see all these exotic women from Thailand, Peru, Taiwan. Swiss men find them on their exotic travels and, after they marry, whisk them away from their homes. They come here and they are miserable, I tell you, and homesick. This is a cold country, *mon cœur*. And I'm not talking about the weather. There are many lonely, lonely women."

"Maybe they will live in Japan?"

"I doubt it." Around the corner was the meat section. "I doubt he would leave. His mother still lives here. She's American, *tu vois*. But she stays for Yves. They are close, I hear, since her husband died. But I tell you, never, ever marry a Swiss man or you'll be stuck here for the rest of your life."

Lainey didn't think Switzerland was such an awful place. So far it was scenic, sunny, and clean. Really clean. Chilly maybe.

"And," Marie Claire continued, picking up some bone-in chicken, "Swiss don't have a sense of humor. I've never seen any of them so much as crack a smile."

Interesting. Lainey had seen M. Claremont smile, at least a half-smile, at her. She didn't mention it. Marie

Claire enjoyed her opinions.

"So, Lainey, you are the only one I don't know about. Tell me more about your boyfriend, Aaron, is it?"

"I—" she began. Hadn't she told her they had broken up? Why did Marie Claire still think they were together?

"First, tell me where you met."

Aaron was her least favorite topic right now. The painful incident at the going-away party had ruined their relationship forever. He was such a different person than the guy she'd met in the co-ed dormitory bathroom her junior year. "You see, I had washed my face, water dripping from my eyes. At the next sink, he watched me feeling around for my forgotten towel and let me borrow his. It was such an intimate gesture for a stranger. I was struck by his thoughtfulness, his awareness of my needs." They dated until two weeks before she left, when he said this was the perfect opportunity to "take a break" from each other, a codeword for a break up. Then the going-away party sealed the deal. They still hadn't talked about it. What defined "taking a break?" Breaking her heart?

Lainey was about to explain more when they arrived at the last aisle.

Her heart pattered against her rib cage.

A whole aisle dedicated to chocolate.

Even with their wrappers on, the chocolate smelled delicious. First were the plaques. Various wrappers stretched out along the aisle, as colorful as a rainbow. Rows upon rows of 100g plaques of chocolate. Farther on were blue boxes of shaped chocolates, chocolate bars with nuts, powders, candies, sticks. Lainey loved living in a country where they believed chocolate was good for you. Nay, a food group essential for life!

Reverently, as if entering a sacred shrine, Lainey gaped for several minutes before even touching a bar. It was so beautiful, she almost cried.

Marie Claire nodded with understanding and waited at the edge of the aisle as Lainey paid homage at this holiest of altars. Lainey grabbed a small basket at the end cap. Now the dilemma, which ones?

She had to buy several bars for her to eat, for snacks, to eat at work, for breakfast. A *pain au chocolat* minus the pastry. She needed to sample one of each, just to see which one tasted the best. When in Switzerland, eat like the Swiss. They ate at least two pounds a month. She converted kilograms to pounds and decided just to round to four hundred grams to a pound.

Oh, and then she needed to buy some for Nadine. She'd be mad if she came all the way out here and didn't bring her home any chocolate. Lainey had forgiven her. Everything would end well.

She chose a variety pack of five: two milk, two hazelnut and a dark chocolate, wrapped together in plastic.

Her parents, of course, needed some. A box, perhaps. She moved down to the boxes. They were considerably more expensive, though they had truffles, sea shapes, milk mixed with white chocolate, fillings of pralines, caramel, ganache, liqueur. After comparing price to weight, she went back to the bars. Her dad only ate white chocolate. Easy. A few bars of white, some with almonds, some with hazelnuts, some with peppermint. Her mom loved nuts. She grabbed a few varieties for her.

Aaron didn't deserve any chocolate.

For herself? She stood back to take it all in. What should she choose? Dark? Extra milk? With mint? Orange? Hazel nuts? Almonds? Pralines? Citrus and pepper? Pear? Raspberry? Blueberry? With or without crispy rice? Bits of cookie? Malted? Her mom would enjoy those. She grabbed her a couple. She giggled with delight. This was too much fun. Her basket weighed so much, it left a red mark on her forearm.

When they checked out, Marie Claire's food passed on the belt. When it was Lainey's turn, she had nearly forty plaques of chocolate. The middle-aged cashier didn't even blink an eye. Luckily, Lainey's paycheck was going to be big.

****

Before bed, she tallied her daily score of how many bad things happened to her.

46. Twenty CHF blew away in the wind

47. Knocked over some lady's cart. Don't ask how it happened

48. Burned myself making the pasta for dinner while separating the pasta from the water without a colander.

Chapter Four

02-10-19 22:36 (GMT +2)

Chocophile: You there, Nadine? It costs money to use the Internet here at the cafe. Can you believe I don't have Internet access at work? I guess it's because they found people were more productive if they didn't access the Internet.

Nadine: Lainey! How are you doing??! How's your internship???!

Chocophile: Great, I have a sadistic boss who's a total control freak. He doesn't like me, and I don't like him, even if he is hot.

Nadine: He's hot, huh?

Chocophile: Yes, but not in a good way. Like "I'm too hot to even look sideways at you."

Nadine: And it bothers you?

Chocophile: I thought we were talking about my internship.

Nadine: Oh, yes! Tell me all about it.

Chocophile: Mostly I've been doing data entry. It's like my boss doesn't trust me with anything important. He hovers over me whenever I do something.

Nadine: Maybe you need to be worthy of his trust.

Chocophile: Thanks, Nadine.

Nadine: What's your plan to get to Chocolate from here?

Chocophile: Work hard. Get the Devil a.k.a. M.

Claremont to write me a good recommendation, if he doesn't fire me first.

Nadine: He won't fire you! You are the hardest worker, the smartest person I know, Lainey.

Chocophile: Wanna fly here and tell my boss? He thinks I'm a dolt. He's the most exacting, punctilious, anal-retentive person I know. He has to have control over every little detail.

Nadine: Sounds like someone else I know. *Cough* (Lainey Peterson)

Chochophile: Ha, ha, Nadine.

Nadine: All I'm saying is you guys sound perfect for each other.

Chocophile: Uh, he's my boss! You can't be interested in your boss.

Nadine: Didn't you say he was hot?

Chocophile: Yeah, but devoid of all humor and straitlaced is not attractive to me.

Nadine: Ooooookaaaaaay, if you say so.

Chocophile: Tell me more about your wedding plans. How did Martin ask you to marry him?

Nadine: OH LAINEY! At Comic-con! At his "Ironitron"—you remember the game he invented right?—booth, the Ironitron had "Will you marry me, Nadine" flashing on its letter board.

Chocophile: How romantic. *Eye roll* Martin is such a nerd. Have you set a date?

Nadine: We're still discussing it.

Chocophile: I'll get home the first week of December. I'll then be able to perform my maid-of-honor duties. I am your maid of honor, aren't I?

Nadine: Of course!!!

Chocophile: If I'm not too beat up from this stupid

internship. If my boss doesn't kill me! Or as long as I don't kill him! I could just strangle him with his own designer tie.

Nadine: You want to strangle your hot boss? Sounds suspicious.

Chocophile: What? Why?

Nadine: It's not love unless you want to kill him.

Chocophile: That's the most ridiculous thing anyone has ever said.

Nadine: You keep bringing him up.

Nadine: Lainey, are you still there?

Nadine: It says typing and then it stops, then typing again.

Chocophile: He's a power freak!!! He's demanding!!! I do NOT like him!!!!

Do not, not, not, not like him!!!

Nadine: Martin says the even number of "not" cancels each other out. You like him.

Chocophile: Gah! Fine! I hate him!

Nadine: Don't say hate, Lainey. It's an awfully strong word.

Chocophile: You're right. I shouldn't use hate, if there was a word stronger than hate, I'd use it! I am not in any way, shape, or form attracted to M. Claremont. He thinks I'm a klutz sent to ruin his career! We are as opposite as, as white and dark chocolate.

Nadine: But they go well together. And you keep saying how hot he is.

Chocophile: NADINE! You'll not bring it up again!!!

Nadine: Okay, okay. Geez, it just sounds suspiciously like you're trying not to like him.

Chocophile: ANYWAY! He has a girlfriend.

Nadine: Ah, see, the fact you know he has a girlfriend—you like him, you like him!

Chocophile: I'm ignoring your last comment. I have to go. Let me know what I can do to be the best maid of honor ever! I can organize the dinner, help with the decor. Oooh! I'll make specialized chocolate truffles with gilded initials, wouldn't you love them? Maybe make one with a Star Trek logo on it for Martin.

Nadine: Tee-hee. He'd love it. :)

Chocophile: I've got your back, I am your woman. This is what I do best. TTYL

Nadine: Thanks, hey, enjoy your internship. I'm sure things will get better.

Chocophile: Let's hope so.

Nadine: :) hugs :) hugs :) hugs :)

Chocophile: Thanks.

****

Lainey entered the cubicle room, leaving the brisk fall air of October outside the windows. Sabine piled a small Washington Monument of folders on her desk. With no explanation. A smirk parted her lips as she left. She might actually derive pleasure from the one-two punch of leaving Lainey with an obelisk of work without any directions.

Flipping back a folder, Lainey inhaled deeply, diving in, trying to figure out what was required. Luckily, she had a minor in Mind Reading and Divination. She scanned a few pages on a new line of dog treats. They wanted her to review these product details and distill them into marketing-speak.

Ha, ha! She rubbed her hands together, suppressing a giggle of glee. With a degree in English, she was prepared for this. She could finally shine. Even if the content was less than interesting. And translating it into French might slow her down, but she was up to the task.

By ten o'clock, she was smoking. She had reviewed three products, written three brochure mock-ups and sent them via email to Sabine for M. Claremont to review. She unwrapped a small corner of an Alpine Foods Milk Chocolate with hazelnuts from her stash and slipped a square into her mouth. She was on fire!

At precisely ten-o-five, by Lainey's Swiss timepiece, Sabine, in her pencil-line skirt and polka-dotted shirt, approached her with the three printed papers in hand.

"M. Claremont says he is not satisfied." She slapped them on the desk and left, the back of her skirt flapping like a doggy door.

"Did he say what I should fix?" Lainey called after her. Of course, there was no reply. Then she glanced down. The top of the first one had "*Trop long*" written across it.

Too long?

She faced the word processor. The first product was Treat Spheres, an organic ball-shaped dog treat. As the dog retrieved the ball, bits of treat would fall into its mouth to encourage games and exercise. She reviewed the product specifications, wondering what she could cut. Iron content, fiber content. She examined the competitors' similar products, compared prices and condensed.

The second was a vitamin water for dogs, called Doggie Delish. M. Claremont had written, "*Pas assez précis.*"

Not specific enough?

She studied the material Sabine left on her desk. There wasn't much to work with. It was water. It had vitamins. What more could she say? She threw her hands into the air. What was she doing? She didn't own pets. In the end, she revamped it with a sales pitch, saying it was the perfect vitamin supplement delivery system.

Next one, Canine Canines, a bone treat/toothbrush. "*Sec comme un os*."

Dry as a bone?

Was this a joke?

Marie Claire said the Swiss didn't have a sense of humor. What was she supposed to write? Eat these treats, and you will never have to floss and rinse? She pepped up her writing and emailed them to Sabine.

When Lainey returned from lunch, her three papers sat on her desk with a huge, "*Non*!" written on two of them. The last one had, "You can do better." The English was a slap in the face.

What did he want?

Yanking open the one and only drawer, she ripped open another bar, stuffing squares of chocolate in her mouth between growls at her boss. She scowled at her computer. Not only did she have to work with dog food instead of chocolate, she had to work for someone who expected her to be a mind reader. Fine.

She opened her email client, found M. Claremont's email address and typed him this:

De: Elaine Peterson@alpinefoods.ch

Á: Yves Claremont@alpinefoods.ch

Sujet: Further enlightenment.

M. Claremont,

I need specific feedback if you are to reject my

product reviews. To write something meeting your meticulous standards, I need further enlightenment.

Elaine Peterson

No sooner had she sent the email than she regretted it. Surely, she would figure it out in a few hundred more drafts.

Within a few minutes, her cell phone buzzed, moving sideways across a stack of manilla folders. A text from Sabine. "M. Claremont wants to see you in his office. Now."

Even in French it sounded harsh.

There was something intimidating about M. Claremont. Not his charisma or his self-confidence. There were plenty of men who had both of those qualities who didn't make Lainey shake. His eyes caught every detail, every move, every emotion. When she entered his office, she felt as transparent as the wall of windows behind him.

"Please sit down, Mademoiselle Peterson." A cufflink clicked on the desk as he folded his hands in front of him, interlocking his fingers.

She sat. He was motionless. Only staring at Lainey. His gaze bore into her soul, unearthing every thought about him. She blushed.

"Mademoiselle," he said. "Why did you choose to intern for Alpine Foods?"

The question caught her off guard. Weren't they talking about pet food product reviews? And hadn't she answered the question in the interview?

Under the weight of his deep, penetrating gaze, Lainey stammered. She wanted to glance away, but she couldn't. When other people asked her, *Why Alpine Foods in Switzerland? Why not stay in the States?* she had said, "The Swiss eat two pounds of chocolate a month. Where else would I want to go?" Which was the truth. But she had a feeling he didn't want a flippant answer about the Swiss diet. Lainey would never please M. Claremont enough for him to recommend her to Chocolate.

"Alpine Foods is the top producer of chocolate in the world. I only wanted to work for the best."

He rose suddenly from his desk to face the window, his back to Lainey, gazing out to the afternoon sun sitting over the Dents du Midi, sunshine filling the Swiss Plateau. "The moment you told me about each individual you helped in your non-profit, I wanted you in our department." He spoke this one compliment over his shoulder to her. A compliment from *him*?

He focused again on the scenery. His dark hair settled perfectly on the back of his head. Even from the back, he radiated confidence. He stalked back to the desk, staring at Lainey directly, anger flashing in his eyes. "I thought someone with your care and passion would give me something better than this."

Ouch!

Her heart burned to her face. She wanted to lower her eyes, but she continued staring straight ahead.

From his desk he retrieved copies of her reviews. He shuffled through them and slapped them on his desk, causing a flutter of other documents.

Her voice cracked with shame. Her face smoldered in embarrassed heat. "I don't understand."

"Let me tell you about the importance of the Pet Care Department. In Switzerland, one in every four people is a pet owner. Those people have needs. And we, in the Pet Care Department, must meet those needs.

For some of our aged customers, their pets are the only pleasure of company they have, to whom they are number one." He emphasized his last point with a finger. The pointer, thankfully. "We need to show them we care for their pets as much as they do. We are not casting for customers. We are helping people." He paused, picking up her papers. "This is selling. We need to be helping." He searched deep into her soul. "It needs to come from our heart, not our bottom line. See it the same way you saw Homemade Meals and you will succeed. You can do this, Mademoiselle Peterson. I know it is within you. Now, go. Please me."

Embarrassed, humbled yet encouraged, she slinked out the door. Those words, *please me*, echoed in her ears, inspiring her.

Back at her desk, she cleared the other folders to the ground under her chair. She considered what M. Claremont said. He was right. She hadn't given her heart. She deleted everything. From her drawer she removed an Alpine Bar, white chocolate-*cassis*. She broke off a corner, letting the blackcurrant flavor smother her tongue as she revamped her work.

Starting fresh, she pictured the elderly ladies and men with their pets. How could this product help them? She meditated, slowly devouring the bar.

At last, she wrote a short essay for all three products in French. She searched words on the English-French dictionary she found shelved amongst other dictionaries of every language imaginable, laboriously searching for the perfect, succinct word to describe the details. She emailed them to Sabine and M. Claremont.

M. Claremont replied, "Perfect. Now I need these in German, Italian and English."

"What?" she said aloud in English when she received the email. Was he crazy? She slapped down the lid of her laptop and stalked around the room to stretch her legs. Did he think she was a linguist? She decided to march right down to his office and tell him he asked the impossible.

Halfway to his office she stopped, her anger spent. She had finished many other difficult tasks. She'd earned a scholarship to one of the most prestigious universities in the United States. She never backed down from the impossible. She would show him she merited her degree. Of course, she succeeded by never giving up a challenge.

She would do the translations. Britta could help her on the German one, so she started with the Italian.

She spied an Italian/French dictionary in the bookcase underneath the window. This would be helpful, since there was no Internet access. She lugged the book over to her desk and searched for the first word. The grammar should be similar since they were both romance languages, right?

With a snap, she broke off another piece of chocolate, opened a new document, flipped through the pages of the dictionary, searching for "canine." This was going to take all night.

Near six p.m., she finished the first bar and reached for another. The other employees left for home and family and the lights dimmed. Several entries in the dictionary for certain words had multiple meanings. Neither tongue was her native language. She flipped, searched, wrote, ate.

Around nine, she took a break to stretch. She was creeped out to be alone in this big empty building.

What if something happened? In the stillness, noises echoed in the hall. She was not alone. Lainey, curious, approached the doors, the voices growing louder.

Lainey peeked through the doors. Gui and Luc passed through the hall.

"Stop worrying," Luc said, his back to her. She smelled cigarette smoke. Had they been smoking? "Yves will get his. Come on."

Nearing midnight, she was halfway through the translation, flipping and searching, not really sure if her translation was correct. She couldn't find *scrumptious.* It should have been, right after…Oh wait, she was in the Italian side, not French. She threw the book across the room, wishing to hit M. Claremont's head instead of the cubicle wall.

She wouldn't let him break her. She had tough professors at Stanford who demanded thirty-page theses on metaphors. Tonight, she only had to translate a simple essay into Italian.

She retrieved the book and continued. Powered by chocolate and adrenaline, she pored over the dictionary, searching for words and usage, reading over her paragraph, hoping it made sense.

By sunrise, she was sweating chocolate. The lights flickered on, and she finished the last sentence of the last essay. Her neck ached from bending over the dictionary all night. Noises stirred in the building. Her eyes drooped.

****

At eight a.m., the door opened to the cubicle area. She awoke with wrappers stuck to her face. M. Claremont, with his calfskin briefcase, stalked in and stood before her.

Lainey struggled to lift her eyes to him after the terrible things she thought about him all night, in case he had power to read her soul. How she wanted to cut off every extraneous appendage and throw it in the lake. Sleepiness clouded her eyes. And her brain. Bits of chocolate were smeared in her wild hair, since she spent the last four hours pulling it out.

His eyes widened. "What are you doing?"

"Translating your reviews." She didn't mean to sound so bitter. She hadn't really slept all night but she was fluent in Italian—that was the chocolate speaking. Finally, she lifted her gaze to his, just to emphasize the grandeur of what he had asked of her.

He carefully examined her desk with twelve empty chocolate wrappers. He scrutinized her hair, unkempt and greasy. At last, his gaze landed on the Italian dictionary, well-thumbed and used, even smeary with chocolate. "You've been here all night translating your reviews with a dictionary?"

She snorted. What a jerk to ask. Even ruder to suppress a smile. "What else was I supposed to do? I didn't know Italian."

Gracefully, he slid beside her—how did he smell so divine?—and with the tap of the mouse, opened an application labeled STS. He copied her original French document and pasted it in there, scrolling over a drop-down menu bar in alphabetical listing of languages. "Italian" right above "Japanese."

In a few seconds, the French she'd spent all night translating magically transformed into Italian.

"Didn't Sabine train you on the Simple Translation Software?" He opened the new tab and translated the same paragraphs into German.

This was wrong on so many levels.

All the work, the whole night, wasted. All the evil, horrible, awful things she thought about M. Claremont while she translated—all wrong.

She flipped back to her original translated document, glaring from her screen to her paper, comparing translations. They were almost exact. Back and forth she glanced.

"Ha! This word, I looked this up. It's actually better translated as *sostenere* not *nutrire*."

M. Claremont blinked, his lips a wavering line. "Go home, Mademoiselle Peterson. You've worked hard enough for today. Go home and get some sleep. Tomorrow you can finish the rest in STS. Sabine will show you how to use it."

She stood, crumpled her chocolate wrappers into a ball and shuffled down the hall. Somewhere in her sleep-deprived, addled brain she noted his amused expression contained a hint of admiration.

****

Yves' gaze followed her as she parted the coming crowd of workers, then he let out a raw chuckle. There were still globs of chocolate on the desk. He removed his hanky from his suit pocket and wiped it off, folding it over a few times until the desk shone. He couldn't help but smile. He had never seen such dedication in a subordinate. An admirable quality. Perhaps his lecture yesterday inspired her.

Still. He sighed, opening the door. Something must be done about Sabine. Sadly, he couldn't terminate her, as she was a protegé of M. le President. He might've underestimated her jealousy.

Yves stopped short, surprised at his word choice.

Sabine wasn't jealous. How could she be? She was careless. And perhaps resentful.

Yves unlocked the door to his office, and set down his briefcase near the coat stand, where he removed his coat. At his desk he opened his laptop, smiling again at the thought of Lainey, her red eyes and frazzled hair. Her innocent translation of the reviews by hand. This was an incident he needed to write to his mother. She needed a good laugh.

But he couldn't use Lainey's real name, even in his private emails. It would never do to link his name with hers. It was just an amusing story. Something to cheer up his mother.

While he was typing his email, Luc tapped on his door.

Yves glanced up, setting the lid down on his email.

"Yes?"

"I was wondering if I could borrow your car tonight." Luc swept back his hair. A cloud of cigarette smoke followed him.

Yves cringed at the thought of him driving his Maserati. He loved the finely tuned V8. He bought Italian shoes, suits, and cars. Because Italians made the best.

"What do you need it for?"

"I have a date with this new girl, and I hope to impress her."

Yves would rather he carried turnips. "I am sorry, but I will be working late tonight." He opened his laptop and began writing down the latest sales reports.

"No other excuse?" Luc slapped the wall. "You need a life, man."

Yves glanced up at him. "And what do you expect

me to do, waste it as you do?”

“You think you’re better than me?”

“No. I know I am.”

“Not for long.” And Luc disappeared around the corner. “Not for long.”

Chapter Five

"Wake up! You can't sleep the whole day." Marie Claire pounced on Lainey's bed, jarring her awake.

"I'm never working late again." Stiff and groggy, her body ached when she moved. "What time is it?"

Marie Claire shook her again. "It's five p.m. Where have you been? You didn't come home last night."

Lainey explained to her what happened and instead of laughing, Marie Claire's eyebrows peaked with sympathy. Her long curly hair forming a halo of an angel of mercy.

Marie Claire's nose ring shone. The draping sleeves of her gold top passed over Lainey's forehead as she stroked her hair. She had told Lainey she could borrow anything from her closet, but Lainey couldn't imagine wearing anything of hers. The Euro-Gypsy style was too bold for her.

"*Ma pauvre*," Marie Claire cooed, stroking her hair.

Lainey extracted herself out of bed and stumbled to the bathroom. Marie Claire followed her in.

"The *soldes* are tonight. I thought we'd go shopping for dresses while they're on sale."

"*Soldes*?"

"You know, when everything is cheaper than the tag price."

Clearance sales. She perked up. Shopping might

cure her. "Let's go." Lainey brushed her extremely fuzzy teeth.

"Then we'll search for some furniture for your room."

Even better. She finished brushing. Her toothpaste spittle was almost completely brown from the chocolate. With some persuasion, her body moved again. She gathered clothes from her bin to take a shower.

"And maybe some new clothes." She cast Lainey's clothes a sideways glance as if seeing at them full-on would hurt her eyes.

"What's wrong with my wardrobe?" Lainey stared at the ensemble she picked out, paranoid.

"And we'll do something about your hair and *oh, là, là*! those eyebrows."

Frowning, Lainey tucked a bundled shirt under her arm. "Now you're getting personal."

****

Lainey followed Marie Claire through the Boutique Soirée as she flipped through formals on a rack filled with vibrant taffetas sprinkled with rhinestones and sequins.

After grabbing a quick bite, they'd hopped a train and coursed along plunging grape-vined hills to Lausanne. Marie Claire dragged Lainey up the steep cobblestone hills to find a dress. Historic buildings with red tiled roofs lined the streets. On every street corner loomed a dominating cathedral.

Lainey oohed and awed at the showcased clothing and jewelry in the windows. Marie Claire tugged her away from fabulously displayed *vitrines* luring customers into their shops. Lainey soaked it in, from the yeasty aroma of fresh bread from the *boulangerie* to the clanging sound of street bands.

If chocolate was Lainey's first love, shopping was her second. In the dress shop, Lainey gaped at the *soldes*. Prices were slashed all over the store. And lots of inventory. She grabbed a tag and did some calculations. These items were a steal. She snagged colorful silk scarfs for Nadine and a wide-brimmed hat for her mom. Gloves for winter, hosiery, shoes. A whole basket was brim full with accessories, jewelry, underwear, and they hadn't even started on the dresses.

Biting her lip, Lainey searched for dresses of a particular style. No backless gowns. Her shoulders must be covered.

Marie Claire spotted a dress with tulle netting gathered around a split in the skirt and held it out to check the tag.

After rehanging the dress saying it was not her size, she snagged a ruby red dress with golden glints. Marie Claire showed Lainey. "The red would go great with your dark hair and your figure."

Since it met her standards, Lainey separated it from the others and hung it over her forearm. The red dress reminded her of the velvet box. "M. Claremont gave me a watch."

Marie Claire didn't stop searching, her eyes intently focused on the dresses she raked across the rack. "What kind?"

"Something costing about 200 CHF."

"Men who make over half a million Swiss francs a year, as does Yves Claremont, would never notice two hundred missing from his wallet. It meant nothing."

Lainey burned inside. Her cheeks flamed.

"If he really wanted to attract your attention, he'd give you designer watches, costing thousands of Swiss francs. He gave one to Hiroko."

"Ah." Lainey's lungs tightened.

From the rack, Marie Claire removed a turquoise sheath and tossed it over her shoulder, shrugging. Lainey found another dress her size with her particular requirements. She was slightly too tall and too bulky for these styles. They headed to the fitting rooms.

Lainey entered the stall, mulling over Marie Claire's reveal. "So, he's with Hiroko?"

Marie Claire entered the next stall, chatting through the divider. "They spend a lot of time together on the merger."

"For business or pleasure?"

Lainey wasn't sure if Marie Claire responded or not because she caught a view of herself in the mirror. She was too tall for the dress. Her legs showed far too much thigh to be attractive. She tugged the tiered skirt down, covering more of that unsightly region. She awaited Marie Claire's opinion. "What do you think?"

"I think they are together. She's refined and wealthy. They are a perfect couple."

"I meant about the dress."

Marie Claire's head split the curtain, and she flashed a smile of approval.

Satisfied, but weirdly disappointed, Lainey returned to her stall to change, pleased with her choice. Fully dressed, she emerged, her dress over her arm.

Marie Claire was in the common area, preening in front of the mirror. "What do you think?" she asked, twirling in a tight-fitting dress.

Lainey responded thoughtfully. "I think M.

Claremont shouldn't mix business with dating."

"I agree." Marie Claire eyed her from the corner of her eye. "But I meant about the dress."

"Oh." She flushed and observed what Marie Claire was wearing. It was the first dress she picked out, the tulle eddying around her legs like sea foam. "It looks great."

Everything flattered her. A spiny, green sprig of jealousy sprung within her over Marie Claire's slim, trim figure, her perfect height.

With their dresses over their shoulders, they attacked the rest of the store. A hot pink cashmere sweater, gray fitted pants, and black flats joined Lainey's collection. Then two more fitted shirts, cropped pants, boots, and several scarves as well. Marie Claire piled outfits on Lainey as if she was her own personal dresser. Lainey tried not to think of her credit card balance.

"From now on, no sneakers in public," Marie Claire said. "And no denim. Not even on your day off. You look like a tourist."

While the sun set, drawing up a chilly wind, Lainey carried the bags out the door, following Marie Claire, who quickened her pace to a stylist next door. "Now your hair," she said.

The stylist had short cropped hair with each clump dyed a different color: magenta, bleached, blue, and orange.

"Keep it long, nothing drastic," Lainey said to Marie Claire.

Surely there would be some misunderstanding, and her haircut would turn out horrible.

The scrape of metal on metal, snipping hair,

echoed in her ears as the beautician blocked Lainey's view of the mirror. The tugs and cuts lasted forever, far longer than a trim should have taken. Long strands of hair covered the floor underneath her feet.

When the beautician finished, she stood back, allowing Lainey to view her reflection for the first time.

No way.

It was actually cute.

To admire herself, Lainey lifted her chin in every direction, the energy bursting through her short locks. Cautiously, she grasped the blunted ends.

"You like?"

"I love it!"

After they embraced, Marie Claire declared eyebrows and legs were next. "Upkeep," Marie Claire said, hauling Lainey into another room where molten wax bubbled lavender scent into the air. "Being a woman is all about upkeep."

****

By Lainey's watch, it was nine o'clock when they returned to the apartment. Lainey figured they had missed their opportunity for furniture. All the shops in Vevey closed before eight p.m. Instead, she'd bought new clothes, new shoes, got a new haircut and was waxed smooth as plastic. She couldn't be disappointed about not buying furniture, too.

Marie Claire unlocked the apartment door. "We'll drop off your purchases and head out to search for furniture, if you're up to it."

"Tonight? Sure. Where?"

"You'll see."

After locking up, they stepped into the night air. A scarf really did keep a neck warmer, Lainey discovered.

Marie Claire continued down Avenue du Général-Guisan instead of waiting at a bus stop. In the faint glow of the street lamps, people huddled together wearing coats against the wind. Five or six men crossed the street and a few women congregated around in an indistinct group.

"What is this?"

"Every other Tuesday, people throw stuff in a pile for anybody to have."

And they didn't get fined? What kind of a crazy country was this? Finally, the pile came into view. Lainey eyed earmuffs, a boom box, and a baby bouncer on the edge of a massive pile of discarded household items.

"Man, this stuff is in perfect condition." Lainey touched a toaster, wondering if Marie Claire had hauled her mattress from the side of the road.

Underneath pots and pans, clothing, bicycles, nightstands, land telephones, hangers, footstools, irons, and other small appliances and junk, Lainey spied something, something she wanted, something she needed to extract out of this junk pile and drag home. A microwave.

"Oh, Marie Claire, can we keep it?" She set the appliance on a coffee machine and opened the door, inspecting it. It was spotless.

"What do you want a microwave for?"

Oh. So many things. Microwaving quesadillas was quicker than using the stovetop. Reheating leftovers in a minute instead of heating up the oven. A microwave was easier than a double boiler for melting chocolate. But to convince her, Lainey said: "It's easier than boiling water to make tea. Just put it in, press a minute.

Voilà, tea!"

"Fine, but you have to carry it."

Lainey nodded, hugging the small appliance to her chest.

Marie Claire extricated a nightstand with a small drawer. The knob was missing, but it could be easily replaced.

The best treasures were getting picked clean by others who swiped armfuls of finds. This was the Swiss adaptation of a yard sale. But it was all free. Lainey giggled with delight.

Marie Claire kicked away a fallen sweater. "Doesn't have what we want. Let's move on."

Lainey wasn't sure exactly what they were searching for, but she agreed and, loaded with her microwave, not daring to part with it, continued down the street.

Apartments lined the streets and about another six complexes or so was another pile.

Marie Claire found a poster of a boy band that was popular five years ago in the US. She tucked it under her arm, motioning to move on.

At the third pile, Lainey's arms ached, and she sat down on top of her microwave, claiming it, as she sifted through stuff.

At the end of the street, there were fewer people crowded around a pile still containing serviceable discards. Marie Claire picked up a small chest of drawers and a towel rack, since Lainey hung hers on a door knob to dry and it constantly smelled funny.

At the last pile, Lainey danced up and down, daring to leave the microwave for a second to inspect something she found. It was hers. No one else had claimed it.

An oyster microsuede recliner with pillow-top arms and tufted back, identical to the one her dad had, sat at the far end of the pile. A surge of homesickness overpowered Lainey. She could almost smell the vanilla scent her mom used to deodorize her dad's fish-frying quirk. Tears tingled at the edge of her eyes. She sneezed.

Setting the microwave next to the recliner, Lainey sat in it, maneuvering the lever to prop up her feet. She smoothed her fingers over the arm rests, the microsuede changing colors. A piece of home. And still in excellent condition, too. Not a tear or a spot or wear. Lainey begged Marie Claire with the most pitiable expression possible. But Marie Claire shook her head, tsking her teeth and wagging a finger.

But Lainey persisted. "Oh, please, Marie Claire. I'll push it home."

She pinched her lips together. Carrying a picture, a towel rack, and a dresser was nothing compared to dragging home a recliner.

"It reminds me of home."

Marie Claire caved.

Lainey convinced Marie Claire to load up their findings on the seat of the chair. First the chest of drawers, the nightstand, then the microwave balanced on the very top. She slid the towel rack and the poster behind them. Lainey pushed. It didn't move. Lainey shoved it with her shoulder and the microwave began to slide.

Marie Claire caught it, resting her hand on top of the appliance. "I'll just keep the microwave from sliding off."

So they progressed down the street, Marie Claire holding the microwave, Lainey shoving with all her might. The return trip seemed much farther.

Her bed would feel comfortable and soft tonight. Her back ached. They stopped to rest. With her long sleeve, she wiped her sweating brow and glanced at her watch. Ten o'clock. They were almost halfway home. She sighed. Maybe they should've come another night. But then she wouldn't have found this great chair. She patted it, to remind herself she loved it.

At their apartment, they stopped in the glow of the lobby lights shining through the glass double doors. Lainey had to rest before she pushing it any farther.

"How are you going to get it upstairs?" Marie Claire opened the door, catching it with her foot.

"The elevator." Lainey gestured to it.

"I don't think it will fit."

"Sure it will."

"It will barely go through the door."

Lainey attempted to slide it through the frame, but the bottom caught on the threshold, blocking it. Lainey's muscles ached, shaking as she pushed.

Marie Claire squeezed past her, allowing the door to spank Lainey on her side. Setting her poster on the floor, she tugged the recliner on both armrests while Lainey pushed on the back.

"I think you are going to have to lift it," Marie Claire said.

"Maybe you could lift your end, and I'll push it across."

Before Marie Claire responded, a car on the road made a screeching U-turn in front of the apartment complex. Headlights cast shadows against the cement building.

Probably someone dropping off a passenger. Lainey hoped they didn't need to get in.

"*Puis-je vous aider*?" a man asked behind them.

Lainey stopped and cocked an ear. His voice sounded familiar.

"Mademoiselle Peterson?"

Lainey's heart contracted at her name. Parked on the sidewalk was an unforgettable, steel-gray Maserati.

No, no no no no no no no no no! Didn't he ever sleep?

****

Yves leaned against his opened door, trying to hide his amusement. He almost couldn't believe his eyes. His intern was moving an overstuffed armchair into her apartment at ten o'clock at night. "May I help you?"

"No, thank you," Mlle Peterson said as Marie Claire said, "Yes."

They exchanged glances.

He glanced between them.

Marie Claire folded her arms and said yes again.

"No. We're fine." Mlle Peterson glared at her companion. Marie Claire elbowed her.

"But you are tired. I'll just park the car and return to help." He ducked into his car and drove off in search of parking.

A few minutes later, he approached them from behind, folding his driving gloves into his pockets, overhearing their conversation.

"We can get it upstairs ourselves," Mlle Peterson said.

"When a man offers to help, accept it. Truly, is chivalry dead in America?"

"I am happy to help," he said.

Shrugging in defeat, Mlle Peterson attempted to slide the microwave off, to lessen his load.

"*Laissez-le*," he said. "Leave it. Just hold it, so it won't slide."

She moved to the side while he grasped both sides of the chair, hoisting it over the threshold.

"Thank you," Mlle Peterson said once inside.

"This is quite a large chair." He set it in front of the elevator.

"Lainey wanted it because it reminded her of home. She's homesick."

"Ah." He focused on Mlle Peterson for the first time under the fluorescent lights of the lobby. "Are you very homesick, then? You are not pleased with Switzerland?"

Her face brightened.

He had never remarked her radiant smile. Something in her appearance had changed but he couldn't point to what it was.

"No, I love it here."

Yves relaxed at her contradictory statement. He didn't want his intern homesick.

"My dad has the same chair."

"Will you be able to get it up to your apartment?" He motioned to the stairs.

"Yes, the elevator." Mlle Peterson pointed at the silver doors. She pushed the button and the doors slid open.

"I don't think it will fit." Yves sized up the bulk of the chair.

"I already told her." Marie Claire gathered up the extraneous items.

"It will fit," Mlle Peterson insisted.

Hugging a rolled poster to her chest, Marie Claire leaned up against the frame of the elevator, impatient for this to be over.

Yves held open the door while Mlle Peterson attempted to push the recliner in from the back. It didn't fit. It was just inches too wide.

"Maybe try turning it," Yves said.

Mlle Peterson shifted it, shoving one of the arms. Blocked again. This time by almost ten centimeters.

Mlle Peterson wiped her face. "I've grossly underestimated how small the elevators are in Switzerland."

"It doesn't fit," Yves said, just to rub it in. But a smile crept to his lips.

"So now what?" she asked. "Leave it here?"

Marie Claire sprang off the wall. "I have not let you drag it all the way down here, just to leave it sitting in the lobby. Come on."

She crossed the foyer to the steps, resting one foot on the first tread.

"The stairs?" Mlle Peterson arched a skeptical eyebrow. "I can't imagine hoisting that thing up the stairs. It weighs a ton."

"Yes, the stairs," Marie Claire said, impatient. "Hurry. It's late."

As Mlle Peterson and Yves persuaded the stuffed chair to the staircase, Marie Claire placed the extraneous items in the elevator and ascended, leaving Mlle Peterson alone with Yves in the foyer. The buzz from the fluorescent lighting filled the silence.

"Did you just come from work?" she asked.

He faced her. "Yes, I did." He didn't want to bore

her with his long lists of to-dos and deadlines.

"Ten o'clock. It's pretty late."

He deadpanned. "I, at least, prefer to sleep in my own bed, and not use my desk for a pillow."

Mlle Peterson opened her mouth to protest, but before she could speak, Marie Claire bounded down the stairs.

"*Bon*." He focused on the recliner at the base of the stairwell. "*Allez-houp!*"

Yves and Mlle Peterson went first, hoisting the rear of the chair, each grabbing a corner of the heavily padded back, while Marie Claire heaved it up by the footrest. Yves practically carried the weight himself. Mlle Peterson struggled for a firm hold.

"Grab it under the arm." Yves indicated a spot.

"Not so fast," Mlle Peterson said to Marie Claire. "You're going to push us over."

"Are you even holding anything?" she asked Mlle Peterson. "I am carrying the whole weight myself."

"It's hard to grip." Mlle Peterson crouched down, gripping underneath the armrest. No good. Her fingers pinched the material, but they slid.

Marie Claire pushed it up another stair, right into Mlle Peterson's face.

"Ow." She held her nose

"Are you all right?" Yves rested the base on a stair, examining Mlle Peterson's burgeoning nose.

Marie Claire stopped and peered around the padded chair.

Out of the corner of his eye, something moved.

"The chair!" Mlle Peterson yelled as it pitched forward.

In a flash, Yves caught it, and with great effort,

balanced the whole chair by grappling the backrest. His muscles strained as he wrested it back.

Mlle Peterson leaned into him to help, instead knocking his cheekbone with her head.

Marie Claire lunged and righted the chair, keeping it from toppling down the stairs. “Sorry,” she said at the same time as Mlle Peterson apologized to Yves.

He shook his head and smiled faintly, rubbing his cheekbone where a throbbing dull pain commenced. “It’s nothing.”

They continued on. Mlle Peterson apparently found a reliable handhold, for they reached the first landing, climbed twenty stairs, the second landing, twenty stairs, third landing.

His thighs ached from the constant crouching, even though he had been working out consistently at the gym. But he also suspected he was carrying the bulk of the chair. Yves focused on the rhythm of the stairs, counting each set before the landing.

Marie Claire grunted on the last few stairs to their floor. Almost there. Nineteen stairs. At the last landing, he forced it up. Mlle Peterson’s foot slipped, upsetting the whole rhythm. The chair faltered under the unsupported lift.

Sproing! echoed off the brick and plaster walls.

“Arg!” came from far side of the chair. Marie Claire used the “word of Cambronne.”

With wide eyes at her profanity, Yves peeked over the top of the chair. Marie Claire was in an unbecoming position, lying on her back on the stairs, staring up at him, and Mlle Peterson was surprised. The footrest had somehow deployed.

“Oh, oh!” Mlle Peterson glanced between Marie

Claire and the outstretched footrest, her hands covering her mouth.

"Are you all right?" With the chair safely on the landing, he held it in place.

"What happened?" There was a bit of fury in her wonder.

Mlle Peterson stepped forward to help her up. "I'm so sorry. I was holding the lever, and when I fell, it dislodged the footrest."

Attempting to stand, Marie Claire shook her head at Mlle Peterson's offer, placing a hand on the bannister. "No, no." She recoiled as if Mlle Peterson were an overpriced evening bag. "I'll get up on my own."

And as she stood, Marie Claire cursed at Mlle Peterson, which she no doubt did not understand.

Hiding a smile, Yves collapsed the footrest into the chair and hoisted it up the last stair, pushing it to the door by himself. Marie Clare and Mlle Peterson followed him.

Marie Claire popped open the lock and stalked inside, carrying her stuff, clacking on the parquet floors.

Mlle Peterson halted at the threshold with the chair. "Want to come in? I can put something on your, er, boo-boo." She winced at the sight of his head. "The Journal of Scientific Findings says melted chocolate spread over a bruise will help it heal. If you want to try it…" She bit her lip in thought. "I think I have a couple of chocolate bars left."

Her sweetness was so endearing. "No, thank you. I prefer to use traditional remedies."

"But I bet they wouldn't smell as delicious."

Her smile was beguiling. He almost caved.

"Or taste as wonderful."

Imagining a chocolate compress on his head encouraged the edges of his lips to curl upwards. "Perhaps another time."

She cocked her head. "You mean another time I hurt you, or another night?"

"Yes." From his pocket he retrieved his keys and gloves. "It's getting late, Mademoiselle Peterson. Until our department meeting tomorrow."

"Oh, yes."

He backed down the hall. "I have something interesting to announce."

"Oh?"

"You'll just have to wait and see." He stopped again, examining his American intern. He figured out what she'd changed. "Your new hairstyle is becoming." Then he disappeared around the corner.

Chapter Six

"*Allo*?" Lainey answered the phone, her voice grinding with the subtlety of a mill stone.

"Lainey?"

"Mom?" She forgot she gave her mother her number in an email.

"How are you doing, honey? Wait. Your dad was just going to bed. Say hi to him first."

She waited to hear his familiar voice. Ever since his business had declined, his voice had a heaviness to it, a salmagundi of tiredness, stress, and bitterness. Sometimes the injustice of the world really infuriated Lainey. Why did his business have to bottom out right when he was gearing up for retirement?

"Lainey? How's my little cocoa bean?"

Wow. He sounded cheerful. Not what she was expecting. "Great." Her mind raced. What was the change? Why did he sound so happy? Did her family win the lottery? "How are you?" She really wanted to know.

And her dad, being who he was, didn't take long to answer. "Did your mom tell you we're moving?"

Nothing prepared her for this. "Moving?" She lowered her voice. Marie Claire was already out of the shower. "Where to?"

"Costa Rica." Her dad was not known for his tact, nor his clarity of speech.

"I'm sorry. I think I misunderstood you. Where are you moving to?"

"We've decided to retire in Costa Rica and live out the rest of our lives on the shores, lapping up the waves and the sun."

"Ha, ha, very funny."

"Not a joke. Reviewing our budget in the current economy, we can live longer, have better quality of lives in Costa Rica. Jim"—his landscaping business partner—"says he's willing to buy me out. And since the last bird has flown the coop, so to speak, the time is right. It has always been your mother's dream to live in the Caribbean."

Lainey couldn't face news without some chocolate. She needed chocolate, and she needed it now. She stretched the phone cord to its limits, reaching across the room to where a half-eaten bar sat in a bag. Almost there. The cord tied her to the wall, just out of reach.

"But you don't speak Spanish." Shocked, Lainey barely pushed the words out of her mouth.

But he didn't answer; he handed the phone off to her mother.

Lainey's fingers grazed the edge of the wrapper. She needed the chocolate. This was too much to take without its help.

"If you can move to a foreign country, so can we," her mom said, just as cheerful as Dad. It was almost an unnatural cheerfulness, as if Dad had returned from one of those turn-a-hundred-bucks-into-a-million seminars. A cheerfulness lasting only until he realized he'd been swindled. Her parents sounded so optimistic on the phone, Lainey knew this was going to end badly. "You're an inspiration to us."

Her? She inspired them to do this? She wanted to tell them they were crazy. "When do you leave?" She strained the receiver away from her ear, hoping to gain the needed distance to reach the chocolate.

"As soon as we sell our house. Isn't it wonderful?" Mom continued with details of selling the house and searching for properties online in Costa Rica.

Lainey held the phone away from her ear, giving her ample room to catch the bar. She unfolded the wrapper with her teeth. The sweet chocolatey goodness filled her buds, warming her, calming her. What were they going to do with her stuff? She finished two squares. She tuned in to hear her mom say, "…sell the house by Thanksgiving."

"What? You want to be gone by the end of November? Don't you think you're being a little hasty? Don't you think you should wait a bit, reconsider the options? The spring is a seller's market." Lainey wouldn't return home before they had left.

"No time but the present. Lainey, you've taught us to act."

"But I won't see you when I get home." The full weight of the consequences sank in as she crammed the last of the bar in her mouth. She caught a sneeze in her nose.

"Fly there! Is there any better way to spend Christmas than on the beach?"

She wanted to yell at them to stop, but her mouth was stuffed full of chocolate. She finished the second half of the bar. Even with all the chocolate coursing through her veins, she couldn't stop the growing pit in her stomach.

"We have more news." Mom grew serious. "Did

Nadine call you? She's getting married."

"She mentioned something when we spoke briefly."

"I was just wondering how you would take it."

Wait, her parents were moving to Costa Rica, and Mom wondered how she'd take her best friend getting married. Was she crazy?

Lainey settled back down into bed. "I'm fine, Mom. I'm happy for her. Yay! Wheee. I'm doing the happy dance."

"I was worried you'd be upset since you'll be missing her wedding."

"What?" Lainey bolted upright, her blankets holding her in bed.

"Her wedding will be over Thanksgiving weekend."

"Wait, wait. She's getting married in two months? But I'll still be here." So soon? Ever since they first noticed boys had attractive eyes and plump butts, they promised they'd be each other's bridesmaids. Of course, chocolate was Lainey's first love and her amorous relationship with it started waaaaay before boys.

Maybe she could have the wedding in Switzerland or maybe Lainey could fly home for the weekend. It was only a twelve-hour flight.

"You'd better give her a call."

They hung up. In the dark, Lainey fumbled around for a calling card she'd bought last week. She punched the numbers and called her best friend.

"Lainey!" Nadine said once she was on the phone.

Lainey came right to the point. "How come you're getting married over Thanksgiving, Nadine?" Her throat had a lump, as if she'd swallowed a whole truffle. "No matter what, I have to be there for the wedding!"

"Martin received a job offer from a Silicon Valley start-up which starts as soon as he graduates in December. This is the last break we have before then because he wants me to go with him."

The same weekend as the gala. "I can't make it, Nadine." Her voice trembled, almost squeaking. "I want to be there for you."

"I know. Oh, Lainey." Nadine's voice vibrated in a pre-cry tremor. "I want you to be here, too."

Lainey sneezed, unable to speak through her swollen throat. "But can't you wait one more month for me to come home?" No friend would ask them to postpone their wedding until Lainey come home. The wedding was about the couple.

"We still want you to be maid of honor."

"But I won't be there for the honorable duties."

"You'll just have to send your measurements."

"My measurements for what?"

"For your dress?"

"You're going to send me a dress even though I'm not going to be in the wedding?"

"It was Martin's idea. He feels so awful you can't be here. He suggested we send you a dress, and you take a high-rez shot of you wearing it. We'll blow it up and stand it in the receiving line with us. You've seen those life-sized cut-outs at Comic-Con."

What a stupid idea. Who wanted a life-sized picture of Lainey anywhere? "I'm not a super hero."

"Come on, Lainey."

"All right. I'll do it for you. Ship me the dress. I'll

find someone to take a picture of me. But I'm so disappointed not to be there for you."

"Me, too."

"Hey, Nadine, make me a promise."

"Yes?"

"If you ever get married again, better make sure I can be there. Deal?"

"Deal."

****

At precisely ten o'clock a.m., the Pet Care team assembled in the conference room with the white board. Yves combed his hair forward to distract from the bruise purpling on the side of his cheekbone. Maybe he should've accepted Mlle Peterson's chocolate bruise cure. The thought made him smile, but he quickly dismissed it.

He stood at the head of the table with a reusable grocery sack, waiting for his subordinates' attention.

"Last month," he began, pacing back and forth in front of the whiteboard, "I mentioned we have lost touch with our customer base. I have been thinking all week of a way to reclaim it, to personally connect with our consumers. I'm not talking about polls or formal surveys. I'm talking about you, each one of you, personally connecting with the pet owners in the French-speaking Swiss *Romande*. Then, if this scheme works, I'll expand it to all of Switzerland, maybe all of Europe, ha! The world."

Luc glanced at Gui with extreme boredom, while the rest of the room sizzled with excitement and curiosity under Yves' enthusiasm.

"I propose in the next month, we do a different type of work." He waited for this to settle on them. "For two days out of the week, instead of clocking in here, I want each one of you to spend ten hours a day talking with everyone you meet."

A buzz went around the room. He was delighted to shake them up. He dug into the bag, retrieving the bi-folds. He tossed one to each of them.

A groan came from Luc as he held it.

"I bought these bus passes"—he paused to glance at Gui and Luc—"with my own money. I want you to be out talking with the people. Talk to them in the parks, in their homes, in the street, on the buses, and the trains on your ride home. I want you to stop people walking their dogs, ask them about their cats."

A smile spread across Gui's face. He was thinking he was going to get out of work. Yves corrected him. "Ah, you think this will be an easy assignment." He stuck his hand into the bag again, revealing hand-sized notebooks, or *carnets,* and passed them around the room. "You will need to record your findings in this book, which I will check and review at the end of each day.

"Ask questions—not these exact ones, but something similar." He spun and with a snap, flipped off the cap to the marker and began writing questions on the board. "How many pets do you have? Ask if they own any pets, first. What do you want most for your pet? How old, what's the pet's name? Care about them, let them know you care. Just don't tell them you are from our company. I want them to give honest answers, not what they think you want to hear."

Luc's face reflected his disgruntlement.

Yves clicked the lid on the marker and faced the table. "Any questions?"

Britta tossed her bus pass between her hands with eyebrows constricted.

Luc finally raised his hand. “Asking questions for ten hours?”

“Yes, those of you who thought you’d be doing less work on this assignment are wrong.” Yves glowered at Gui. “You’ll be crawling back the next day, begging to come back to work full time in the office. It will be both mentally and physically taxing.”

Gui’s unfaltering smile finally faded.

“You will have to get out of your comfort zone, most of you. You are not used to speaking with strangers. I will give you partners to make it easier. I think. Britta and Sabine, Gui and Luc. We’ll meet tomorrow morning at the *gare* at seven a.m.” Yves paused. “Any questions?”

Luc grumbled, and Gui bowed his head to his chest, but Yves took no notice.

“Until seven, then.”

As he proceeded to gather up the bag, Mlle Peterson raised her hand.

“Yes, Mademoiselle Peterson?” He barely glanced up as he folded the bag. “I have not forgotten about you. You will go with me.” He left the room in two strides.

As he stalked to his office, he barely acknowledged co-workers greeting him. Should he have paired Mlle Peterson with someone else? Perhaps he should’ve paired her with Gui or Luc. Pairing her with one of those would have been tedious for her. Maybe with Britta. Sabine never would have given her a chance. No, he was clearly the best choice.

His father taught him not to second guess his

decision. To stick with it even if it was the wrong one. To waffle was weakness. This way, at least he would be assured she was working hard. She was his responsibility after all. His intern.

****

Gui was the first to speak after M. Claremont left. "I think I'll just meet there and then go home, make up my responses in my book. And have myself half a week of vacation."

Luc scowled at him and motioned for them to leave.

After they had left, Britta, unmoved, unemotional until now, raised her head to speak. "I think M. Claremont has a great idea. We sit here in our big building when we should be more in touch with our pet owners who make our job possible. Do you want to do it?" Britta asked Sabine.

Sabine had an elven figure next to Britta, who was tall and broad with sharp cheek bones. Sabine only sneered at her *carnet*, tucking it into the pocket of her swing jacket.

"I think it's a wonderful idea, but I'm afraid to talk to people," Britta said, before Sabine launched some disparaging remark. "It would be easier if we said we were from the company."

Lainey hated to listen in. And the better part of her screamed for her to leave the room. But she stayed. She pretended to be preoccupied by her papers. They ignored her completely.

Britta spoke to Sabine. "What do you think?"

"I think he's a fool. Monsieur le President will be interested in knowing his new methods of research." Her giant eyes squinted with an evil glint. Despite her evident flair for fashion, she was still a jerk.

"Don't tell him." Britta rounded the table to Sabine's side, pleading. "You know, I have respected Yves Claremont since he came. He has used many unique and different techniques to turn the Pet Care Department into one of the top departments at Alpine Foods. For my own mistakes, he had reasons to terminate me many times but did not, for which I am grateful. He continues to give me more praise on my employee reviews than I deserve."

Sabine snorted, flaring her porcelain-smooth nostrils, but said nothing.

Britta continued, "He has earned his reputation here. But this, I worry this will be his undoing."

"It might be. People don't appreciate companies sniffing into their business." Sabine's eyebrows wrinkled darkly.

"Please don't get Yves into trouble. He's doing wonderful things for the company."

"No," Sabine replied. "He's doing wonderful things for himself."

Britta prickled. The quiet German straightened herself up. Her height was intimidating. There was determination firing from her eyes.

Sabine stepped back.

Britta addressed her with fire in her voice. "He is not selfish. Just remember this, if Yves soars, we soar with him. If he fails, we will be dragged down with him. Just keep it in mind, Sabine. Remember, if you sabotage him, you take us all with him." She thrusted her chin in the air. "Until tomorrow."

****

Just before seven a.m., the sun cleared the

mountains, causing a haze to rise off the lake. Lainey crossed the lawn in front of the train station, wetting her shoes in the dewy grass before she reached the *gare.*

Outside Albertos, Britta and Sabine waited and chatted. Britta tugged at her scarf, covering more of her long neck. In America, they both would've been drinking coffee with whipped cream, but Europeans didn't have to-go. Enjoying a *café* while chatting, yes, but "to-go" wasn't Swiss.

Lainey joined them. Her Swiss watch said it was ten till seven.

M. Claremont, dressed in his standard suit, stepped out of Albertos with a paper bag under his arm. Every time she met him, Lainey was struck by his appearance. Not just the planes in his face, but the intensity in his eyes, his focus, his drive. The wind-whipped scarf around his neck reminded her he was European, her boss and therefore, off limits.

"Where are Luc and Gui?" In the cool morning, steam rose from his lips when he spoke. When no one answered, his jaw muscle flexed as he checked his watch. "Do you all have your notebooks?"

Lainey's was identical to the one she had bought for her list. She shook, either from the chill in the air or from nerves. Seeing they all had their notebooks, he clapped once. "*Bon*, remember, talk with people, as many people as you can. Ask them the questions we discussed yesterday. Do not write the information down until after you've parted. Don't show them your notebooks. Write as many details as you can about the person, for example how old you think they are, income, and so on. Just an estimate, don't ask."

M. Claremont handed Britta and Sabine the two

tickets on the 7:05 train to Fribourg, the eastern border of the *Suisse francophone.* With the rumble of the locomotive, an influx of people gathered on the *quai*. Their train entered the *gare* and the two women set off.

M. Claremont faced Lainey. His stare was perhaps softer today, but intimidating all the same. An awkward silence settled between them.

Then Gui and Luc, smoking, sauntered up from the street and joined them on the cobblestone near the shaded entrance to the *gare*. Gui inhaled a long drag from his cigarette as if he never ate, subsisting only a steady nicotine diet.

Luc stamped his cigarette on a stone bench before joining M. Claremont and Lainey, releasing a strong stream of smoke from his nostrils.

Gui, after inhaling into his broad chest, flicked his butt into a grate encircling a fall-colored sapling. He spread his arms as if he were being frisked by the *gendarmes,* his thick coat hanging from thick shoulders. “We forgot our notebooks.”

Without a word, M. Claremont produced two more notebooks.

Luc met his accusing glare with one of equal force. Face to face, the men stood, locked in a competitive stare. Lainey glanced between them. M. Claremont was all harshness again.

After a few seconds of silence, Luc grabbed the two *carnets* without losing his deadlock stare, tossed one to Gui, then tucked the other in the pocket of his woolen pea coat.

Eyes still holding a steady glare, M. Claremont produced two tickets to Lausanne, the second largest city in French-speaking Switzerland, a fifteen-minute westward train ride.

Luc made no movement but kept his hands in the pockets, his eyes still steady on M. Claremont.

A voice over the speaker announced the arrival of the Lausanne train.

Lainey hopped from one foot to the other. *Just go*.

"Your career depends on it." M. Claremont stared him straight in the eyes, still extending his hand with the tickets.

"I think you're mistaken." Luc returned his stare. "*Your* career depends on it."

Although Lainey might not understand every French nuance, she read body language. M. Claremont's jaw bulged as he clamped his teeth. His keen eyes continued their unyielding focus on Luc.

In exaggerated coolness, Luc snatched the tickets with a swipe of his hand, retreating from his superior. He tapped Gui's shoulder and motioned to go. They disappeared into the crowd boarding the train.

After they boarded, M. Claremont relaxed, exhaling audibly.

"If he is such a bother, why don't you fire him?" Lainey asked.

M. Claremont studied the departing train from the platform through the thick lashes shading his eyes, his expression thoughtful, distant. "It's good to have opposition, so you don't go too far off in one direction. Those who oppose us prevent us from making mistakes."

"Is this a mistake?"

Perhaps M. Claremont asked too much of his subordinates. Perhaps this broke some unwritten Swiss rule: Don't ask questions, don't speak to people unless you are introduced.

At Stanford, people accosted Lainey all the time on campus. Activists petitioned for a Student Union expansion or smaller class sizes. Perhaps it was a cultural thing.

He didn't hear her or if he did, he didn't answer, but spun on his well-shod heels and strode toward the *centre-ville* without another glance toward Lainey.

Chapter Seven

Day four of street contacting and M. Claremont combed the city with indefatigable energy, speaking with anyone who allowed him a few minutes on the bus, on the street, everywhere in between.

Lainey enjoyed watching him. He was a master people-person. Who would've thought the harsh, abrupt manner he used with his subordinates—or just Lainey?—melted away to charming pleasantness when conversing with customers?

An elderly lady flashed too-white teeth and answered all his questions. Now, a young woman with wide-set eyes gushed and blushed under his interested eyes when he asked her about Didier, her dog.

Lainey wanted to tell her he wasn't always pleasant; try working for him sometime.

The young woman made him laugh in return.

Lainey glanced away. The girl was frumpy. Yet he lavished attention and smiles on her until she descended at her stop. After she left, he jotted a few scribbles in his notebook.

"Your turn." He nodded to Lainey, tucking the notebook away into his lined trench coat, his gaze severe upon her.

At the next stop they descended, waiting in the alcove of the plexiglass shelter of the bus stop on a tree-lined street. A steady drizzle sogged the remaining browning leaves off the limbs.

They sloshed to the arriving bus. Lainey glanced at him again as they ascended the stairs. The glare of his eyes told her to go solo.

Lainey lost track of him when he sat next to a slender Asian woman while she slinked to the back of the charging bus, swaying with its movements, and slumped into the seat next to an elderly lady.

Large hands poked from her down-filled jacket, her graying hair tucked under a cap. Her aged eyes begged to examine her properly, but propriety kept her focus at the front of the bus. Lainey sensed the lady knew she wasn't native Swiss.

Clearing her throat, Lainey made an attempt at conversation in French. "A rainy day, *n'est-ce pas*?"

Shallow conversation never led anywhere. Since coming to Switzerland, Lainey sometimes yearned for deep conversation. Politics, ethics, spirituality, whether or not CEOs made too much money. Something. Anything!

The elderly lady raised a brow at Lainey's accent. "You are English?"

"American."

Now the lady regarded her properly. Her eyes, shining behind thick-rimmed glasses, tactlessly evaluated Lainey's outfit, her hair, her accessories, as if wondering what an American was doing here. But she tolerated Lainey's lousy French and listened.

"On a sunnier day," Lainey said, hoping she didn't sound too contrived, "it would be perfect to take a dog on a walk around the *bord du lac*."

A smile and nod. But she didn't shoo her away.

Lainey was encouraged. This was so

uncomfortable. "Do you have a dog?" Lainey asked with the goofiest fake smile on her face.

She shook her head, her eyes still transfixed on her.

Lainey leaned closer, as if sharing a secret. "Cats are better anyway. Do you like cats?"

"*Non.*" She tsked and shook her head.

Great, where could she go from here? Data entry all of a sudden sounded horribly interesting. Stuffy? Boring? Yes, but at least she wouldn't have to interrogate random people. M. Claremont was the devil. Her frozen smile thawed.

"You've been in the country long?" Her question broke Lainey's thoughts.

"About three months."

"You speak well." The Swiss were too polite. To the point of lying.

But secretly, her ego expanded. Lainey smiled. A real one this time. "Thank you." Lainey scrambled to make conversation, just so the lady wouldn't think she was weird. "I'm here on an internship at Alpine Foods." Oops, she wasn't supposed to mention the company. She hastily asked, "So, what do you do for work?"

"I used to work as a pastry chef, but I've retired."

Finally, something worth interrogating someone about. Lainey scooted to the edge of her chair, facing her. "That's awesome. What would you say is your specialty?"

"Oh, this and that."

Avoidance technique. Lainey vowed to penetrate the stoic Swiss. "You know what I've always wanted to learn how to make?"

A vague shake. Her eyes were wandering.

Lainey was losing her. "Chocolate mousse," she

said triumphantly.

"Really?" An insincere question, but Lainey continued.

"I've only had the powder kind you add milk to."

The lady was horrified—a real emotion. And she was hooked.

"I'd love to learn how to make real Swiss chocolate mousse."

Light shone in her eyes. A smile parted her lips. And Lainey broke the stoic dam. *Cha-ching*.

The lady waved her hand. "Oh, it's so easy. I can tell you how."

"Really?" Lainey grabbed her notebook, the one with all the bad things written in it, careful not to confuse it with the one M. Claremont had given her. "Okay."

"You need chocolate, cream, sugar, and eggs." She counted the ingredients on her fingers. "First, take a 100g plaque of chocolate. Melt the chocolate in the *bain-marie*."

"*Bain-marie*?"

"Double boiler," she said in heavily-accented English.

Lainey raised her eyebrows in understanding. Ah-ha! She could use her microwave. It was so worth dragging home. She scribbled in her notebook. She planned to cook this tonight.

"Okay, next?" Lainey asked, her pencil poised.

"Next, you beat the cream."

"How much?"

"Two deciliters."

Scribble, scribble. "How long?"

"Until it is fluffy."

"What type of cream?"

"Liquid."

Right, whipping cream. She tapped her pencil on her chin. She could pick up some on the way home from work. Ah, chocolate mousse. Something between hot chocolate and chocolate pudding. Light enough to almost inhale. Would it work with white chocolate? Oh, with peppermint or amoretto flavoring? Mmmmmm. So much to experiment with.

"Then mix in the chocolate." She stopped to examine what Lainey was writing.

"Mix the chocolate. Okay, and then?" Lainey asked. "Then?" She persisted one more time. The elderly woman didn't continue. Had Lainey lost her?

She glanced up. The woman was staring over Lainey's head. Lainey spun in her seat.

M. Claremont had a censuring scowl across his face. "Mademoiselle Peterson, I believe we are at our stop."

One could light a cigarette from the heat radiating from her face. "Thank you," she mumbled to the lady as she rose out of the seat. "I must go." She crossed the aisle and hopped out of the folding doors.

****

Once on the street, Yves faced her. "What are you doing?" After the training, he couldn't believe she deviated from the script. He paced in front of her. "Why are you writing in front of her?" He pinched the *carnet* from Mlle Peterson.

"I wasn't asking her about pets."

At this confession, he stared at her in disbelief.

"I mean, I began the conversation about pets. She didn't have any. So I asked her about work and would you believe it, she's a pastry chef."

He glared at her.

Her voice grew smaller when he didn't react. "Retired, now."

He consulted her notebook. "And so you asked her how to make chocolate mousse?"

"What was I supposed to do, move and sit next to someone else on the bus?"

"Yes, if you want to be the most effective."

"I thought it rude." She tapped her foot on the ground. "Can I have my notebook back, please?"

He didn't mean to be so harsh. The harshness came from the intensity, the drive, the passion—love—for his work. He was disappointed in her. Mlle Peterson squirmed under his gaze, but didn't flinch her eyes.

Finally, he flipped the pages, letting them fly by without reading and relinquished her notebook.

"You care too much about candy." He waved a dismissive hand.

"Candy?" Mlle Peterson stepped back.

Perhaps he was patronizing her, purposefully provoking her.

"Chocolate is not just candy. The type of chocolate you eat determines who you are. The kind you give tells what you know about them, how much you care for them. It even has a whole language of love."

"Love?" he asked, intrigued. "How is chocolate a language of love?"

Mlle Peterson stammered, her cheeks deepening to a becoming shade of pink. "Well," she began tentatively as if waiting for him to cut her off.

But he stood with his hands in his pockets, patiently waiting for her to continue.

So she did. "Chocolate is more than understanding *couvertures*, Dutch processing, cleavage, undertones. Chocolate is extremely emotional. It carries nuances plain candy does not. You must discover which chocolate lights up your lover's emotional center, the pleasure-seeking part of the brain."

"How do you find out? By asking him?"

"Oh, no. Asking is for amateurs. First, I observe, learn something about him, know his tastes and dislikes. Then apply what I know to his personality. Nine times out of ten, I'm right about which is the favorite."

Yves stepped closer, his eyes still on her, challenging her. "What would you predict is my favorite?"

Mlle Peterson met his stare. "You're baiting me."

"Perhaps." Then tilted his head down and whispered. "Or perhaps I want to see how well you have been observing me." He scrutinized her reaction.

"I've totally pegged you," she said, not even hiding her confidence.

He cocked his head. "You think you know me?"

She thrust her chin upwards with confidence. "I know chocolate. And I've been on the streets with you for four days."

"Then guess." This would be entertaining.

"Well." She stepped away from him, adopting an air of indifference. "Judging by the car you drive, your penchant for passion, and Merino wool suits, I'd guess Mandorie Noir?"

He blinked, unable to believe how accurate she was. She *had* been watching him. He straightened and brushed some drops from his trench coat. "Good guess." He continued down the sidewalk under the dripping trees.

Mlle Peterson followed him.

"I do enjoy Mandorie, probably my second favorite. In fact, my father was a close friend to Signore Antonio Figgerelli, the CEO."

Mlle Peterson's jaw dropped momentarily, but she recovered quickly.

He cast her a sideways glance. "But not my favorite. See, you are too cocky. Don't be too quick to judge."

Her brow furrowed. "I'm usually right. All right. Alpine Foods Exclusive Dark?"

"Nope."

"Reganwald?"

"I eat Reganwald occasionally." A tasty German chocolate.

"Damville Chocolate?"

"Mmmm. Very good, but no."

"Criollo."

"No."

"Fairly."

"Delicious. But nope. I don't think you know me very well, Mademoiselle Peterson." Nothing gave him more pleasure than to see her squirm, to shake her confidence a bit.

"I give up. What's your favorite chocolate?"

He glanced up, savoring the tease. "Chocolate chips."

"No way! You're making this up just to prove me wrong. They don't even have chocolate chips in Switzerland."

"True. And you're right; chocolate is an emotional

thing. Growing up, my father didn't allow me many sweets. He was a hard and exacting man. Sweets were strictly forbidden."

For the second time, Mlle Peterson's jaw dropped.

He noted it with a nod. "It was a great exercise in discipline—something I learned from my parents, for which I am grateful. But one summer, my mother and I visited her family in Evansville, just outside of Chicago. I think my father was on a business trip to New York. Anyway, my aunt decided to make chocolate chips cookies for a picnic and let me help her."

For a brief moment, Yves was somewhere else, somewhere in his memories. Instead of buildings, the cityscape of Vevey, rows and rows of corn stretched from horizon to horizon, green lawns spilling over hills. He smelled corn and fertilizer. "I remember sneaking into the bag and shoving a handful of morsels into my mouth." He refocused his gaze on Mlle Peterson. "The perfect blend of milk and chocolate."

Yves stepped closer. He had never shared anything of this sort with any of his subordinates. The autumn wind whipped the silky strands of her auburn hair across her lip gloss. He had the temptation to brush the strand away. But he restrained himself.

"Chocolate chips aren't what I consider chocolate." She brushed the strand away. "They are mostly sugar and have additives to make them into those shapes. So it doesn't count."

Her lips shone in the milky light. Her light brown eyes danced with delight. A warm glow, almost unfamiliar, burned in his chest. Ah, but she was an intern.

"Do you know what you need?" he asked,

changing the subject abruptly to snuff the feeling. "Focus. You need focus."

"Focus? I do focus, just not on pet food."

"Yes." He faced away from her, refocusing on the road ahead of them. He charged on ahead.

Mlle Peterson jogged to catch up.

"You need to discipline your mind."

"And you are so self-disciplined?"

"Yes."

"You never get distracted?"

At an intersection, he finally stopped and faced her. His eyes searched her. How could he tell her all he had sacrificed, what he continued to sacrifice?

"Rarely. Distractions interfere with my goals. You are constantly distracted by chocolate."

"I am not distracted by chocolate. It's the reason I came here. Why I crossed the ocean, left my family and friends. Chocolate isn't a distraction, it's my destination!"

"Then change your destination."

"What if your distraction is what you want?" she asked.

He paused, confessing yet another hidden secret. "Then I discipline my mind until it is no longer what I want or it is no longer a distraction. I have only one desire."

"Oh?"

"To succeed." He whipped around and marched off.

"At the sacrifice of everything else?"

"If need be."

"Even personal relationships?"

He stopped near an *épicerie* and examined the

groceries placed in crates under the awning.

Mlle Peterson bumped into his back. She was goading him on.

"Yes."

"See, I told you—wait. Are you serious?" She stepped back, nearly whacking her head on the awning protecting the crated squash.

"I could never be with someone who doesn't understand the passion to do one's best."

Cars pressed up and down the road behind him, pedestrians crossed the streets all around them, but he was oblivious to it all for one second. He focused on Mlle Peterson. "Don't you agree?"

Mlle Peterson was somewhere else. "I wanted to study, get the top grades, and Aaron wanted to have fun, go spin broadies in the sand dunes. Instead of going to the library to study, I read my books at his baseball games. I was always arranging my study schedule to please him. To do things with him."

"Aaron is your boyfriend?"

Mlle Peterson frowned. "Marie Claire told me all about your girlfriend. Does Hiroko understand your passion?"

Yves stepped back, surprised, not noticing he nearly trod on a passing lady in a mink stole, who eyed him darkly. He recovered quickly.

"I'd like to keep my personal life just that, personal." He meant to silence the conversation.

But Mlle Peterson didn't stop. "She says Hiroko is the daughter of the Atatakai International CEO."

The lids of his eyes closed, his body tensed with constraint.

"So surely she must understand the importance of

success."

Suddenly his eyes flashed open, a boiling within him bubbled over. If anyone suspected he was dating Hiroko, it would ruin everything he had worked for. "Let me be perfectly clear, Mademoiselle Peterson. If you value your internship, you will never broach this subject with me or with any other employee of Alpine Foods again, do you understand?"

Mlle Peterson trembled.

"Do you understand?" he asked again.

She nodded.

"And I will ask Marie Claire not to discuss my personal life with employees."

****

Church bells chimed, signaling the middle of the day. On day one, Lainey hoped to stop for lunch, but by day four she knew better.

M. Claremont kept right on trucking.

At one point, while he was conversing with a man walking a small breed, Lainey stopped in a store to buy a baguette and a *branche,* a stick, of chocolate. He didn't even scold her when she rejoined him. Since their conversation earlier, awkward silence prevailed. Lainey endured his severe stares. So painful. Like a zit on the inner nostril.

At the next stop, a young woman attempted to mount the steep stair of the bus, struggling with a child in a stroller. Lainey moved to help her, but M. Claremont beat her to it, lifting the carriage up over the stairs and into the bus.

"*Merci,*" the young woman said with an accent, through a bit of breath.

"*Je vous en prie,*" he said, then charged to the front

of the bus to speak with a woman holding a small dog breed pup on her lap.

The young woman stood by the pram.

"Here you go." She stuffed a crust of bread into the kid's mouth.

Lainey jumped when she spoke. English. A strong British accent. Lainey had to speak with her. "Hello," she said to the young woman.

The young woman jerked around so quickly her tiny wisp of a pony tail whipped her face. To Lainey's surprise, she didn't smile, just returned her hello, quickly.

"Where are you from?" Lainey asked.

She stared hard for a minute, then continued to feed the child. "England."

"What are you doing here, in Switzerland, I mean?" Speaking English was like eating chocolate cake with ganache icing. Lainey's ears tingled with familiarity. Were headaches language induced?

"I'm a *fille au pair*."

People stared at them from the sides of their eyes, but Lainey didn't care. Although the young woman seemed uneasy with the attention. She glanced around to the others.

Perhaps Lainey should be quiet. But she couldn't. "What's that?"

"While Mum and Daddy are working all day, I take François to the park instead of watching Babar on the telly." She stuffed more bread into the toddler's mouth. He gummed it and spit it out.

Before Lainey asked another question, two men in dark clothes and caps stepped onto the bus at a stop. A bit of nervous tension sizzled through the bus.

A shabby, dark-headed man, seated by the window, ducked his head.

The two men passed through the benches, observing people, sometimes requesting something.

"What's going on?" Lainey asked.

"The *gendarmes*. They're checking permits." She dug around in her bag to find a purple bi-fold smaller than a bus pass. She flashed it to show Lainey a permit.

"I don't have one of those. I've only been here a few weeks."

"Can you prove it?"

Sweat gathered at her brow. Lainey's heart thundered until it strangled her breath. Was this even legal?

But the police never reached them. Maneuvering down the aisle, they tapped the slumped, dark-headed man on his shoulder. When he didn't respond, they tapped him again.

They exchanged words in French. The man nodded and patted his pockets. He rose and moved out of his seat, walking in the aisle, the police following after him.

When the bus stopped, the man seized an opportunity to swing around a pole and out the door, running up the street. But the police were faster. One caught the man, wrangling him down to the ground as the other called for assistance on his radio.

Everyone watched out the window. But from where Lainey stood, it was difficult to see. As the bus left the curb, the police escorted the dark-haired man between them, his hands bound behind him.

"What will happen to him?" Lainey asked.

"Deportation or fined."

Lainey reminded herself, *Get my permit.*

****

On a different bus later in the afternoon, M. Claremont approached a young lady with olive skin and attractive, large attentive eyes. She smiled coquettishly at his attention.

Lainey wanted to yell he was only interested in her dog resting on her lap. Instead, she stumbled to the back, sidling next to an old lady with a doggy in a carrier.

The doggy barked, startling Lainey. M. Claremont was so paying for her therapy after this. Concentrating on her French, she didn't notice two black-clad men enter at the front of the bus.

In full conversation about the papillon lap dog, she was interrupted by a tap on her shoulder. Thinking it was M. Claremont, she paid no heed until an expression of horror passed on the elderly lady's face. Lainey spun in her seat.

"*Votre permit, s'il vous plâit.*" A very serious-looking policeman waited expectantly for her permit. How did they guess she was a foreigner?

"I don't have one," she said in French, guilt burning her face. "My boss is just up there. You can talk to him, and he'll tell you I'm employed here."

The *gendarme* didn't even turn his head. M. Claremont was fifteen feet away, and they wouldn't ask him.

Lainey waved to M. Claremont, whose suited back was to her as he talked to another young attractive girl—was everyone here a supermodel, or did he simply choose the supermodels to talk to?—oblivious to her plight. It would have been a time for *less* concentration on the porcelain-skinned beauty and *more* distraction in her direction.

Should she call out to him? No. Imagine the lecture she'd get if she embarrassed him. All of Alpine Foods would be shamed, their company and brand tainted. She would just talk this out. Surely the *gendarmes* weren't going to treat her like a common criminal.

He asked for her passport, and she handed it to him. Shame on her for being so compliant.

"Please follow me, mademoiselle." The taller officer gripped her upper arm, pushing her in front of him off the bus. Her face was red hot, heat rising from her jacket.

Inside the bus, M. Claremont still conversed with the coquette. How long would it take for M. Claremont to notice she was no longer with him? At the end of the line? This evening? The bus left the curb. Evidently, she was so important to him he didn't notice the police hauling her off the bus. He possessed some serious focus.

They needed to revisit this topic.

The bus halted at a light up the road. At the bus stop, the officers grilled her. How long had she been in the country? Was she living here legally?

She remained quiet, unsure if her answers would reflect poorly on Alpine Foods. Did she have Miranda rights? Where was the US Embassy? She imagined being imprisoned in a dark cell with flickering fluorescent lights and a crusty yellow bidet in a corner. She sneezed. Hot tears flowed from her eyes. She didn't dare raise her eyes to the officer's. She decided to talk.

Focusing on the buttons and silver looped key holder on the officer's uniform, she answered the questions. They said they would transport her to the *Hôtel de Ville*. A hotel? What a relief.

When they paused, she glanced up to see the light change and the bus lurching forward. As the bus chugged up the hill, M. Claremont, his mouth open in shock, stared at her through the bus window.

With only her fingertips poking from her cuff, she waved, smiling wryly.

He shook his head.

Chapter Eight

The *Hôtel de Ville* was a misnomer, a false cognate—not a hotel at all but City Hall in a limestone building with decorative cornices. If she hadn't been there on official detention, she might have enjoyed the architecture.

The *gendarmes* allowed her the dignity of ascending the granite steps unaided. Once through the doors, though, they grappled her shoulders to guide her through the crowd. Department of Motor Vehicle-type lines compassed the frescoed walls of the front foyer, applicants for permits.

Weaving around the lines, the *gendarmes* escorted her across the polished wood floors of the lobby, interrupted by four great columns. In a seating area, a woman with dark hair and several children completed paperwork on her lap, constantly quieting the interrupting children.

Beyond the lobby, down a floor, and through a few doors was a sort of holding cell. The *gendarmes* deposited her there with only one small window carved out of walls made of foot-thick blocks of gray stone. As if she was going to make a run for it.

An hour passed as she sat on a hard, wooden bench, alone, lost, and abandoned. She had left her cell phone at her desk and didn't have anyone's number memorized.

A fluorescent light flickered above her. She contemplated her sentencing. Deportation? What if they suspended her passport and forbade travel to Costa Rica to see her parents? Fear tightened her chest halting her breath. The sun had set and the *gendarmes* had not returned.

Footfalls sounded in the hall. The door opened. An officer stepped in with M. Claremont.

The mere sight of M. Claremont sent large tears down her cheeks, just to see someone, anyone, she knew. At least she didn't drop to her knees and blubber odes of gratitude, which was what she had planned if anyone came to rescue her.

The officer handed her a stack of papers to complete, bawling out Lainey in French. She hastened through the questions of name, address, employment, with M. Claremont's careful eyes observing her self-consciously check the "single" box. Signed, sealed, paid, and dated. She was now permitted to live and work in Switzerland.

By the time Lainey and M. Claremont descended the steps of the *Hôtel De Ville*, the bells of the church were chiming seven o'clock. Previously, M. Claremont had called the others, directing them to bring the *carnets* by his office for review. Since the buses ran less frequently at night, they strolled back to headquarters.

It was the first night they had missed the rendezvous with the others. He said nothing as they passed lighted windows of the boutiques lining the main street in *centre-ville*.

Lainey stared into the windows, admiring the luxury and the richness of the furs, jewelry, evening gowns, shoes, releasing her mind of the tiring day. A *boulanger* was just closing shop; the pastries and bread visible from the street made her tummy rumble.

The wind picked up from the lake and blew her hair around her face. In vain, she tucked it into place.

"You caused me a lot of trouble today." M. Claremont spoke with exasperation about how he had to convince the officers to allow him to come and help her apply for the permit. Because she'd already been picked up, they wanted her to pay the fine. Of course there was a fine.

"I risked our reputation for you today. I put the company in danger for your neglect."

Should she say sorry or thank you? Gratitude swelled in her heart, but an awful pit grew in her stomach. She'd apologized to him so much, she sounded like a broken record. So she said thank you.

"I almost let them deport you."

She faced him. "Oh, no, M. Claremont. I want to be here, honest I do."

"You want to be here? You don't take Pet Care seriously." His eyes burned into hers.

She hung her head in shame. He spoke the truth.

"Sometimes I think you are sent here to ruin me."

"No, it's not that." Rubbing her hands across her face, she must staunch the flow of tears before she sneezed. "I'm…It's…This doesn't usually happen. I'm not usually like this. I'm usually much more with it."

"With it?"

"On top of things, more together, productive."

His brow hung heavy over his dark eyes.

How could he understand all the trials she had been through? She waved her hands around for drama, searching for the right words, the right feeling. She had reached the breaking point. "I am being beaten down. Every time I get up, I get beaten down again. I'm being conched."

"Conched?"

"Yes, it's a term used in chocolate."

He was almost amused. "Why am I not surprised."

She gave him a long sideways glare, but he listened attentively.

Apartments replaced storefronts as they continued west on Avenue du Général-Guisan. Lights shone from apartment lobbies, spilling onto the sidewalk. This late at night, few cars passed them.

"So what does conched mean?" he asked in earnest.

"There's a story of how Rodolphe Lindt discovered the secret of making exceptionally smooth milk chocolate. You see, before then, milk chocolate was too grainy to be enjoyable as a bar. Here in Vevey, Daniel Peter mixed chocolate and milk after Henri Nestlé popularized sweetened condensed milk, but people mostly consumed chocolate only as a drink."

"Sounds interesting."

Lainey decided he wasn't mocking her. His expression was serious, curious even. Why was she so paranoid about boring him? Because Aaron never listened when she discovered something interesting about chocolate. He only mildly tolerated her passion for chocolate. Whenever she grew excited about a new idea, like lemon poppyseed white chocolate or chocolate covered ginger, he would either interrupt her to praise their local baseball team or give her the glazed-eye stare.

She peeked out of the corner of her eye to see if M.

Claremont's eyes glazed over. He was attentively listening. Weird. "As legend has it, M. Lindt left the factory for the night forgetting about the *mélanguer*, the mixer, which was still beating the chocolate. When he came in the next morning, he was quite distressed."

"A waste of production and materials."

"Yes," she said, pointing to him. "Exactly what he thought, until he tasted it."

"And what did he find?"

"He found extensively beating the milk with the cocoa fused the two ingredients, previously grainy and inedible, into a creamy, addictive substance suitable to be molded into a bar."

In front of her apartment, he stopped. He was so close his breath tickled her face. In the dim glow of the street lights, his stare intensified, reaching down to the depths of her heart. His lashes shaded his eyes. "So you are saying beating two incompatible substances over a long period of time can make them not only compatible but superior?"

"Yes."

"Remarkable." He stared off over her shoulder as if contemplating the meaning of his statement.

"Yes, it is. Wait, remarkable I know this or the process is remarkable?"

His eyes gleamed when they rested on her. "Both." A corner of his lip lifted.

"So conched came to mean the continuous and long mixing of the chocolate. And I'm being conched, beaten over and over again."

"Yes, but Mademoiselle Peterson, what happens when you are conched?"

"I get fired from my internship?"

"No."

What a relief. She thought for sure she would be fired for being arrested by the *gendarmes*. What was worse than getting fired?

"You become better." He held out his hand. "Now please, Mademoiselle Peterson, your *carnet* for the week."

She opened her purse and handed him her *carnet*.

He cracked it open and perused under the light glaring from above the double doors. "What is this?" He stopped at a page and read. "'Number Sixty-Seven: Flushed Aaron memorabilia down the toilet. Had to call plumber to undo blockage'?" He glanced over the top of the pages to her. "Mademoiselle Peterson, what are you recording?"

Nooooooo! Wrong notebook!

She jumped for the *carnet*, but he blocked her, holding it above his head in his gloved hand, still reading her list!

"That's not…" she began, jumping to retrieve her *carnet*, but she missed it.

He flipped to the beginning. "Number seven: Going away party went bust.' I must hear the story. How does a going away party go 'bust'?"

"Can I have my notebook back?" She held out her hand.

With crossed arms, M. Claremont tucked it under the arm of his coat, his eyebrows set. "Not until you tell me the story."

Was he serious? His expression said yes. Lainey sighed. "Okay, fine. My best friend Nadine threw a going away party for me the Thursday before I came."

"At Stanford?"

Lainey shook her head. "I'm from Arizona. I only went to school in California."

"Ah."

"But she sent the invite via text message." She expected him to empathize, to grasp the meaning, to understand, but he just stared at her. "Over two hundred people showed up!"

"You should be happy you have so many friends."

He missed it completely. "They weren't all my friends. Some of my friends texted it to their friends who texted it to their friends, and then someone brought out the citrus shooters and oranges were going everywhere until the cops came. It was a mess. And the same night, I found my boyfriend in bed with another girl."

She wasn't planning on confessing the last part. She hadn't realized how raw those emotions were until now.

M. Claremont was silent. Though she focused on a piece of lint on his jacket, his gaze was on her. "I'm sorry, Mademoiselle Peterson, I shouldn't have pried."

"No, it's not your fault. I am just a dumb American." As soon as she said it, she cringed—instant regret. She pinched her lips together. Maybe he didn't hear it.

"Dumb American?"

Nope.

The sides of his usually straight and serious mouth bent upwards. His flashing eyes beamed humor, not irritation.

She waved her hand to signal dismissal. Walking down the street, she hoped he would forget it. "Nothing."

"No, this is very interesting." He quickened his pace to step in front of her. "Please, Mademoiselle Peterson. Elaborate. What do you mean?"

She stopped and face him. She hesitated.

"I tried to learn everything about Switzerland before I came, but I keep making mistakes. Anyway, I've been keeping track of all the mistakes in this notebook."

"And you think you're unprepared?"

"The notebook speaks for itself. I've recorded everything. And numbered them."

"Oh, really? What number are you on now?" His gloved hand flipped through her notebook. "May I?" he asked.

She nodded reluctantly.

He thumbed to the end of her writing. "Two hundred and fifty-six. Incredible."

"You might as well start from the beginning." She nodded her permission for him to peruse her personal record.

In the dim streetlight, he flipped the pages back and read down the first page, then the second. He laughed. And kept laughing for some time, garnering sideways glances from the other passersby as he continued to read. He didn't notice.

Lainey loved his laugh. It was not pity nor ridicule, but a simple chortle, the sound of sharing a joke with your best friend.

"I'm glad you find this so amusing," she said, hoping Hiroko didn't make him laugh with as much gusto. Impatient with the cold, she paced to keep herself warm while he continued to read.

"Panty hose?" he stopped, raising his head.

"Hosiery?"

He laughed again, tilting his head back, elongating his Adam's apple and showing his beautiful teeth. He continued reading. "I remember." He must be where they were street contacting. "Wait, what is this? 'Number sixteen: Displayed my granny panties in front of my uptight Swiss boss.'"

The panty show. Oh no! She'd forgotten she wrote about it later.

Her body sprang into action. "No!" With all her might, she lunged at him, like a woman searching for chocolate when she was PMSing. No holds barred, she wrestled the book from his hands, twisting his wrists.

There might have been bloodshed. And definitely some serious body contact, making her giddy.

In a short snatch, he tried to grab it back, but she blocked him with her back. Too slow. She clawed at the pages, ripping them out, crumpling them and stuffing them in her pockets.

"Mademoiselle Peterson, what are you doing?"

"You cannot read those pages." Satisfied with her censorship, she returned the book to him.

"Are you embarrassed about something in the dressing room?" He blinked his eyes expectantly. Were his lips just twitching into a smile?

"Did you see?" she asked. Maybe he didn't see her underwear. Or he did, and he was nobly allowing her to keep her dignity by not making a big deal about it. Either way, she didn't want him reading about it.

"You are asking if I read what you wrote?"

"Did you read it?"

"I did not read it—all."

"But did you see?"

"Did I see what?" His face was so deadpan.

"If you didn't see, I'm not going to tell you." She relaxed. If any other guy had seen her underwear, it would've been fair game for ridicule.

But M. Claremont didn't even hide a smile. "But it involves your uptight Swiss boss."

She bowed her head in shame. "Please forgive me. I didn't know you then."

"And now that you know me?"

She provoked him. "You're still uptight."

He laughed. "I see. May I continue?"

Lainey nodded.

With a few chuckles, he continued reading until the end. When finished, he slapped the book closed and handed it back to her. Their hands touched as she retrieved the book. He didn't let go at first. "I'm sorry, Mademoiselle Peterson, you have had so many trials. I hope I was not too insensitive by laughing."

She shook her head.

"But really, you should focus on the positive."

"Oh?"

He continued. "Do you not believe in the power of attraction? Like is drawn to like. Positive to positive. Whatever you focus on, you draw closer to." He finally let go of the book. "Now, I must return to Corporate. And you still owe me a notebook."

"It's back at my desk. I'll transfer what I accidentally wrote in this notebook and turn it in."

"Shall we walk together then?"

They walked together in silence.

****

Yves brooded in his thoughts until they reached the corporate building. Once inside the gray doors, they parted ways, Mlle Peterson to her cubicle and Yves to his office. To his surprise, M. le President greeted him.

His large frame filled the doorway. "I heard you are trying something unconventional again."

Yves rounded his desk to the chair. "Oh? Says who?"

M. le President squinted at him, and brushed his salt and pepper hair back. "I have my sources. Just remember everything you do reflects on Alpine Foods."

"It is in my thoughts one hundred percent of the time."

M. le President glanced at the stack of notebooks on his desk. "What is all this?"

"I am asking real people real questions of what they need in Pet Care. I want my team to understand the customer base."

"How are you paying for this?" M. le President demanded.

"With my own money. I didn't use a *centime* of corporate funds." Yves continued to read through the notebooks, almost pretending the President wasn't standing in his office, standing over his desk yelling at him.

"I don't want our name associated with such tactics. I worry about public opinion. The last thing we need right now at this critical point during negotiations with Atatakai International is scandal. You, of all people, should be conscious of the consequences."

"I have already informed my team about the sensitive nature of the questioning."

Yves' calm reply to M. le President's gruff accusations broke the anger in the older man's voice.

M. le President gazed thoughtfully at Yves, then

spoke with more sensitivity. “Your methods are unusual, Yves.”

“Thank you. I’m glad you approve.”

“I don’t approve,” he snapped, breaking the recent aura of peace between them. “But they produce results.”

“And you are interested in results.”

M. le President took this as an insult. “Be warned. Promotions are not set in stone. The Board does not appreciate wild cards. Don’t forget it.”

With a calm steadiness, Yves raised his gaze to meet his superior’s. “I will not, M. le President, I assure you.”

“Other people have worked just as hard to get where they are. They don’t want to lose what they’ve worked for.”

Yves bowed his head slightly without breaking eye contact.

M. le President wished him a good night and blustered out the door.

A few heartbeats passed before Yves spoke again. “You can come in now, Mademoiselle Peterson.” Yves had spotted her hiding outside the door during the confrontation, listening in.

She jumped slightly.

“You know what will happen if you eavesdrop, don’t you? Your ears will fall off.” He laughed stiffly. Yves didn’t realize he was still shaking from the confrontation with M. le President. “Then you could write about it in your notebook.”

“I wasn’t eavesdropping. I was waiting to give you my *carnet* for review.” She left it on his desk, then retreated.

"Wait, mademoiselle—"

She faced him, her eyebrows arched. "Did you know you are the only person at Alpine Foods who calls me Mademoiselle Peterson?"

"I'm sorry, Elaine—"

She laughed. "I think after being together for several days we know each other well enough for you to call me what everyone else calls me."

"What's that?"

"Lainey."

A strange barrier was broken, one he had purposefully erected. Once he called her by her first name, he could no longer hide behind the distance. It pleased him and scared him at the same time. "Lainey, then." He reached under his desk lamp to turn out the light. "I'll read these at home as there are constant interruptions here." He gave her a teasing glance.

They paused in the lobby before parting ways.

"Now I have a favor for you, *Lainey.* If I am to call you Lainey, then you must call me Yves."

She avoided eye contact.

His eyes narrowed, scrutinizing her, teasing her. "Haven't you noticed no one else at Alpine Foods calls me M. Claremont. But you insist on calling me M. Claremont. Why?"

Instead of answering, Lainey raised her gaze to him, sticking out her hand. "All right, goodnight, *Yves* Claremont."

He arched an eyebrow at her outstretched hand. Someday he would have to teach her the *bise*, a true Swiss parting. But he shook her hand in goodwill, a smile creeping on his lips. "Goodnight, Lainey Peterson."

****

The next morning in his office, Yves and Lainey prepared for their usual day of street contacting.

Lainey—it was easier than he imagined to call her by her first name—wrapped a scarf around her neck. She slid into her coat and flipped her auburn hair over the collar. Even in the fluorescent lighting there was a hint of fire in it.

Britta stalked in. “Yves, read this.” She slapped *Le Temps du Temps* on his desk, surprising him.

Yves dropped his pen and drew the newspaper close, his leather chair creaking. “What is this?” He read the title “‘Alpine Foods SA Engages in Door-to-Door Selling.’”

Britta’s eyes widened with horror. “Someone must have told the press.”

Lainey peeked over Yves’ shoulder to read the headline with him.

While he read, his face flamed. “This is absurd.”

“What does it say?” Lainey asked.

Britta faced her and translated the more difficult French for her. “It says we were engaged in *porte à porte* selling dog food.”

“But we weren’t.”

Yves chewed on a cuticle as he read, ignoring them. “Ah, but it doesn’t matter what we were doing, it matters what they perceive we were doing. Perception is greater than truth.” Yves slapped the paper together and threw it to the recycling bin but it fluttered to the floor instead. Just as he retrieved his phone, it buzzed. He picked it up and read the text. From Luc. “Thank you, Britta.” He hesitated before responding to the text. This should be dealt with face to face.

"Shall I tell everyone to go ahead as usual today?"

"Yes, and to leave the *carnets* here on my desk for review at the end of the day. But wait, first come with me. You," he said to Lainey, startling her, "wait here." Yves stalked through the door. "He got his way, anyhow," Yves said to Britta as the two left together to go find Luc.

Yves and Britta found him by the copier. "You texted me?"

"Yeah." He glanced at Britta. "I thought we would talk privately."

"Whatever you say to me you can say to anyone."

Luc stared at Britta who thankfully didn't back down either. "I want to be done with this ridiculousness."

Yves faced him. "We are doing this as a department."

Luc mulled this around as he glanced at the ceiling. "You are spending a lot of time with the new intern." His gaze returned to Yves. "It would be a shame if you two became too close."

Yves' cheeks warmed at his insinuation. He glanced at Britta to gauge her reaction. But she was impassive.

"Don't worry. There is nothing between Lainey and me."

"Lainey? Oh, I see you're on a first name basis now." Luc smiled. "I want the street contacting to be over."

Yves regained his composure, arched an eyebrow and stalked away, Britta trailing behind him.

"What are you going to do?" she asked.

As fond as he had been of combing the streets,

surveying people, perhaps it was time to call it quits. Too much was at stake. "We have already gained valuable insights. Perhaps it's best to continue working on making the best products. Monday will be our last day."

Britta nodded her understanding. Yves was grateful for her support. Once back in his office, he grabbed his overcoat and scarf off the coat rack near the door.

"What was that all about?" Lainey asked.

He most certainly wouldn't tell her about Luc's veiled threat. "Someone leaked we were doing personal surveys, street contacting. Someone told the press we were from Alpine Foods and, shall we say, elaborated a bit on the truth?"

"And you know who it was?"

He nodded. He clearly underestimated how much Luc hated the project.

"Was it me? I accidentally told the pastry chef I worked for Alpine Foods."

Yves, surprised at her confession, laughed. "Oh, no. It wasn't you, Lainey. You have no reason to hurt me." He remembered his conversation with Luc. "No, I know who it is. Monday will be the last day with the project. Just as well, I think we've learned some valuable things."

Like who your friends were. And who were your enemies.

****

"A package came for you," Marie Claire said when Lainey returned home after a long day of contacting. When Lainey crossed the hall to her room, Marie Claire gestured to a large box on the floor.

Heart-speckled tape held the box together.

Homesickness overtook any ache in her feet. Seeing all the blue and white USPS American eagles on the First-Class Priority Mail stickers pasted *all* around it—it had to be from Nadine. With her Swiss Army knife she tore the tape, hoping for something to lift her spirits.

She flipped open the flaps to see what was inside. Across a vacuum-sealed bag, as heavy and as hard as a boulder, was a note: "Call me when you get this, Nadine."

From the land line, Lainey dialed her number.

"Did you get my package?" Nadine asked.

"What is it?" Lainey poked the boulder with her finger.

"It's a formal dress. It cost us twenty-two bucks just to send it."

"A formal dress?"

"You're my maid of honor, remember? Put it on and take a picture and send it to me."

"Ugh."

"We're going to enlarge it for a full-sized cardboard cutout."

Egad! Lainey was hoping she forgot. "So you're serious? You really don't want to see an anything of mine enlarged."

"You promised."

"All right." She hung up. With the mini-scissors on her Swiss Army knife, she cut away the plastic, letting air into the compacted vacuum-sealed bag. It expanded like an air mattress, letting loose a swirl of chiffon and taffeta. She stared at the contents. "Uh."

Marie Claire clacked across the hall. "What is it?" She poked her head inside Lainey's room. "It's a hideous color."

Inside the shrink-wrapped package was a fabric root beer float. Cutting the rest of the plastic, Lainey released the brown taffeta dress from its prison. Shaking it free, she held the strapless frilly thing at arm's length to examine it.

"Let me see." Marie Claire snatched it from Lainey, examining it. Below the waistline, a peplum split over layers upon layers of creamy flounces. She held the plain straight neckline across her chest. Marie Claire asked, "Is this in style in America?"

Lainey nabbed the dress and threw it on the bed. "No, my friend just has interesting taste."

The color wasn't even a gorgeous copper or a dark chocolate brown. It had too much red in it.

Marie Claire arched an eyebrow. "You'll look like dog plop covered in Chantilly cream."

"Thank you."

Marie Claire shrugged. "I speak the truth."

At least Nadine remembered to include a bolero jacket the same color as the creamy chiffon to cover Lainey's shoulders.

"I have to take a picture of me. They're going to make a life-sized cutout of me for a wedding."

Marie Claire stared at her incredulously. She must not have understood.

Lainey's flip phone didn't have a camera. "Does your phone have enough megapixels to enlarge a picture to life-sized?"

"No." Marie Claire showed Lainey her beat up old phone.

"Who has a top-of-the-line camera?"

Lainey thought it, but it was Marie Clare who said, "Yves Claremont."

****

Marie Clare paced the hall, her ear pressed to her phone, while Lainey nearly dislocated her shoulder ironing wrinkles out of the taffeta. Shrink-wrapped wrinkles were pretty stubborn.

Marie Claire entered the room. “Yves has a camera and can come take pictures.”

“When?”

“Right now. Get dressed. Put on your makeup.”

Right now? Lainey’s heart lunged. She replaced the iron. It fell onto her bed. She snatched it before it scorched her comforter, burning herself. “Ow!” She tugged on the plug. The smell of burnt feathers tinged her nose. “You mean, right now, right now?”

“He was just finishing up some work at Corporate and will stop by shortly.”

Of course.

Behind her closed bedroom door, she stripped and dressed. Nadine thankfully included all the undergarments she needed, a petticoat and a strapless bra. But no shoes. No one was going to see her feet anyway underneath all this frill. With the near ear-deafening rustling of taffeta, netting, and flounces, she slid the dress over her head, wiggling and gyrating to move her fat around to the right spots, as a snake might slither out of its shed skin.

Even utilizing various yoga positions, she still couldn’t access the zipper. She needed help. With her elbows pinching the dress in place, she worked on her face, applying more than normal street makeup. Eye shadow there, rouge here. Done. She was a mix between a street whore and a prom slut, but she wasn’t repulsive. When she finished, she kicked the hem of the dress to open the door.

"Here," she called from the doorway. "It's tight. Zip me up?"

She rounded the corner to see Yves standing in the hall, in his suit, absorbed in his phone.

Marie Claire must have opened the door for him while she was dressing.

She stopped short, her breath hard to draw, and she hadn't even zipped yet. Thankfully, she was still in shadow, her exposed shoulders hidden.

He glanced up. Their gazes locked.

"Not you," she mumbled. "Marie Claire, I mean."

The globe light above them cast harsh shadows across his beautiful face. But he didn't smile. She didn't expect a smile. He was M. Claremont after all. But he didn't give her any chastising remarks, either. After a brief second of heart-pounding silence of locked eyes, his returned to his phone.

Marie Clare emerged from the kitchen. Lainey motioned to her to help her zip in her room.

It took some major inhaling. She hadn't gained much weight living here, had she? Finally, all done up, bolero over her shoulders, she emerged from the bedroom and into the hall. "Okay, ready," she said.

"What is this for?" he asked.

"My best friend is getting married at the end of November but since I'm here, she sent me this"—she kicked yards of fluff entwined in her legs—"as punishment."

"Where should I take the photo?" he asked, producing a DSLR.

She spread her arms wide, motioning around her, anxious for him to leave. "Uh, just snap one here in the hall. They're going to cut away the background anyway."

Yves shook his head. "We need someplace with better lighting. Your apartment casts too many shadows."

"Sadly, it's too dark outside." Marie Claire motioned to the windows.

"I have an idea." He opened the door. "Follow me."

With a quick turn, he headed out the door and without waiting for the elevator, bounded down the stairs.

More slowly, Lainey followed him. With a rustle comparable to a Midwest thunderstorm, she carefully trod downstairs after him. Marie Clare tiptoed after her to avoid stepping on the dress.

"Wait here," he said, once they were downstairs.

"The lobby has better lighting than our apartment?" Lainey stared dubiously at the blinking fluorescent lights casting funky yellowed shadows across the room.

"No, Mademoiselle Peterson." He leaned close to her, almost within kissing distance. "I'm retrieving my car." He stepped out into the dark, the glass doors swinging shut behind him with a swoosh.

His car? While they waited, Marie Claire ran upstairs, returning with a few hair clips. She twisted and wrapped Lainey's hair, using the glass doors as a mirror.

A few minutes passed before they heard the heart-stopping sound of his Maserati. He jumped out to open the doors for them.

Surprisingly, Marie Clare fit in the back comfortably.

Just as surprising, the dress—and Lainey—fit up front, and they could still see out the windows, although Lainey felt like an inverted mushroom in the front seat, the frills about her ears.

They rode for a while, Lainey stuffed up front between the gear shift and the door, Marie Clare still tugging her hair in silence, as they drove through *centre-ville* eastward, toward Montreux. The buildings became more extravagant and more ornate.

At last, they arrived at a large, cut-stone building with decorative cornices and many glowing windows, and parked under a pillared pagoda.

"We're going someplace public?" Lainey asked, slumping in her seat, staring at the Bentleys and limos shining under the lights of the Grande Hôtel de Vevey. She'd already been in the dress longer than she anticipated and had been seen by far too many people.

Instead of answering, Yves was already out of the car, popping open Lainey's door, allowing her to spill out of his car.

Which took some doing.

After rocking back and forth, attempting to find her feet under the frills, Lainey glanced up to see Yves' outstretched hand. "Thanks," she murmured, accepting his help, and stepped out onto the cobblestone in her sneakers. His hand was warm and strong.

But he released it almost immediately, helping Marie Clare extricate herself from the backseat.

A gloved man in a dove gray, short-waisted, double-breasted coat, jumped from behind a pulpit and all too delightedly took the keys from Yves.

He didn't notice the barely-contained glee of the valet, who caressed the dashboard before easing the machine into gear. Did Yves ever worry a valet would take off with his car?

No, no. Without a backward glance, Yves bounded up the stone stairs to the massive glass doors where another gloved man, in an identical uniform, held open the door as they entered.

Immediately, Lainey was out of her element. She had never seen so much gilt. It was everywhere—on the mirror frames, the marble-topped sideboards, legs of chairs, in the chair railing, candlesticks, crown moldings, baseboards, and around the marble-topped reception desk. The dress, and sneakers, in the lobby, made her a pretender, a fraud. But surprisingly, surveying the other patrons, her makeup was not overkill here.

And Yves was right about the lighting. Huge chandeliers dripped with crystals reflecting light and refracting rainbows around the room. Around huge marble columns hung wall sconces, highlighting richly upholstered furniture and plush carpet. Behind the desk, a polite receptionist recognized Yves at once, calling him by name.

Yves asked in formal French if they would allow them the honor of photographing their lobby.

The receptionist, in a stiff tuxedo as if he was going to prom, too, assented and led them to a seating area, off to the side.

The three of them marched through the pillars and furniture as if they owned the place, Yves searching with his ever-attentive eye for the perfect background.

Marie Claire plopped in a chair, legs crossed, arms folded.

"Stop," Yves said when Lainey passed one of the

great marble pillars. “Right there.”

Startled, Lainey stopped and faced him, skeptical. “Right here?”

“Yes. But don’t make a face.”

She relaxed, facing him straight on, like a driver’s license mug shot.

“This is not a passport photo, Lainey.”

“What do you want me to do?”

“Here.” He handed his DSLR to Marie Claire. He strode toward her, deep thought in his eyes. “Turn here.” He wrapped his arm around her waist and twisted her until she faced the pillar.

“Yes, my backside. This is definitely better.”

He ignored her. “Chin over your shoulder, here.”

She obliged him. It was unnatural and contorted; her senior pictures all over again.

Reaching around her, he gently lifted her left hand, planting it shoulder height on the pillar. His touch was warm, the marble cold.

Her body prickled.

He pressed against her, warm and alive. He placed her right hand on the pillar near her breast. He studied her eyes, slid a strand of hair away from them, then slowly tilted her chin down.

“You don’t need so much makeup.” He stalked away.

“What?” She broke her hand from the pillar.

“Don’t move,” he said sternly, his back to her. How did he know she moved? “You don’t want me to reposition you.”

Actually, she did, but she pretended not to.

At his upturned hand, Marie Clare returned his DSLR. He adjusted the lens to snap a photo. “Wait,” he said when Lainey moved. "I have not even begun." He pressed a button and snapped another without the flash.

"I think they're going to be standing this up in a reception line, so I think it would be silly to be coyly smiling over my shoulder. Probably better to do a face on."

He lowered the camera, shrugging. "Then face me. Turn your foot out so you are at a three-quarter angle. Like this." He approached to arrange her shoulders. His warm touch on her shoulders made her stomach jump. "Stand straight. Place both hands behind your back. I'm sure the bride doesn't want you to be so limp. Might think the better of her idea."

"This was actually the groom's suggestion."

"Have they been together long, your friend and her fiancé?" Another picture.

"About three years. But they just became engaged last month."

Snap again. "And they are getting married next month? Why so soon?"

She wanted to say it was because Nadine was so sweet and lucky. And Lainey was unlucky. Maybe if she hadn't left, she would still be with Aaron. Though the last thought didn't comfort her much.

"Smile, Lainey. Or is this wedding a horrible event?"

Lainey forced a smile. "No. She's my best friend. I'm ecstatic."

"But you are disappointed you can't be there for their wedding."

"I'm supposed to be the maid of honor. But I'm here instead."

"Are you sorry you came to Switzerland?" Click.

"No."

"That was not the best. Smile, Lainey. You don't look happy."

She smiled again. "I am very happy and grateful to be here."

"Your smile is forced. Then you're sorry you have an internship in Pet Care? If you had returned home in September, you could be there for the wedding. Perhaps it was a mistake to stay."

Through the next series of snaps, she didn't reply. Her feelings were hard to discern. If Yves didn't give her a smashing recommendation, then this whole ordeal would be a waste of time. Not true. It had been educational. No learning experience was ever wasted.

He stepped forward, his camera resting in his hands. Now he was staring straight at her. His lashes fringed his eyes. The color of his lips matched the color of his cheeks when he flushed. His voice was low and controlled. "I should not have hired you, then."

His questions were driving her nuts. They were not questions, they were statements. He wanted her to contradict him. He waited for her answer. Then suddenly, Yves broke from his stare, stepping back to snap a few more half-hearted photos.

Finally, after a few more minutes, Yves lowered his hands. "I will email the pictures to you, then you can send them to whomever you want."

"Thank you for taking time from your weekend to do this," Lainey said.

But he had already approached the receptionist's desk to thank him. Lainey wrote out her personal email address on hotel stationary before rustling back into his waiting car to be chauffeured home.

Once the high gears of his Maserati faded from their hearing, Lainey gathered up her skirts and opened the lobby door.

"I think he likes you." Marie Clare removed bobby pins from Lainey's hair.

"Who? M. Claremont? No."

"He fusses over you."

"No."

"As an outside observer, there was definitely some chemistry going on there."

"No."

"Why do you keep saying no?"

"He's my boss, and I'm an intern."

"So?"

"So, no." Lainey shook her head. "We are always disagreeing."

"Men like Yves show their affection differently."

"By constant fighting?"

"By fighting himself."

****

Later, Lainey trekked to the Internet café, loading in her pre-paid card to use the computer. There was an email from her parents and five emails from M. Claremont with the pictures in a zip file. He was efficient. But then again, he probably didn't want to leave her pictures on his camera in case his girlfriend happened to find them. Might cause some misunderstanding. She clicked on his first email.

They were so big, he explained, he made thumbnails to preview.

Wow, he must have touched these up. Lainey leaned closer to the screen, her eyes absorbing the pixels. He did an amazing job. Her senior pictures weren't this professional. She didn't even recognize herself. After clicking through and previewing all five email attachments—thirty-four pictures in all—she picked out the best one to send to Nadine. Now her parents' email:

Lainey,

We sold our house and put an offer in on a bungalow in Costa Rica. There was some confusion with our new house so we'll have to stay in a hotel right on the beach for a few days until closing. We plan on swimming every day, so your dad is running every morning so he can show off his bod in a swimsuit. I packed all your stuff in a rental unit. I'll mail you the key so you can get to your stuff if/when you come back.

I'll call you when we are packed and on our way so you can track the flight if you want. We're so excited to get on with the next phase of our lives!

XOXOX Mom

Dear Mom and Dad,

You are crazy. Thanks for abandoning me here in a foreign country depriving me of a home to come home to. Now I can't even call you. I hope you get bedbugs.

No, how about…

Dear Mom,

Congrats on selling our house! I'll be home after the gala. I doubt I'll get a recommendation from my boss, so I'm not going to get a job at Alpine Foods, and I'm going to work a menial job and die a lonely, lonely old maid.

Delete, delete, delete.

Dear Mom—

Glad to hear you and Dad are doing something interesting now you are free. Sounds lovely. A run on the beach sounds great right now, as it is turning cold here. My internship is better. There's a big fancy dance and dinner with awards and promotions and stuff next month. Supposed to have a date.

I need a date to the gala.

Anyway, let me know when you get in a house and have a phone and we'll figure out the time difference so we can talk.

Sure love you guys,

Lainey

Chapter Nine

The sun sagged to the west, casting long shadows across the valley as Yves and Lainey ended their last day of surveying pet owners together. Standing across the street from Corporate headquarters, Lainey hugged herself against the wind from the lake slicing through them.

Lainey wrapped her coat around her tighter as she waited for Yves, speaking in French on his cell phone, to cross the street. The wind played with his scarf, ruffled the dark fringes of his hair, and blew his bangs off his forehead.

As much as she thought she hated this project, a twinge of sadness crept into her heart. Speaking with all these people in French had been tedious. But she was more fluent now, and she had learned to love the people here. And clocking miles each day had fatigued her, but strengthened her.

And made her hungry. The day was over, and she waited to give Yves her *carnet*, then go home and eat.

When he joined her across the street, he pocketed his phone. "There's one last stop I need to take you before we end our time on the streets. You have not met any real Swiss. I cannot have you go home with an unfavorable opinion about us."

"I don't have an unfavorable opinion about *all* Swiss."

"Just me, then?"

She didn't reply. Did he think she disliked him? At one point she thought she hated him. But now?

At his car, he beeped the keyless entry and opened the door for her. As the sun set, they drove out highway number nine, built high above the city traffic, like a giant roller coaster through the rolling hills. In his car, it was more like flying than driving, given the smoothness of the road, the altitude, the quiet hum. They coursed through the mountains, barely speaking. She stared out the window to the darkening valley below them.

The scenery astounded her. The setting sun bathed the mountains and valley in an orange glow, the reflection of fire on water.

Fire on water. An impossible mix. Just as impossible as the two of them.

They didn't have a relationship. He was her boss. And yet, here she was, driving with him to some unknown destination. Alone together. After work hours. But he always distanced himself.

Night settled upon them like a sheet when they exited the freeway at Monthey. They continued on to a road which led to a smaller road, then to a smaller road. Finally, he drove up a gravelly path almost on the far side of the lake. Pebbles *tinked* the underside of the car. His tires crunched gravel as they ascended higher and higher until they reach a little, oh so little, house.

In Switzerland, one was taxed for square footage of the ground level and not by how high you built. Even in the countryside, where there could easily be suburban sprawl, people still built up.

The house resembled a boot. The old woman in the shoe might come out of the large wooden front door.

The roof extended over the balcony ornamented with cut wooden details, like something out of a picture book of fairy tales.

After turning off the motor, Yves propped his hands on his steering wheel while he removed his gloves. "I want you to see a different part of Switzerland, a traditional side, not just the city dwellers." He nodded toward the house. "These are true mountain Swiss."

A man in coveralls, barely visible from the porch light, stepped from behind the house and waved, motioning for them to come.

Yves unbuckled his seat belt and cracked the door. Light flooded the interior. Yves' eyebrows gathered again in the middle as he stared out the windshield. The always cool Yves hesitated for once. "These are simple people, Lainey. Good people."

Before she asked what he meant, Yves lithely slid from the car and strode across the gravel to the large man. She clicked her seatbelt and followed him. The sound of the door slamming was swallowed by the small forest and the vastness of the sky.

Beside the house, the thick man squatted, turning a small cage over a fire, like a spit. Inside the cage, the delightful sound of clashing chestnuts reminded Lainey of pebbles washing up on the beach. The sweet smell of smoke burned her nose when the wind shifted.

"Sorry, I just had to turn them so they don't burn. Hope you enjoy them. We gathered them from the woods this fall." His French was rough and slow, with an exaggerated sing-songyness.

He stood, dusted soot from his large hands, and kicked a stone closer to the fire with a worn boot. "How're you doing, Yves? We haven't seen you for a while. How's work at your fancy factory?"

Yves smiled. In the half light of the small fire, he relaxed.

Lainey stepped closer to him, bewildered. *Who were these people?*

Yves was overdressed in his suit up here. "Very well, very well."

The man's gaze flickered to Lainey. Yves motioned to her, but didn't meet her eyes. "This is Lainey, our new intern. She's from the United States, so you'll have to excuse her French." A tease. "Lainey, this is Christophe, one of the best carpenters you'll find in the Swiss *Romande*."

Christophe grinned but didn't contradict his compliment, nodding in her direction. He then crouched to open the latch of the cage with a stick. Opening the latch allowed one of the nuts to tumble out. Christophe cracked the nut when it cooled, and danced it from hand to hand before popping it into his mouth.

Marrons. On the streets, venders sold the warmed chestnuts from carts, wrapped in paper cones for a couple of Swiss francs.

"Not quite done." He tilted his head to the house. His haircut was too short and uneven, as if he were a child who wouldn't sit still long enough to get a smooth cut. "There are chairs over there."

Yves retrieved two plastic chairs from a pile leaning against the house, first for Lainey, then for Christophe. Lainey sat close to the fire.

When Yves returned to the pile for a third, he stopped, examining something. "Is this your work?" he asked, running an admiring hand over the intricate scrollwork on a bedstead footboard.

Christophe glanced up, but returned his gaze to the fire. "*Ouiah.*" His accent was long and drawn out in natural exaggerated undulations. "Took me nearly three months, but it split on the last turn. Damn waste of birch. Out here for firewood now."

"It's beautiful." Yves continued to admire the piece.

"The headboard's inside."

"May we see it?" Yves asked.

"*Ouiah.*"

Christophe moved the cage away from the fire, motioning for Lainey to come, too. He cranked the handle of the heavy wooden door.

From behind Yves, she glanced around. Almost the whole first floor was a workshop. Flying bugs buzzed around the naked light bulb.

Inside the dimly lit workshop, lacquer and smoke tinged her nose. Over a cluttered and sawdust-covered bench, a bank of opaque windows faced the twinkling lights of the valley. Spiderwebs and dust covered nearly everything, from the large wooden beams of the ceiling to the concrete floor. There was no drywall or plaster. It was all exposed studs. Lainey tripped on a few planks of wood lying on the ground.

Yves grabbed her elbow, righting her. "Are you all right?" There was a hint of tenderness in his voice.

"Yeah." A scrape reddened along her ankle, sawdust dotted her socks. "Just a scratch." She bent to brush the sawdust away and thumb-lick her wound.

"Sorry. You have to watch your step in here." Christophe raised his eyebrows in concern.

"Do you need a bandage?" Yves gently inspected the scrape.

"I'm fine." It stopped bleeding with a bit of spit.

More carefully, they followed Christophe around as he showed them some of his projects at Yves' insistence—a bookcase, a set of drawers, and finally the headboard on the lathe.

Yves ran his hand along the grooves. "You could still use the headboard, yes?"

"*Ouiah*. But they command a higher price with the matching footboard."

Lainey followed the curves with her finger. The smooth scrolls bent and curved to make a heart shape in the center. Never had Lainey seen such craftsmanship. This piece alone could cost hundreds, if not thousands, of dollars.

When Yves was satisfied, they returned to the smoke-filled yard. Christophe replaced his tumbling nuts on the fire.

"How was the apple crop this year?" Yves nodded toward a sloping pasture filled with trees.

Christophe followed his glance to the edge of the mountain where a darkened orchard blacked out the lights of the valley. He nodded to Yves. "Pretty good this year. Anïse pressed apple juice with the first harvest of the season."

"Ah, Anïse. Where is my cousin?"

"Inside. Feeding the babies before bed. Go in. She's expecting you."

Yves motioned for Lainey to follow as he crossed the yard and knocked on the dark wooden door with heavy carving. Without waiting for an answer, he entered.

A small entryway was filled with coats overflowing from wooden pegs on the wall and shoes heaped on a small rug.

"Should I take off my shoes?" she asked.

"Yes."

In front of them, gleaming wooden stairs climbed to the second level. Whining and a woman speaking informal, incomprehensible French came from upstairs. Scuffles, thumps. Then a cry.

Lainey glanced at Yves uncomfortably. He motioned for her to climb the stairs ahead of him. When she reached the top, she waited for him, the sound of cries growing louder. They rounded the corner.

"Yves!" At the table, a curvaceous woman held a baby at her breast. She poised a spoon mid-air to feed a four-year-old with a clamped mouth. When the boy spied Yves, he shoved himself away from the table and ran to hug his knees, nearly knocking over his older cousin. A dog in the corner rose up, barking and pawing.

Lainey used Yves as a human shield. Then she recognized Futé. But she still hid.

With dinner forgotten in the distraction, Anïse gave up, dropping the spoon and scolding her son instead. "Enough, Jean-Christophe. Run and get ready for bed."

The dog still clawed at Yves' pant legs. Yves patted his head.

"And take the dog upstairs," Anïse said.

The boy faced upward to Yves for an appeal to authority, but Yves tousled the boy's hair and sent him on his way, Futé at his heels.

With all the noise, the babe unlatched from the breast, a bit of milk dribbling down at the corner of her lips. She was at least two. Her smile was full of teeth. The child slid down from her mother's lap and toddled over to the chair, banging a cup on the wooden seat.

When Yves greeted Anïse, they kissed each other on a cheek. This was the first time Yves had shown any sort of affection.

"And this is your friend?" Anïse wiped her hands on a colorful towel after washing them.

Lainey blushed slightly.

"Yes." Yves cleared his throat. "Anïse, this is Lainey. She's an intern from the States. My cousin, Anïse."

"Pleased to meet you."

When Anïse approached, Lainey braced herself for a warm hug, but instead Anïse gave her a *bise*, just one, on the cheek. She smelled of sour milk and cereal.

Lainey admired Anïse right off. She was different from the Swiss women she'd met in town. It wasn't the added poundage around the hips and thigh area, either.

She happily cleared the table, asking Yves about work and his mother. Her eyes weren't bored; they even glowed and not from eyeshadow. In fact, she wore no makeup, and her hair was held in a simple ponytail. Her smile warmed Lainey. Whatever dreary, boring thing Yves was saying about work, she smiled and listened pleasantly, seeming genuinely interested in his drivel.

"Sit down, sit down." She motioned to a small but ornate table. Her kitchen was small, with beautiful wooden cupboards reaching all the way to the high ceiling, made by her husband, no doubt. Unsurprisingly, no dishwasher. Neither was there a microwave or any counter space. Certainly different from the gourmet kitchens and granite countertops back home.

Anïse washed off the table with a dish rag, clearing the plastic dishes.

Yves picked up the youngest child and sat her on his lap facing Lainey. She smiled at the baby. The toddler returned it with a toothy grin. Lainey tickled her under the chin. The baby laughed. Then she spit up on Lainey's slacks.

Anïse glanced up in time to catch the damage. "*Desolée.*" She wrung a rag from the kitchen sink. Lainey wiped her pants, laughing. Anïse lifted the babe from Yves' lap.

A door opened somewhere upstairs. Shortly after, an older girl came in. She sucked on a piece of chocolate. Lainey's stomach rumbled at the smell.

"Can I color in bed?" the girl asked.

"No, it's time to sleep." Anïse clunked plates on the table with finality.

"Not fair. You said Jean-Christophe can read until you come up. Why can't I color until you come up and tuck us in?" The girl was about six, judging from her missing front teeth—a cultural universal.

"Tell your brother he needs to put on his pajamas and brush his teeth."

"Hello, Cousin Yves." The girl threw her arms around his neck, leaving a smear of chocolate on his white collar.

He patted her forearm.

"Can I stay up and eat with you?

"No," said her mom.

The girl eyed Lainey carefully. "Is this your new girlfriend?"

What? A dozen questions popped into Lainey's head. Heat poured from her shirt. She resisted the temptation to peek at Yves' reaction, but she laughed it off. Maybe too much. Okay, she needed to stop laughing.

Anïse interrupted Lainey's insane laughter. "Jacqueline, to bed."

Before leaving for bed, she offered Lainey a square of chocolate embossed with her fingerprints. Lainey gladly ate it to shut up her mouth.

"Even if you're not his girlfriend, I think you're pretty," Jacqueline said before thundering up the stairs.

Lainey didn't dare glance up, but focused instead on the hardwood floors.

Jean-Christophe pattered down, complaining about a stuffy nose.

Sighing, Anïse shooed the kids up the stairs, baby on her hip, leaving Yves and Lainey alone to listen to the sound of a noisy bedtime routine.

"Wow, is it warm in here?" Lainey said in the awkward quiet.

"Yes." Yves removed his jacket, tossing it over the washing machine behind him, already piled high with laundry. It was the first time Lainey had seen him without a suit jacket. He loosened his tie. His face softened, his strict manner dissolved into total comfortable relaxation. Transformed.

H-O-T!

And this time it was not the room temperature.

He was her boss. He was her boss. He was her boss.

She had to think about something else. Where was Anïse, anyway?

Soon silence reigned upstairs, perhaps because of a threat. Anïse returned, childless, and resumed setting the table with Yves' help. Lainey jumped up to help her, happy to have a distraction, something to take her mind off what she wanted to rest her eyes on.

From the fridge, Anïse found a large cruet of cloudy orangish liquid.

"Anïse makes her own apple juice." Yves set it on the table.

"So said Christophe. Awesome. You'll have to show me sometime." She was too nervous to say more. Her voice might have cracked. Jitters shook her.

Anïse removed a platter from the small fridge to hand to Yves. "Sorry. The cheese and meat were purchased at the store."

Yves set down the thin-sliced dried meat alongside a wheel of cheese. And butter, not yellow but white, in a dish.

"What we're having tonight," he whispered to her in English, tickling the hair on her neck, making her heart thunder, "is a traditional meal. Anïse and Christophe are some of the last Swiss to eat off the land. As you can see—" he indicated each dish with his butter knife—"it is not calorie-free." He grinned wide, setting the knife on the dish. The up-tight boss was gone. Actually, forget the boss. She preferred this version of Yves Claremont.

Her eyes lingered on his lips, wondering what kind of kisser he was.

Lainey!

Christophe entered the house, stomping, calling for Anïse to bring a bowl down. The earthy aroma of toasted chestnuts preceded them up the stairs, and Lainey's mouth watered. Christophe placed the wooden bowl filled with charred chestnuts in the middle of the table.

They sat and said grace.

Lainey had never eaten chestnuts before. Using her fingernails, she tore at the X cut on the flat of the shell. The ends curled up, making it easier to pry them open. But the nuts were too hot to hold them long. She plunked the nut on her plate.

The noise attracted Yves' attention. "Not like that." Yves took her hand. "You will burn your fingers."

"I think I already did."

He inspected the reddened tips with dismay. His hands were warm and soft. "I'll show you." Taking her stubborn nut, he slipped his knife under the cut. "Use the blade to get under the skin." He cracked the shell with his knife, extracting the nutmeat, and handed it to her.

She held it in her hand. Slathering it in butter, as others had done, she popped it into her mouth. She hoped to always remember the taste. So wholesome, so earthy, yet delicate and simple, like homemade bread. Everything they served was tasty. Cheese, nuts, meat. Some greens from the garden. Freshly pressed apple juice. After a few helpings, she was full. She listened to the conversation around her. It was so casual, she only caught half of it.

Anïse was the last to speak to Lainey at the table. Perhaps she was nervous, not knowing what to expect from an American, wondering if she understood French well enough to hold a conversation. She spoke slowly. "So, Yves tells me you are the new intern in the Pet Care department."

Lainey nodded. She was mid-bite of a helping, which was probably more than she should have eaten.

"What made you decide to go into Pet Care?" Anïse asked.

Yves shifted in his seat. But Lainey finished the bite quickly, patting her lips with a rough napkin.

"Well, I originally applied to Chocolate, which is where I really wanted to work, but there was some miscommunication and M. Claremont, er, Yves—" She glanced at him. His eyebrows rose, pleased, and he nodded as she continued, "Yves agreed to take me in Pet Care."

She had never thanked him. In the pause, their gazes locked. Lainey absorbed every detail about him. His smooth skin on his fine nose, his defined jaw, lightly stubbled, his thick dark lashes, his black hair. And his penetrating eyes. They shone for her.

"I think I would want to work in Chocolate, too." Anïse broke the spell, speaking at her normal speed.

Lainey bowed her head, staring at her plate, her heart hammering.

"Too bad Yves didn't work for Chocolate." Anïse stood to clear her plate. "We'd get all the free chocolate we wanted, but then we'd have to buy dog food again."

Surprised, Lainey glanced at Yves.

Yves shrugged. He lifted his plate to the sink and rolled up his sleeves, pocketing his cufflinks and watch in his trouser pocket. Anïse protested but he told her to go sit down.

When Lainey finished, she carried her plate to the sink. "Can I rinse and dry for you?"

He nodded to another dishtowel. He tucked one towel into his pants to protect them.

Oh, to be the dishtowel. Lainey shook her head. *Focus, Lainey, focus. On the dishes.*

She rinsed and dried the plates as Anïse cleared platters off the table.

The baby cried.

"There's Vivianne." Anïse thanked them for doing the dishes before heading upstairs.

Christophe swiped his face with his napkin. "I better make sure the fire is all out." After dropping off his plate and clasping Yves on the shoulder, a wink in his eye, Christophe descended the stairs with heavy footfalls on the tread and snapped the front door shut.

They were alone in the kitchen.

The house was silent except for the clanking of dishes. Yves washed a pot and scrubbed stuck-on food with a cloth, his jaw set as when he tackled any problem, his eyes focused.

He was not just attractive. A man could be attractive and have the personality of…of…a bar of soap. And anyone, even a homely person, could be attractive, depending on the type of person they were inside. Yves was both physically and emotionally attractive; any girl would go ga-ga for him. And Lainey was no exception.

Stupid, Lainey, stupid. She must not be attracted to him.

Marie Claire said employees were fired when they were found fraternizing. It was fine to think your boss was hot and desirable. It was not okay, however, to act upon it. Besides, didn't Yves have a girlfriend? In Japan?

Clank. The sound of a pot dropped in her sink revived her from her thoughts.

He tugged at the towel at his waist and wiped his hands. "All yours." He smiled.

Oh, if only it were true.

He retrieved his watch from his pocket. With a flip,

he snapped it back into place.

Lainey caught the mark. A pricey timepiece.

He folded his towel and drained the sink, watching her as she rinsed and dried the last pot. Satisfied with her work, he found the broom and was sweeping when Anïse came downstairs.

"You don't have to sweep." She nodded toward the drying dishes, all completed, including several there before they arrived. "Thank you."

"No, thank you." Lainey folded her towel. "For a wonderful dinner and a great memory of Switzerland."

"And now, I'm afraid, we have kept our guest far too late." Yves finished the floor. "We must go."

A round of parting *bise*. This time, Lainey was ready for it. One kiss near the cheek.

Yves unrolled his sleeves and stuffed them in his jacket. They headed to the door to don their coats.

Lainey checked her watch. Nearly ten o'clock!

Christophe entered as they slid on their shoes. "Goodnight." Christophe's lined face was haggard with the day's work. He closed the door behind them.

Once they were outside, the wind blew hard. Lainey hugged her jacket around her, staring up into the clear sky. "The stars are bright up here."

"And it's a beautiful view."

"Yes."

His eyes were focused, not at the stars or at the city lights below, but on her. He stuffed his hands into the pockets of his unbuttoned wool trench coat.

Lainey wandered farther, her neck still cocked back, overwhelmed by the brilliant stars, her mind abuzz with what he meant, if he meant anything at all. Almost to the car, her foot slipped on loose gravel, and she fell backward, completely on her back. “Ow.” She clutched her elbow, where most of her weight fell.

“Needed a more comfortable view?” He stood over her, holding out his hand.

She remained on her back, scanning the stars and then him. “Did you make a joke? Because I think I’ll get another notebook and write down all your jokes. Marie Claire says the Swiss have no sense of humor.”

He frowned, retracting his hand. “Marie Claire should not make collective statements about any group of individuals. She will always be wrong because people as a whole act differently than individuals.”

“Wait, you’re ruining it.”

“What?”

“Nothing.”

“What am I ruining?” He crouched down to her level.

Lainey sat up, their faces inches apart. His perfect lips, curved in a bow, were only a breath from hers. The front porch light shone into his eyes. They were deep, full of concentration and curiosity, and they were staring right into hers, searching for meaning. Every avenue of her soul opened for his inspection, allowing him to know every secret desire of her heart. She could tell him anything, and he wouldn’t reject her. A closeness more than physical.

And he was her boss.

And she was an intern.

And they could both be fired.

She closed her eyes. And she had to stop it.

When she opened her eyes, his arms were resting on his knees. His jacket fell away from his wrist, exposing his watch.

“Nice watch, eh? Pretty pricey.” His watch was a perfect target. Clearly, she was not in his league. She must punish herself for even raising her thoughts to him.

Instead of replying, he tugged his coat sleeve over it.

“I’d guess your watch cost as much as a car.”

He was unprovoked.

She glanced at his Maserati. Its sleek lines, with the strong trident in the middle of the grill, was out of place next to the tiny shack of a home.

“But of course, not *your* car.”

His expression altered to a frown.

There, she annoyed him. Tension gone.

Still crouched next to her, he pivoted on his feet and picked up a handful of pebbles, tossing them one by one across the driveway. “There is nothing wrong with buying a well-made machine. Quality, passion, precision, and practicality are attributes I believe in. If I did not, I would not be working for Alpine Foods.”

“Practicality? When do you *need* all that horsepower?”

He gave her a quick glance. “When I pick up girls who are running late. I am partial to being on time.”

Lainey blocked the tease. “But can’t you find something better to spend your money on?”

Tilting his head, he considered her seriously. “And what should I spend my money on, Lainey?”

“Your cousin, so they don’t have to live in this place, eat off the land.”

He stopped tossing pebbles. “First off, they love what they do, the life they have built. Second, just giving them money will not help them. Third, you don’t know how proud Christophe is. Fourth, they remain here even when it's hard. Fifth, they accept help from no one." Pebble tossing again. "And for that, I applaud them."

"But they do take dog food."

"Only because I convinced them dogs should not be eating table scraps, enjoying, instead, the benefits of sound nutrition found in Alpine Foods dog food." He finished by throwing all the pebbles and dusting off his hands.

She'd never heard of anyone, even executives, receiving enough free samples to support a dog. Light flashed in her brain. "You don't get free dog food. You buy it for them," she whispered. "You use the excuse of free samples as a ruse for them to take it. They think they are doing you a favor." This man gave a family, too proud to receive help, a handout and made them glad to do it. Brilliant!

And he didn't protest; instead he bowed his head.

"You're amazing." It popped out of her mouth and hung there a few seconds.

Yves blinked. He stood abruptly, his eyebrows contracting. "What?"

She backtracked. "You're an amazing boss." Heat rose to her cheeks. Her heart lunged. But he stood there.

She had ruined it. She had crossed the line. He was going to think she liked him. She swallowed. "I mean, I admire you as a boss. Your methods may be unorthodox, difficult and trying to the body and spirit, but you make things happen. I'm a better person having worked with you. I'm even kind of glad I didn't get into Chocolate. You didn't have to hire me. Thank you."

She was babbling without meeting his eyes.

Without a word he pivoted, beeped his car, and climbed in. The engine hummed.

Lainey still sat on the ground, illuminated by the headlights. What just happened? Lainey stood, brushed off her bottom, lest she leave gravel dust on his leather seats, and climbed in the car.

In the dim light, his mouth flattened to a straight line. His jaw flexed several times when he glanced behind him to reverse. His gathered eyebrows hung low over his eyes. There was not going to be much conversation on the return trip. Down, down the mountain they drove, in utter silence except for the sound of the rocks flipping up to hit the car.

Curse these stoic Swiss men. He should just say what was bothering him. Did she cross some forbidden line in Swiss business? She pinched her lip to keep her nose from tingling and tears from burning her eyes.

On the freeway, he opened up the engine and sped across the top of the mountains. The speedometer read over 130 km/h.

Ninety miles an hour. Even though no one else was on the road at 10:30 at night, Lainey gripped the seat. The scenery passed too quickly in the dark to give any pleasure. Giving up, she stared out the front window, watching the approaching lights of the city.

At the Vevey exit, he finally slowed, but his harsh expression didn't change. His eyebrows met together, his jaw set, yanking on the gear stick. He relaxed when they approach her apartment.

"Thanks for the interesting insight to the Swiss psyche," she said, opening the car door before he came to a complete stop. She didn't care anymore.

"Lainey, wait."

"Goodnight, M. Claremont." Without a backward glance, she jumped from the car and slammed the door. Even from inside the lobby doors, the sound of his car tearing down the street, shifting into high gears, echoed against the buildings.

Marie Claire must've been in bed already. She stumbled, squinting, into the hall when Lainey came in. "Where have you been?"

Lainey threw her coat down and stormed into the bathroom, picking up her toothbrush and paste. "I can promise you, Marie Claire, I will never marry a Swiss man. They're all psycho."

"Have you been out with Yves?"

"No." She plastered paste on her toothbrush, not caring it made a mess. "Yes, but not a date. We just ate dinner." Not an outright lie. They did eat, but she didn't want to tell her he took her to meet his family. In case dinner with family was cause for termination.

****

What was he thinking, taking her up to the mountains to meet his family? Clearly, he was losing his focus.

Yves opened up the throttle and sped out of town. He had told himself the whole time they were merely friends. What happened?

He shifted into high gear to merge onto the highway.

Under the starry canopy, he craved her. It astonished him. He who was so careful. He who had refused dozens of other propositions from women within the company. Sabine was not the only one who had wanted to be a part of his life.

Without thinking, he laid on the gas. Lainey was

supposed to be safe. Didn't Marie Claire say she had a boyfriend?

She was aware of it, too, he was sure. A connection. A closeness. She understood him. But then she ruined it by trying to provoke him.

Yves glanced at his watch, his father's watch. When his father begged the Board not to lay off workers, during the recession, he worked tirelessly to maintain the company. At first, the Board humored him, and he was able to maintain and even prosper during hard economic times. However, when his health failed, the Board voted against him, and he resigned. And it killed him.

The watch was only a symbol. His father had grown up poor, like Anïse's mother, country folk. After studying and working hard, he earned his own way through university. He went to the States to attend an MBA program and met Yves' mother, considered a gracious beauty, who even after all these years of living in Switzerland, still yearned for her home in the corn fields of Illinois. Yves never wanted someone he loved to pine for a home he couldn't give her. And what about a relationship with Lainey?

He didn't need this complication right now. Not before the merger deal. Alpine Foods had a strict policy on relationships. The consequences were dire. He could not, would not risk it. He owed it to his company and to the Japanese company to make sure this merger went smoothly with no complications.

Perhaps after the deal. Then he could explore what happened up there on the mountain.

Unless he gave her a recommendation for Chocolate. The realization crashed upon him. She would be an official employee and therefore even more off-limits. But if he didn't, then she would surely return to the States, and he would never see her again.

Either way, he would lose her. It must end now.

He glanced down at his needle. 120 km/h. Not nearly fast enough. The engine roared as he sank the pedal to the floor.

Chapter Ten

Yves stood at the front of the small conference room, his face drawn, possibly from lack of sleep. He held the newspaper with the accusing headlines. "M. le President asked us not to continue with our street contacting. He feels we have violated the trust of the Swiss people."

Lainey wanted to laugh at his seriousness. Did they really tarnish the reputation of Alpine Foods by street-contacting people? The article said they were selling but it was not true. They didn't even mention they were from Alpine Foods.

"Perhaps we can turn it around." Britta snapped her pen cap. She was meticulously dressed in formal office attire, a suit coat and black skirt. And very high heels.

"Elaborate," was all Yves said, turning on her with his keen hawk-like eyes.

"Earn their trust. Show them we do care about the community."

"How?"

Britta shook her head to indicate she didn't know.

"Offer free dog food." Gui slouched in his seat.

"Resembles a pitch still," Yves said, tilting his head to face him. "We want to avoid pitches."

An idea floated in the back of Lainey's head, itching the back of her brain. It hovered there for a while, but she hesitated to bring it up.

Yves had exhausted this team. Even the usually straight Britta sagged a bit at the table. Gui intermittently fell asleep between conversations. Even with makeup, Sabine couldn't cover the dark circles under her eyes. Being out on the streets the last few weeks had drained them. They were grateful to be back in the office. Even Yves seemed ready to forget what happened on the streets, especially Monday night at dinner. He hadn't said anything to Lainey since parting that night, hadn't even made eye contact.

Lainey's attention was drawn to him, capable and in charge at the front of the room, as he controlled the discussion and probed for solutions. Perhaps her idea wasn't so bad. But it would be another risk. Would Yves be willing to make the sacrifice? She decided to try out her idea.

She raised her hand. Everyone glanced in her direction. Everyone, except M. Claremont. Finally, Yves raised his gaze to her.

"Mademoiselle Peterson?"

"I have an idea."

The room prickled with curiosity.

"*Alors,*" Yves said, avoiding her eyes as he reviewed his notes in front of him. "Go ahead."

"Maybe we could give away pets."

Luc immediately scoffed. "Ha! The biggest gimmick of them all." He held out his hands in front of him, mocking her. "Here is a free pet, now buy our pet food." He shook his head and laughed, Gui joining him with his guffaw.

Yves stopped their laughter with his glare. "Continue, Mademoiselle Peterson."

"If the newspapers say we're selling, maybe we

should go one step further. Instead of skulking away with our tails between our legs, so to speak, we should be more visible by giving away pets."

"Where would we get the pets?" Yves asked.

"You're not seriously considering this, are you?" Luc asked his superior.

"I am asking for more details. That is all," Yves responded.

"Does the *canton de Vaud* have a humane society?"

"Yes," Yves said.

"But the pets will need to have their shots, and Swiss law requires training for each pet owner." Britta set down her pen.

"Can Alpine Foods pay for those things?" Lainey asked.

"You're asking the company to drop all this money for your idea." Luc raised his eyebrows filling some of his large forehead. "You have some nerve."

Lainey bowed her head, her face burning. Perhaps it was a silly idea.

"I love it." Yves dropped his pen with decisiveness.

The mockery between Gui and Luc stopped. "But when are you going to do this?" Luc's mouth fell agape.

"The sooner the better." Yves nodded.

"So, after being accused of selling pet food, you're going to give away pets?" Luc asked.

"I'd even throw in the first bag of food for free." Lainey grew more confident in her suggestion.

"That was my idea." Gui sat up straighter.

"I think it's brilliant," Yves replied, though he had just shot it down a few minutes earlier.

Gui beamed. Luc scowled.

Yves assigned different tasks to the supervisors.

Britta would call the humane society to inquire about available pets, assess cost of shots, training etc. Sabine would arrange for a truck to haul in a load of dog and cat food for promotion. He asked Luc to scope out a spot and secure a permit for a street display in the *centre-ville* and Gui to advertise. Yves would talk to the vice presidents about distribution and promotional budgets.

"What if they won't give you the budget you need?" Lainey asked.

He shuffled his papers and snapped them in a folder. "Then I'll pay for it myself. If it will repair the damage we have done, it will be worth it."

Luc sniggered in the corner, whispering to Gui just loud enough for Lainey to hear, "He'd even pay for it out of his own pocket."

Lainey fantasized about smacking them across the cheeks. Yves sacrificed for his work.

Sabine, already on her cell phone, left in haste. Britta, with her assignment, clicked her pen and strode to her desk. Gui sauntered off to his cubicle, hands stuffed in his pockets. Yves approached Luc. Lainey tried to slip around them to leave, but Yves stopped her.

"Lainey, wait." Facing Luc, Yves held up the newspaper, showing him the front page. "What do you know about this?"

"*Rien.*"

"Nothing?" Yves arched an eyebrow. "Amazing how the press cites Lausanne, not Vevey. And I wonder who told them it was Alpine Foods asking the questions."

Luc challenged him with his eyes. "I told you, I don't know anything." With a glare in Yves' direction, he stalked out.

"Why don't I believe him?" Lainey said, without thinking.

"Because he is lying." He assembled his papers on the table.

"Do I have an assignment for the project?" Lainey asked.

"Yes," he said. "Come with me." With his notebooks and folders tucked under his arm, he strode out of the room. To keep pace with him, Lainey half-jogged to his office.

"Get your coat on." He stepped inside his office and unhooked his overcoat from a rack.

"Where are we going?"

"To buy ribbons."

"Ribbons?"

Instead of answering, he dialed his cell phone. "How come you don't have your coat yet?"

Lainey ran to her desk and grabbed her coat and scarf. When she returned, he was hanging up his phone.

"The VPs commenced their meeting. They will text me with their answer." He strode down the hall.

Lainey followed. "You think they'll go for it?"

He shrugged, illuminating the button to open the lobby door. "I'm not going to wait for them to 'go for it.'"

Out in the parking lot, Lainey squinted in the glaring sun shining off the cars. He paused near his car and pocketed his keys. "It's a beautiful day. Let's walk." Instead of heading to Avenue du Général-Guisan, toward *centre-ville*, he strode toward the lake. "There's a haberdashery down here."

A paved promenade followed the shoreline of the

lake. The scent of wet mud from the rocks below reminded of her California. Even the cooing of pigeons and lapping water transported Lainey to beaches far from there.

While living a short hop from the Palo Alto area, Lainey and her friends spent long weekends at Disneyland, the beach, or taking Highways Eight and Five to San Diego. Ah, college road trips, with chips and soda and so much laugher. Horizon stretched all around the road if they were headed to Las Vegas. A pang of homesickness stabbed her.

As they descended to the *bord du lac*, Yves continued his insane pace, threading through couples, tourists, and walkers, persisting with unwavering concentration on his path.

The beauty, even in late fall, arrested Lainey, but it didn't faze him. Even after being in country two months, she still gaped at the scenery.

On the far side of the lake, mountains jutted upward, perpetually spread with a giant gauze of snow. Their reflection rippled in the water, doubling their impact. All along the *lac*, crowds gazed over the weathered sculpted balustrade. Giant urns full of birds of paradise, red shade-loving plants, giant-leafed elephant ears dotted the wall every ten feet. Opposite the balustrade, facing the lake, sat benches filled with older ladies tied to a dog or two.

Against the balustrade, an elderly man broke off chunks of stale French bread, tossing them into the lake. Ducks and a few pigeons scrambled among the rocks to catch his crumbs. Above him, a sign said, "No feeding birds." He'd probably get fined.

Yves rushed past this scene, speaking of statistics

and calculations, but Lainey couldn't. The contrast of the blue sky, with the dark mountains, the greenery all around, made her dumb as well as immobile.

For several paces he carried on without her. When he finally noticed her missing, he stalked back, an annoyed frown pasted on his lips. He tapped her on the shoulder. "Lainey?"

"I don't get this country."

His lips pressed into a straight line. Yves pivoted on his heel without replying.

She sighed, jogging to keep pace with him.

"You are constantly making fun of the Swiss. Why?"

"Because you work all the time and rarely laugh." Her legs ached maintaining his mad pace.

"Did Marie Claire tell you that?"

Lainey pinched her lips together. Guilt spread through her with warmth.

"Americans don't work all the time?" He slowed to a stroll.

"They do." Except her parents. They might be the only exception. "But they also know how to have fun. Baseball games, NASCAR, quilting, golf, reading."

"And you work during lunch."

So he was attacking America now? "True, we often have working lunches."

"Working lunches? How about to-go and eating in the car?"

"Yes, sometimes we eat in the car. It doesn't make us workaholics."

"But you see, here in Switzerland we take off lunch. It is our time to relax."

"Except you." Lainey stared at him. "I've never

seen you stop for lunch."

He squinted into the sun to stare at her. "Now you see how I am both Swiss and American. In hopefully more ways than just my work ethic."

"In what other ways?"

"Despite what Marie Claire says, I do have a sense of humor."

Lainey snorted.

"See, you laughed."

She did. She clasped her hand over her mouth. She didn't mean to laugh.

"You have been purposefully withholding your amusement. It's not healthy, you know."

Convicted by his statement, Lainey fell silent.

He continued. "Also, I think I have the ability to be more open-minded about how to do business. I don't always follow the Swiss rules. Sometimes it works." He paused. "Sometimes it gets me into trouble."

Giving away pets was definitely an American style of doing business. Would it work or get him into trouble?

"And you, Lainey, are more Swiss than you know."

"What? How?"

"Don't worry. It's not an insult. I'll let you discover how. So what else does Marie Claire say about the Swiss? I find this extremely amusing."

"Marie Claire says never marry a Swiss man."

"Sounds like something she'd say," he mused. "Did she say why?"

She couldn't remember exactly. Something about foreign wives being cold. "Because all the foreigners Swiss men marry are miserable here."

"Why, I wonder."

"It's too cold."

"Then it would apply equally to the men in Finland or Norway."

"No, not that type of cold. Culturally. Women from other countries are used to more sociality, and when they come here, they are shunned."

"Because they don't fit in?"

"I don't know."

"Perhaps because they miss their country or their family."

"Or the sunshine." The sun hid behind a cloud as if on cue.

His eyes burned into her. "You suggest I should only marry a Swiss woman? Or marry a woman who is disillusioned with her country and detached from her family? No, I could not be happy with someone so detached. But a woman close to her family members would not want to leave them. But perhaps if I promise to fly her home to see her family as often as she wishes. Would it satisfy her? Convince her to marry me?"

Why was he asking her? Oh, Hiroko. So he was contemplating marriage. His penetrating stare suddenly made her uncomfortable. "I don't know what other women want."

"Then what do *you* want? What if you were offered to work here after your internship? Permanently. Would you stay? Could you leave all your friends, family, and potential relationships? Or perhaps he would come here?"

"Potential relationships?" Oh, Aaron. "I don't know," she mumbled, which was a lie. Aaron would hate to live there. He would complain the whole time about not being able to find his brand of beer, about how expensive everything was, how early everything closed up. He would mock the old ladies and their mink coats. And he hated the cold.

Yves stepped closer, his gaze still intently focused on her. "Could you live here, Lainey? For the rest of your life?"

His questions shook her heart. Although there were lots of similarities between Switzerland and America, Switzerland was still a foreign country. Beautiful to be sure. But she was lonely when not at work. Lonely and homesick. But what did she yearn for? Her parents were moving to Costa Rica, and Nadine was getting married. What was there to go home to?

"It depends," she said, with diplomacy. "I'd hate living in an apartment. A girl from New York or some big city, like Tokyo, might be used to it, but I'm used to the urban sprawl."

"Okay, so you'd need a house. What else? What would make Switzerland home to you?"

Surely, he was wondering if Hiroko would leave Japan and live in Switzerland.

What made anywhere home? Familiarity? Certainly. Friends, family? Her parents didn't think so if they were moving thousands of miles to a country without knowing anyone. "Why are you asking me?"

"You have the correct opinion of everything. You must know how to please a woman since you are so difficult to please yourself."

Ouch! Her heart lunged. "To feel at home," she said at last, a twinge of sobering reality in her voice. The pain of having nothing to go home to hurt. She lifted her eyes to his. "I'd need to be with the people I love the most."

His eyes softened. “Very well said.”

“Whoa, a compliment? Because if you complimented me, I’ll need another notebook to write it down.”

“What are you talking about?”

“You are hard on me.”

“Yes, I am.”

He admitted it. “Why?”

“Because you are not living up to your potential.”

“My potential? My potential as what? A doormat? You haven’t seen what I can do. This whole internship I have been under your ever-watchful eye, as if you’re afraid if I’m on my own, I might screw something up.”

“That must be why I can’t let you out of my sight.” His voice dripped with sarcasm.

“Give me a chance, please. I won’t disappoint you.”

“We’ll see how this enterprise turns out. If it’s a success, then I’ll find a project for you to do on your own.”

“Really? You mean it? If this works, I get my own project?”

“Yes. But if it fails, then…”

“Then what?”

His lips grew into a tight line. “It cannot fail.”

Too much rode on this project. His promotion and Lainey’s chance to prove to him she was not a bumbling idiot.

****

At the next street, they crossed and mounted stairs leading to a small ribbon and lace shop. They all but ceased to exist in America, but in Switzerland, they were still a protected species.

Inside the store, hundreds of varied colors and widths of ribbon hung on pegs covering every inch of the eighteen-foot walls. Along another wall, ribbon on spools and ribbon wound on cards were stacked in cubbies. A small staircase along the back wall led to a cozy loft upstairs, overflowing with more fabric, ribbon, and lace. A lady came downstairs and greeted them. The shop smelled of dusty rose potpourri.

"Here we are." Yves systematically evaluated the shop.

Lainey tugged at a spool, letting the ribbon fall a short distance.

"My assignment is to pick out ribbon?" she asked, feeling insignificant and underused.

"No." He unwound red velvet ribbon from a spool. "My job is to pick out ribbon. You are here to help me calculate how much we will need."

What a relief. "What is the ribbon for?"

"To put around the animals' necks."

Every exacting detail. He thought of every tiny detail. Before they calculated how much, he sent a text to Sabine asking if the humane society had responded. A few seconds passed before his phone buzzed.

"Eighty pets," he read. "For the cost of immunizations and neutering, they are ours. Find some way to transport them." He texted the words as he spoke them. "Now about the permit." A few seconds passed. "Tomorrow? Excellent." He reposted his phone in its holster.

They bought nearly twenty meters of assorted ribbon. The sales lady placed the lengths of ribbon in a beautifully printed paper bag, reminding them there were no refunds.

"Vice Presidents haven't responded." Lainey bit her lip.

Right on cue, his phone buzzed. He retrieved his phone again, reading his text. He slammed his phone on the counter. "They've said no."

A pit formed in her stomach. And they just bought all the ribbon, non-refundable, too. "What are you going to do now?"

He thanked the woman, his eyes fixed with determination. "Do it anyway." He squeezed the bag out the door.

"Wait." Lainey scurried to the sidewalk next to him. "Are you allowed to do it without their blessing?"

"One thing I hope you will learn, Mademoiselle Peterson, while working with me: you don't go anywhere without taking risks."

"But they could fire you."

"They could."

"Then what would you do?"

He faced her. Since he stood higher on the sloped sidewalk, he towered over her. He searched her eyes as he spoke. "When I came to work for Alpine Foods, I didn't want to be in Pet Care."

But he was so passionate about it. He lived, breathed, and ate Pet Care. So he was only ambitious. Pet Care was just the means to the vice presidency as Marie Claire said.

"I wanted to work in bottled water." He stared behind her to the lake. "I had some great ideas for water long before they came to market. Flavored water, I had the idea. Vitamin water, as well. Yet I let other people take those ideas and run with them."

If there was one thing more boring than Pet Care, it

would be water. "How did you wind up in Pet Care?"

His eyes returned at the question. "Pet Care was a sinking ship, numbers were falling off the chart. It was the albatross of the company. I decided to take a risk, to take on a department I knew nothing about. I tried things never tried before, sold in ways never sold before, and I reached people never reached before and created markets never before achieved. And now we are one of the top selling brands in the world. We are about to expand to the Asian markets. Do you think they will fire me? No."

"But you wouldn't be promoted."

He bit his fingernail, then dropped his hand from his mouth. With worry in his eyes, he spun sharply, climbing the hill. She lagged behind.

"And you want to be one of the Vice Presidents."

"More than almost anything."

"Almost?"

He halted and pivoted so quickly she bumped into his chest, thick and solid. And warm.

"*Pardon.*" She blushed slightly, stepping back, breathing in his fragrance.

"What I want, I keep to myself. Yes, most people have divined I want a promotion. I want it more than almost anything just to prove to myself I can do it. But everything else I want, I keep to myself. And not even Marie Claire has figured everything out."

An awkward silence continued before Lainey spoke again. "I just want you to know I'm not going to be, uh, holding any of the dogs."

"And why not? I expect you to be there with everyone else promoting your idea."

"I can't do it."

r"Why do you hate pets so much? Why can't you just throw your heart and soul into it? You've been recalcitrant every step of our outings and whining about how much you'd rather be in Chocolate. Why can't you accept your lot and be grateful? What is so horrible about pet food?"

Lainey stepped back. Whine? Did he think her ungrateful? Hot angry tears burned her eyes. She fought off a sneeze. She yanked her collar down, threw open her jacket, and opened her collar to expose her left shoulder.

M. Claremont stared, bewildered at her exposed clavicle in the middle of the street on a breezy day. Then he focused on her back, just above her scapula.

Her scars.

Though it had been over ten years, the twisted pinkish scars remained. A source of pain far worse than physical.

"When I was nine, a rottweiler knocked me down and bit me. Busted through a wooden fence. This is just one of seven places where my flesh was ripped from my back. The doctor said I was lucky I fell on my face, and it bit my back where the scars can be hidden. And I hide them. No tank tops, no backless dresses. Always boleros and T-shirts while swimming so people don't ask what happened.

"Every day for twelve years, every barking dog made my heart skitter, my palms sweat. I relive the moments when those giant paws forced me down, trapping me on the hot sidewalk. I relive the moisture of its breath before its teeth tear through my back. So imagine how I feel, having to ask people how much they love their pets, discussing the needs of dogs, when

I secretly despise them."

She covered up her scars. Though her eyes focused on him, scenes from that awful afternoon, the powerful beast charging through the shattered, splintered fence, played before her. The gravel ground into her chin, heat rose off the pavement. Torn flesh throbbed. The physical pain had healed, but she winced at the memory.

"I am sorry, Lainey."

Wow. A man who apologized. But his eyes didn't lose their intensity.

"But you can't let an experience twelve years ago keep you from doing your duty at work."

That was not the response she was expecting. "What?"

"I'm sorry it happened. It sounds traumatic, but when you are at work, you need to leave your personal life behind you. Work is work."

"You think I'm making excuses, don't you?" She wanted him to back down, to say it was okay, to give her a free pass. "I had eight years of therapy."

"I'm not minimizing your pain."

Her emotions jumbled. She'd told him her deepest hurt, and he still wanted her to go through with this pet care stuff. She faced away from him.

"Now you think I'm heartless. I do care, Lainey. I do. Just don't let this experience impede you from giving your all to pet care. You can be better. You are capable of doing great things, Lainey. You have demonstrated your capacity. We all have things we are dealing with, but we can't let our issues interfere with our work."

Lainey faced him. She didn't know whether to be

insulted or pleased he thought so highly of her.

He was about to say more, but his phone buzzed. When he answered it, he handed Lainey the bag of ribbons. She tucked them under her arm and waited.

After finishing his call, he clipped the phone back to his belt. "We have lots of work to do tonight," he said.

Chapter Eleven

The next day, Sabine came to work, followed by a truck. This was not a huge moving van truck. All the vehicles in Switzerland were slightly larger than a hotdog cart. Trucks were no exception.

The smallish truck backed into the alleyway, and Yves and Lainey loaded their supplies for the town square, where Luc and Gui had prepared a table with Alpine Food products and signs advertising free pets and food. Yves and Luc unloaded the first kennels in the square. Gui set out pamphlets.

Lainey was to tie ribbons around the necks of the animals. With trepidation, she approached a Yorkshire terrier with keen eyes and a lolling tongue. She squinted her eyes.

It's not going to bite me. It's not going to bite me.

"Come here, poochy." She clenched her teeth. Facing it, she knelt down. Its ears twitched. It yawned, exposing a full tongue, pink with a hint of purple.

Lainey hesitated, her heart skittering. Its warm breath smelled of dog food. Almost hugging it, she bent and threaded the ribbon through its collar and quickly tied the ribbon into a bow. The red ribbon worked.

Yves strolled by for inspection and tugged at an asymmetrical loop of ribbon but said nothing, his brow furrowed, his eyes deep in thought.

She was rewarded by a kiss on the cheek. From the

dog.

Britta was already conversing with one of their first takers. “They make great friends,” she said, holding a white puppy with dark eye patches, stroking him with her hand. “Here, hold him.”

The woman couldn’t resist. “They’re already immunized?”

Britta nodded.

“And the training is paid for?”

“Compliments of Alpine Foods. Just bring in this voucher.”

“And we get a bag of free food?”

“The best Alpine Foods offers.”

Britta smiled and placed a bag in her hand. Then she removed the certificate for the training and shot records from a folder, handing it to the lady who cooed sweet nothings into the dog’s ear.

It was magic. It created customers. But it was slow. By ten they had only given away a handful of pets.

Yves wandered around with a scowl on his brow, gripping his hands behind his back. All of them were edgy. Even the animals whined a bit, impatiently stamping in their kennels.

At lunchtime Yves bit his nails. Perhaps contemplating how he was going to continue payments on his car if he lost his job. Luc, Gui, and Britta left for a lunch break, leaving Lainey and Yves alone.

He stalked around, as if he was attending a funeral, certainly not attracting potential customers. The shops across the cobblestone square held more interest for the passersby.

“You might as well eat,” he said to Lainey at last, scratching his brow where he stood behind a table loaded with pamphlets and dog food.

"I'll stay."

The pets mimicked their frustration and whimpered from their kennels. There was no place to sit except in the chair next to Yves.

What they needed was to attract some positive attention.

Lainey had an idea. Maybe if they let out a few to show off instead of keeping them in their kennels, their playfulness would attract potentials. Scraping the kennels across the bumpy cobblestone, Lainey circled them to create a small compound. Some were heavy, requiring great effort to push them into place. The whimpers and whines of the dogs inside the kennels almost drowned the sound of the plastic scraping against cobblestone.

Lainey's heart lunged, but her strength continued. Under the watchful eye of M. Claremont, she opened the latch from the first kennel. A Weimaraner-mix raced out, knocking her off balance.

It's going to eat me!

Fearing an attack, she covered her face and shrieked. When she opened her eyes, the pooch stood before her, wagging its tail.

"He wants to play, Lainey," Yves observed from the table.

Shaking, she righted herself.

"It's all right. He's not going to hurt you."

Summoning her courage, she approached the dog.

Yves chortled as he stepped between kennels to join Lainey in the circle. "He won't bite you."

"How do you know?" Lainey shook. She hadn't been this close to a bigger dog in a long, long time. Her throat held a lump of fear, and her heart pounded. She jumped at a tap on the shoulder.

"Here." Yves shook out some kibble into her palm.

Inhaling their earthiness, she inspected the treats, contemplating how to feed them to the dog. Before she decided, its moist nose bumped her and sniffed outside her clenched fingers, making her tremble. She yelped. Then its tongue, wet and warm, lapped the outside of her balled fist. It took all Lainey's self-control not to go running.

She tightened her hand around the treats. Tentatively, she glanced up to see if M. Claremont would chide her for being such a chicken.

Instead, he stepped behind her and slid his hand down her arm, steadying her wrist. Pressing against her, he bent them closer to the dog, a hand on her back. With his cheek near hers, she smelled his fresh scent, his chest warm on her shoulder.

Her heart beat faster. And not from fear.

With warm, controlled hands, he coaxed her fingers open. "He's not going to bite you, Lainey." He whispered low in her ear, as thick and textured as chocolate ganache.

Through a veil of hair, she peeked at him. His eyelashes brushed his cheeks when he blinked. What a perfectly sculpted nose. The curve of his lips only inspired lusty thoughts. He flexed his jaw. With her right hand, she flipped back her hair for a better view.

From the corner of his eyes, Yves glanced down through those gorgeous fringy eyelashes, and smiled at her.

Dog completely forgotten. Town square—gone. Just the two of them as everyone faded away. Their gazes met. A zing went through her heart, all the way to her toes.

Slowly, she opened her fingers, and the dog's moist breath warmed her hand. His textured tongue systematically lapped up the treats, leaving her hand a wet, crummy mess.

She had been holding her breath. She exhaled. Letting a dog lick her wasn't too horrible. When she glanced up, a crowd had gathered around the circled kennels, watching them.

In the crowd, Luc stared at them.

The dog pranced on his paws, waiting. She leaned forward to pet his head.

Bark!

She jumped back, into Yves, who wrapped his arm around her just for a second.

"You can do this." He handed her the opened bag of kibble. "This is exactly what they need."

He meant the crowd, of course, not the dogs. They loved watching her with the dogs. Releasing her, he unlatched more dogs from their confines until they circled her.

With the bag in hand, Lainey held it aloft as the rest of the dogs gathered around, nipping at her ankles, pawing at her legs.

"Down," she shouted. When they stayed down, she dropped a few kibbles for them. Their noses searched through the cracks of the cobblestone, moving their heads sideways to lick up every morsel. At the end of the bag of treats, she shook out the crumbs, which they immediately devoured.

The crowd clapped with delight. There were plenty of smiles. Even on M. Claremont.

Even on Lainey.

This was great! People led away more dogs with papers and pet food.

They must not fail.

Then a Welsh corgi shimmied between the kennels, ran around the square, terrorizing other dogs, and relieved itself on the bike racks. They got fined. But this created such a scene, it drew more curious spectators to them. No press was bad press.

There was also the issue of potty breaks. Since most of the animals were not potty trained, they should've expected accidents. When an older lady in a pill box hat stopped to observe, a white bichon frise-mix squatted right near her foot, leaving a log.

Yves put Lainey on doody duty.

"Are you serious?" she asked, wanting to shake his hand from her shoulder.

"Show me I can trust you with even unsavory tasks." Yves referred her to the bags provided by the city for picking up any warm packages left by the doggies, depositing them in the specially marked bins. For the kitties, Britta bought a litter box for under the table.

The rest of the time, Lainey scooped poop, glaring at M. Claremont.

At the end of the day, all but four kitties were placed in homes. Britta claimed a tabby she named Aurore for her grandkids.

Lainey hugged the other three, while the others cleaned up. Their pink sandpaper tongues licked her fingers. They cuddled into her chest, their hair as fine as duckling down. "I wish I could take you home with me," she whispered to them before Gui loaded them back into a kennel. She waved goodbye as they closed the back of the truck and drove down the street back to the humane society.

It had been a long day. With sunset, the square was completely devoid of people. In the fading darkness, Yves spoke on the phone while he collapsed a table, directing Britta with the posters. When they were finished, they climbed into a car without a backward glance toward Lainey. After everything she did, not even a "Thank you, Lainey. Would you like a ride?"

Her back ached from scooping poop all afternoon. Even though her shoes pinched her swollen feet, Lainey headed home on foot. Luc, the last one, stopped her, asking her to help load the poster board and remaining fliers into his car.

"I see *le caïd* has used you to attract customers." Though Yves was boss, Luc said the term with a sneer. "He's a brilliant man to leverage others' strengths. Your ridiculous behavior out there drew in customers. Brilliant."

Lainey didn't know how to respond.

"I've known Yves Claremont for a long time now."

Her heart jumped when he said Yves' name.

"He's very ambitious." He slammed his door. "It's a shame to see a man so driven by his desire to succeed. Not good for the heart. Or for the health."

This was all so odd. Luc hadn't asked her any questions. She wasn't sure if he expected her to say something.

He whipped out an American cigarette, lit it, and inhaled a drag. "I wouldn't be surprised if he wanted more than a promotion. Yves Claremont only cares about a few things: beautiful women, fast cars, expensive baubles to gratify his ego and power. If I were you"—he paused for a cigarette drag—"I would not get too close to Yves Claremont. I wouldn't want you to get hurt."

What was worse, him blowing smoke in her face or insinuating Yves was using her? Either way, she felt sick.

****

At home, too tired to cook, Lainey grabbed a chocolate bar for dinner and waved goodbye to Marie Claire, who left for Jean's for the weekend. Around eight, Lainey was too pooped to stay up and read any longer. She had crawled into her PJs, washed her face and even brushed the chocolate out of her teeth when her phone rang. Caller ID said M. Claremont.

"It was a success!" he shouted into the phone. "We risked our comfort, and it was worth it. Alpine Foods has been receiving phone calls all day with high praise for this program. In fact, we're going to start our own animal rescue program. Lainey, you're wonderful. Want to celebrate?"

In the mirror, her reflection was a mess. She was already in her pajamas. But too exhausted to celebrate with M. Claremont? "I'd love to."

"I'll be there in ten minutes."

Ten minutes? She threw the phone on the bed and ran to the bathroom where she pasted on some makeup, brushed her hair, then padded around in her jammies, searching for something to wear.

When he said he wanted to celebrate, what did he mean? A night at a *discothèque*? An art gallery? She should've asked him what they were doing. Lainey didn't know what to wear. Where was Marie Claire when she really needed her?

Back at Stanford or Arizona, she would just wear jeans because going out meant bowling or going to the bar to see how long they could ride the mechanical bull. But Yves? What did you wear to a celebration with your hot boss?

Certainly not jeans.

A little black dress? What if he wanted to walk around the lake? Was it too cold for bare legs?

Her watch said she had five more minutes.

She stamped her foot. Why didn't she do more clothes shopping? Or buy something for a hot date? Everything clean was all officey or wrinkly, and she didn't have time to iron. She needed access to an awesome wardrobe now.

From her doorway, the light fell into Marie Claire's room.

Hmmmmmmmm.

Marie Claire said she could borrow anything, didn't she?

Just to be sure, with shaking fingers, she called her. Ahhhhhh! Voicemail. She hung up. She stared across the hall. Surely, Marie Claire wouldn't begrudge her a shirt. For a night.

'Twas easier to ask forgiveness than permission, right?

In Marie Claire's room, she slid open the closet doors to find a shirt to go with her short, black skirt. Hangers squeaked across the bar as she passed outrageously obnoxious fashions until she reached a few stylish shirts. She held out a long flowing white silk one. Too dangerous. Might spill something on it. She replaced it and continued rifling through her packed closet. Too pokey, too avant-garde, too garish, too daring.

After shifting through a few hangers, she removed a turquoise silk shirt, dotted with sequins and a bit of a daring neckline. Dressy, but not too dressy. She held it out, debating. What if this was Marie Claire's favorite shirt? What if she was planning to wear it Monday?

The buzzer rang.

Lainey's heart fluttered.

Forgiveness was sweeter.

She yanked the shirt off the hanger, tossing it over her head and fluffing her hair one more time. A spritz of perfume. She shouldn't keep her date waiting.

No, not date, she reminded herself, stopping in the entry way, calming her heart with a deep breath. A celebration with the boss. The whole pet department might be there, too.

She opened the door.

Yves waited in the dimly lit hallway, no suit jacket on, just his white sleeves rolled up to three quarters, reminding Lainey of a cologne model. He'd missed his calling. Though he was not doing too bad as a pet care Department Head, either.

Languishing at the open door, Lainey struck her coquettish pose, hoping to have some effect on him.

His eyes skittered over her outfit, not resting too long in any one area. A corner of his mouth rose, and his eyes softened.

A twinge of guilt burned at her cheeks when she thought of Hiroko. Hiroko, a faceless lady who had prior claim. He never talked about her, but why would he talk about his girlfriend to the clunky intern?

Swallowing, he bowed slightly, pointing a hand

away. "Shall we go?"

Parked on the sidewalk, with two tires on and two tires off, was his metallic steel-gray Maserati. In a deft movement, he opened the car door, holding it so it wouldn't fall back on her, since the car was tilted. With a push of the button the engine hummed, wrapping them in a quiet security.

"Where are we going?"

"You'll see. There is a restaurant *gastronomique* I want to take you to. You've had a traditional meal. Now it's time to experience the higher eating."

The road was a silver river as they traveled in the moonlight, leaving the sleeping town of Vevey behind them. Darkened vineyards passed beside them until they reached a small village before the thriving city of Lausanne.

Nightlife here meant after eight o'clock there was still a restaurant open.

Before allowing the valet to park his car, he grabbed his suit coat, swinging it over his shoulders, truly European-style. Across the street hung a sign encased in iron scrollwork for the Restaurant Terrasse.

Clustered on the wooden deck leaning out across the steep hillside, were gathered a few of the younger, hipper and extremely well-dressed crowd in Switzerland. With wine glasses in their hands and designer bags clutched at their hips, these were not her typical Friday night cohorts.

While Yves checked in with the maitre d', Lainey absorbed the atmosphere. The plexiglass walls reflected the ambient candles and tea lights while showing off the panoramic view of the lake and valley. Below them, the tiered vineyard stepped down toward the lake.

Tarnished limestone farmhouses with red tiled roofs dotted the fields. Utterly romantic.

"This way." Yves' hand spanned the small of her back, warm through her shirt, guiding her through a space between two tables—some serious boss-intern touching. Surely a friendly gesture. Her heart beat at a sugar-high pace. Despite the outdoor heaters, Lainey shivered, not with cold, but from excitement.

Yves must've noticed her teeth chattering in one of his catch-all glances. "You must be cold." He slid off his jacket and leaned close to place it on her shoulders, filling the very small space between them with his incredible cologne.

People didn't smell in dreams, did they? Because Lainey hoped she wasn't dreaming. If she were, this was the most wonderful dream she'd ever had, and if she spoke, she'd break the spell.

He stood close—a box of chocolate couldn't fit between them, or even a plaque of chocolate—staring down at her. She yearned to know what was brewing behind those dark eyes. Shaded by his thick lashes, his gaze flitted across her face, landing on her eyes.

When a waiter in a fitted white tux brought them two drinks on a tray, Yves backed away, breaking the tension. "To our success." He handed her a glass.

They clinked their rims.

Tilting up his flute to his mouth, Yves never let his gaze leave hers. With his usual confidence, he slid his hand down to hers, stepping to the edge of the deck, gently drawing her closer.

A chocolate wrapper wouldn't fit between them.

Her heart was a subwoofer. Was this fraternizing? Maybe handholding in Switzerland didn't mean the same thing as it did in the US.

Hand in hand, he led her to the railing facing the Alps, inky black against a starry blue sky. He dropped her hand to stand behind her as she leaned over, scanning the lake to the trail of twinkling lights illuminating the mountain side. Yves pressed near her, pointing to a cluster of lights off to their right, across the lake.

"Over there is Evian, France," he whispered in her hair, causing a few strands to move with his breath. At this closeness, she inhaled his cologne and wondered why, after a day of handling pets, he didn't smell nasty.

He lingered close enough that his heat penetrated her clothing. His thigh brushed hers.

Lainey envisioned him brushing the hair away from the nape of her neck to kiss it. At least there. Her whole body quivered.

What if their relationship did progress? She imagined their weekends. She'd start her stunning and prosperous career in chocolates, dragging him all over the EU exploring chocolate boutiques. Yves had discriminating taste. He'd give his opinion about each chocolate, and they'd never agree which one was the best.

Or she imagined them combing Paris in his Maserati for the perfect plaque of chocolate. Afterward they'd eat lunch at some swanky restaurant or maybe a picnic out in the countryside. Definitely out in the countryside. The sun setting across a golden valley of ripened wheat, sitting side by side on a checkered blanket under a tree, a bottle of wine, a picnic basket. He'd reach for her chin…Ahem.

Lainey.

Must be the alcohol.

Just a sip of champagne and *poof*, the frontal lobe broke down. She'd forgotten who she was. *He'd* forgotten who she was. Lainey Peterson, remember? The dorky American intern who was off-limits.

But he was still close to her. His breath tickled her neck, the warmth from his body shielding her from the wind lifting off the lake. She struggled to keep her breath and her thoughts under control.

She needed a distraction. Her gaze flitted around. Farther down the railing, in a darkened corner, a couple was making out.

Not there.

Yves lifted his glass, stepping away from her, leaving her in full contact with the wind. "I owe you an apology, Lainey."

She stood straight, leaving her drink on the railing. "An apology for what?"

As if to give him courage, he sipped again from his glass. "For wanting to get rid of you." He said it so matter-of-factly, not even apologetic.

"You wanted to get rid of me?"

"Only after you nearly cost me my promotion."

"Is that the only thing you care about?"

"Until I get it, yes." He tilted his glass back for another drink. "But there is something else."

"More apologizing?" Lainey faced away, almost hurt.

"No." He caught her arm, searching her eyes with his. He grew serious.

Her heart beat wildly.

Before he spoke, his eyes darted over her shoulder. He dropped his hand from Lainey's arm, the pleading expression gone from his face.

Heels clacked behind her on the wooden decking before hands slid over her eyes. "*Cou-cou.*" Marie Clare's hair blew in the wind. After giving Lainey the *bise,* she nodded to Yves who acknowledged her with a nod. "How are you *two*?"

A few seconds of awkwardness passed when no one said anything. Impatience flashed across Yves' face. But as it came in an instant, so was it gone. He addressed her in French. "What a coincidence we chose the same restaurant tonight."

"Jean and I are celebrating our third anniversary. We are not the only ones from Alpine Foods here."

"Congratulations." A tight smile crossed his lips.

Another pause. Lainey glanced from Marie Clare to Yves, who seemed impatient for her to leave. Marie Clare was the head of Human Resources. And she was prone to flapping her mouth.

Switzerland was such a small country.

A chime broke the silence. Yves reached for his phone, his face contracted in his usual scowl. "This is a phone call I must take. If you'll excuse me," he said to Lainey, phone already to his ear.

"Yeah, sure."

Marie Clare tracked his departure over Lainey's shoulder, then focused on Lainey, but not before recognizing her outfit.

"My shirt." Before Lainey apologized, Marie Claire waved her hand as if the shirt was unimportant. "You're here with Yves?" she asked, her eyes lit from alcohol or from this intriguing discovery, or both.

Shrugging, Lainey blushed.

"This is the second time you've had dinner with

him—" she questioned Lainey with her eyes "—this week." The wind stuck a long curly lock to her lip-gloss. With a finger, she freed it, tossing it to the leeward side. She had the most gorgeous hair.

Lainey shrugged again, tamping down a bubble of excitement. "He's just showing me Switzerland before I leave."

Marie Claire raised an eyebrow.

"It's two co-workers celebrating a successful idea with dinner."

"*Oui. Two* co-workers?"

"Maybe everyone else was busy?"

"*Allez*!" Marie Claire shoved her shoulder playfully. "I've worked with Yves Claremont for the last three years, and I've never heard of him taking *anyone* to dinner."

"What does it mean?"

"It means, *ma chèri*e—what do you think it means?"

Lainey's mind raced with possibilities. But none of them made sense. "I don't know."

"And you. You, dear Lainey, like him, too."

"What? No, I don't."

"I see the way you moon at him. How you constantly talk about him."

"I do not."

"Admit it."

"No."

"You do."

"Even if I did, I wouldn't tell you."

"Aha! Admission. You like him. You like Yves Claremont."

"Shhhhhh." Lainey glanced to where Yves left.

"You are such a perfect couple. Now all you have to do is quit Alpine Foods, and you can be together."

"Quit? What about just not getting caught?"

"Monsieur le President is bearing down on inter-personal relationships at Alpine Foods. As an intern, you would lose your job if he found out."

"And Yves? What would happen to him."

"Despite being a favorite, most likely he would be fired, too, or at least not promoted. But quitting is not the end of the world. He would take care of you. He has plenty of money."

Lainey bit her lip. "I can't quit." She needed Yves' recommendation to Chocolate. Chocolate was all she ever wanted since she was nine years old. To give up now would mean… A pit balled in her stomach. She must've had too much to drink.

Marie Claire grew restless with Lainey's sudden seriousness. "*Écoute*. Jean's getting his car. I must go. I want to hear all about"—she motioned to Lainey and then off to the direction where Yves had gone—"this."

Just as she did when she first approached, she kissed Lainey on both cheeks to say goodbye.

"How come you do two *bises*?" Lainey asked. "I thought the Swiss only do one *bise*."

"You forget, I am French. The French greet differently. Just remember this: one in Switzerland, two in France. *Ciao, ma biche*."

"Ah." She waved to Marie Claire as she strode off, her long hair billowing in the breeze, heels clacking on the wood planking. At least she explained the difference to Lainey. Lainey imagined someone coming in for a second *bise*. Sigh. Could she ever learn to be a native? Adapt to all these cultural codes?

What if he was about to confess undying love for her? He was by far the sexiest thing in a suit she'd ever seen.

She shook her head. Lainey had to give up M. Claremont. She couldn't let him jeopardize his career for her, couldn't even allow him to say it out loud.

****

Yves paced near the restrooms behind a wall of ferns during the phone call with Frédérick Morrel, the Senior Vice President for Pet Care. He requested more details before proceeding with the upcoming pet adoption program. "It was all the intern's idea. Yes, the American intern." Lainey, sweet Lainey, who also wasn't afraid to take risks. Who overcame her fear of dogs. Involuntarily, a smile crept on his lips. Hopefully, Marie Claire was gone.

"Yes, thank you." Yves hung up without any notion of what Frédérick had said. Yves reposted his phone in haste, anxious to return to Lainey, when Luc rounded the wall of ferns.

"Oh, hello." Yves hoped to quickly side-step him.

But Luc blocked him, his arms crossed, a thin lock of hair falling from his usual slicked coif. "A minute of your time, please."

Yves frowned. He didn't want to keep Lainey waiting. Now he understood Marie Claire's statement was a warning that other people from Alpine Foods were here.

"What can I do for you?" Yves clapped his hands together.

Luc grinned from ear to ear but said nothing.

"If you don't have anything important to discuss, I do have someone waiting—"

"Yes, the American intern."

Yves closed his eyes. Of all the people he did not want prying into his personal life, Luc was at the top of his list. He would have to be more discreet. "We're just here as friends."

Luc crossed his arms. "I'm sure."

"Is there something you needed?"

"Yes, I was hoping to help you."

"Help me?" Yves didn't want to play Luc's game.

"Since you are busy with brokering the merger deal, I was hoping to take some responsibility off your hands, lighten your load."

Yves arched an eyebrow. "I can't think of anything at the moment." He tried to side-step him.

But Luc refused to yield the floor. "Are you sure you don't want me to take charge of your new intern? She occupies a lot of your time lately."

Yves halted, understanding the threat. Luc had no accusations, yet. But it was a wakeup call to Yves. He had been awfully unguarded in his behavior with Lainey. Something he needed to remedy. "What do you want?"

"More responsibility. I want to show our superiors I am as responsible as you are. I, too, can make things happen."

Yves clenched his jaw. If Yves refused, Luc would run to his superiors and imply his relationship with Lainey. Nothing had happened. What could he say? Giving in to what he wanted would admit guilt. "What are you after? What do you really want?"

"I just want to be like you."

Yves didn't have time for this. "A restaurant is not the place to discuss work. Come to my office first thing

Monday morning. We can discuss it then." Yves didn't even regard his expression, but instead hastened to where he left Lainey.

Luc called after him. "If a restaurant is not a place to discuss work, why are you here with the American intern?"

But Yves ignored him.

****

Lainey finished off her drink, and when Yves approached, she drank his, too. "How was your phone call?" Her head buzzed, her thoughts jumbled.

His face clouded. "*Pénible*. I hate mixing work with pleasure."

Why did he care so much about his work? Or did she care too much about work? She couldn't remember. "Then I'm sure this 'work' celebration must be dragging you down."

He tilted his head. "Not at all."

"I'm not really hungry. I'm calling it a night. Thanks for the drink." She took a wobbly step toward the entrance.

He blocked her path with his muscular chest.

"We can go somewhere else, if you wish."

"Actually, I'm not feeling well." Not a lie. Her head pounded, and she might throw up.

"Lainey, is something wrong?"

"Yes, there is something wrong." This world was unfair. He would lose his chance at promotion if this carried on. Why couldn't she have her chocolate cake and eat it, too? She had to let him go. Her tears bubbled underneath her calm restraint. She needed to leave before she cried in front of him. She needed to break his heart. And she didn't want to do it.

"Lainey, you are acting so strange. Did Marie Clare say something?"

"Tell me the truth. Did you really try to get rid of me?"

His beautiful face crumpled in disbelief. "This whole time, you've been sitting here stewing over what I said?"

"Your greed, your ambition, your hunger for power and all it buys."

Shocked, Yves stepped back, as if she'd slapped him. He recovered quickly, sharply asking, "Is that what you think I want, what I work hard for? Is that all you think I care about?"

Lainey's eyes flitted to his wrist. His watch.

"What? The watch, the watch bothers you? You are bothered because I wear an expensive watch?" He snapped it off his wrist, letting it slide to the deck with a clank.

Lainey winced, but she did not waver in her goal.

"I do not care about the watch. Or is it the car?" Glints of light hit his keys as he removed them from his pocket, weighing them in his hands. "Perhaps you think I love my car." He spun, and with deft motion, chucked the keys off the balcony into the darkened vineyard. "I don't care about the car or the apartment or anything in it."

"No." She gathered her breath and courage for the final blow. "All you care about is your damn promotion."

Her fierceness rocked him. He couldn't deny it. He didn't attempt to. His chest rose and fell in controlled anger.

Glaring at him, she slid off his jacket and threw it

at him. Not even attempting to catch it, he let it drop to the deck in front of him.

Heart pounding, she spun to go. “Goodnight, Monsieur Claremont.” She focused on the exit. The other patrons stared at her un-Swiss-like display of emotion.

Hot tears streamed down her face when she left the restaurant. She was glad to be free so she could finally cry. She bumped through the darkened and sleeping city, blinded by tears.

Chapter Twelve

Thankfully, there were few people on the streets at nine p.m. to witness her fitful rain of tears. Hot tears, the kind fueled by a deeply wounded heart, as if someone had taken a paper shredder to it.

Yves. She couldn't even think his name without a fresh barrage of tears. If only he didn't need the promotion to be happy, if only she didn't want to be in Chocolate. If only they didn't both work at Alpine Foods. If only they didn't have a rule about co-workers.

She cried even more reading the bus schedule. Of course, the last bus left at 8:50, not even two minutes ago. Curse the Swiss efficiency. Now she had to walk home, instead of riding in a totally hot Maserati.

Normally, a five-kilometer walk was not a big deal. But at nine at night? In heels and the skimpiest skirt in her closet?

She'd handle this professionally. So professional, she wouldn't ever talk about him with Marie Claire. Alone, she must suffer this alone. Oh, the pain. Her heart ached. Why was she such a fool? To think she could love someone, and there wouldn't be consequences. There were always consequences. She'd let her heart lead. She should've been more guarded, seen it coming, and prevented it.

Nearing eleven, she finally stepped under the familiar light of her apartment lobby. Too tired to climb the stairs, she pushed the elevator button. Feet swollen, eyes swollen, heart swollen, she selected her floor and leaned against the cool walls of the elevator, keeping herself propped up. At her door, she unlocked the handle with a click, feeling the heat of the apartment warming her chilled bones.

Not even removing her clothes, she crawled into bed. Huddled under the blanket, she smelled M. Claremont's cologne on Marie Claire's shirt. Tugging it off over her head, she chucked it to the floor.

Chocolate, she needed chocolate.

One arm poked tentatively from under her covers, feeling its way to her stash under her bed. Not that one. That was milk. She identified the wrapper by touch. She needed something dark. 90% Cacao. As dark and bitter as her mood. If she had cocoa nibs, those would have been even better.

She extracted packages of dark chocolate, unwrapping one and stuffing it in her mouth. She barely tasted it as it smothered her molars, melted on her warm tongue, and slid down her throat, coating her soul.

Another, Alpine Foods Exclusive Dark. She unwrapped it, filling the gnawing hunger in her stomach. Something hurt.

She needed more.

Alpine Extra Bitter. The smell of chocolate consumed her, it reached her nostrils, filled her mouth.

It was intoxicating.

Alpine Intense Dark. Metallic wrappers crumpled. Paper wrappers crinkled.

Chocolate would fill the gaping hole.

Tears made it difficult to see the easy-tear packaging, but somehow she managed, stuffing it into her mouth, snapping it, crumbs spraying.

Alpine Extra Dark Premium. A sob constricted her throat. She couldn't eat anymore. But she couldn't stop.

She must squelch the crying.

Alpine Supreme Noir. She ripped the wrapper off. The sobs won, chocolate spilling from her mouth, oozing on her sheets. She curled up on her bed and cried and cried and cried.

****

Yves didn't eat. What just happened? Lainey wasn't seriously mad at him for confessing he wanted to get rid of her, was she? When she stormed out, Yves paced the deck then found the maitre d' and asked for help to find his keys. Giving him something to do would help him forget about the incident with Lainey. Though he picked up the jacket and the watch after she left, recovering the keys proved to be more difficult.

He and Roberto, a waiter in a white short-waisted tuxedo, helped him comb through the field. The grapes had all been harvested in September, leaving the barren stems to brown until they were pruned in February.

"How did you lose your keys out here?" Roberto asked.

Yves didn't answer him, but swiped the earth with the flashlight on his phone up and down the aisles. He wasn't sure who he was madder at, Lainey or himself for getting mad at Lainey.

Already he had listened to his heart more than his head. It was best to reset. To wake up. His promotion was the most important thing. A goal he had set for himself years ago to honor his father. Even if his father was no longer here, Yves was determined to follow through.

With his fingers, he combed the rich soil where any reflection drew his attention. He was not seriously considering jeopardizing everything for her. Was he? In some ways, he was glad this happened. There was no scenario where they could possibly be together. Luc sniffing around only complicated things. Perhaps he would give Luc his wish.

After an hour of searching, he finally called it quits.

Roberto caught up with him.

"Can I come back and search in the morning?" He had the valet key for his car.

"Must be some trouble with a girl."

"What makes you say that?"

"How you react to the problem. If you talk about it, it is work. If you don't talk about it, it is relationship problems."

"I didn't think I was so transparent."

"In all the years I have worked here, *mon ami*, I have seen many couples come and go. But you, you are different. You didn't chase after her. Why?"

Because all these years, he'd only had one goal until he met Lainey. Lainey who broke his heart. Lainey, whom he wanted more than anything, but could not have.

He thanked Roberto, handing him a generous tip for his help, and called the only person who would let him stay at her house at short notice.

****

"What are you doing?" Marie Claire asked, backlit in the doorway of Lainey's room, her hands on her hips.

When Lainey raised her head off her pillow, the rustle of wrappers echoed in her ears. Her microsuede teeth tainted her breath. Oh, and what a headache she had.

"Why do I smell chocolate? What's going on?"

Lainey laid her head back down. "What day is it?"

"Are you ill?" Marie Claire flipped on the light.

Lainey squinted again. Marie Claire, dressed in a fluorescent yellow plastic shirt, electric blue jeggings, and green Turkish elf shoes, floated into view. Lainey pinned the covers over her head.

"Lainey. Did you eat all these chocolate bars today?"

"Depends on what day it is."

"Sunday. It's Sunday night."

She sat up, disturbing the wrappers on her covers. A cascade rustled to the floor with each movement of her blankets. Lainey blinked at the surrounding mess. Dozens of wrappers crowded her bed, scores were buried in her sheets. Chocolate blobs oiled her arms and tummy and, she discovered, her face and hair. She bowed her head. Her stash was finally depleted. "No, mostly Friday night. Some Saturday. Some today."

"Lainey, what is going on?"

Her ears rang. Her head was stuffed with cotton.

"Did something happen at dinner with Yves?" Marie Claire flipped down the covers.

Lainey sat up and snatched the blankets and fell back into her pillow, spraying wrappers like a tree trunk falling into water. His name churned Lainey's stomach. Her eyes hurt too much to cry.

"Come on." Marie Claire grasped Lainey's wrist to haul her from bed.

"Where are we going?" She was still in her bra and black skirt.

"To the bath. You are covered in chocolate." Marie Claire yanked her halfway out of bed. Lainey's legs dangled over the edge. Marie Claire rustled through the wrappers as she staggered to hoist Lainey.

"Just let me die."

Wading through wrappers, Marie Claire guided Lainey to the bathroom where Marie Claire drew water.

"Now take a bath."

Worried, perhaps, Lainey would drown herself, Marie Claire changed her mind and flipped on the shower and let out the plug. When finished, she closed the door on Lainey.

Facing the mirror, Lainey resembled a spotted German short-hair dog, with bits of aluminum foil and chocolate stuck to her. And she stank.

She stripped and stepped into the shower, allowing the warm water to dissolve chocolate, sugar, grease, and her tears into a brown murky mess on the shower floor until it flowed clear.

What did she do? Her heart ached, a literal soreness in her chest. Did she do the right thing? It was best to cut things off before they grew too serious. They both had plans, plans which didn't involve each other. The comfort of knowing she did the right thing helped tie the drawstring tighter around her heart.

Marie Claire knocked. "Don't forget to wash your hair."

Awakened from her trance, she shampooed. When finished, Lainey dried off, brushed her teeth, combed her hair. She shuffled to her room in her towel. While Lainey showered, Marie Claire had cleaned up the wrappers, changed her sheets and set out pajamas. Lainey dressed.

Marie Claire leaned against the doorway. "You hungry?"

Lainey shrugged. "Not really. I think I have a stomach ache."

"I made you some soup."

Lainey's tummy gurgled. Chocolate overload or hunger?

Around the four-foot-square table in their tiny kitchen, they ate a simple and refreshing meal of butternut squash soup squeezed from a box, and a warm baguette. After wiping the residue of the soup with the soft *mie* of the bread, the angry monsters in Lainey's tummy were vanquished, or subdued. But once the soup was gone, Lainey slipped into a languid stupor.

Marie Claire stared at her over empty soup bowls. "Are you going to tell me or do I ask Yves?"

"You wouldn't."

"Oh, I just might. 'Yves, Lainey came home and gorged herself on chocolate, and it wasn't out of euphoria. Can you please tell me why my roommate went out with you and then went all crazy?' "

"Please don't."

"Tell me."

Lainey shook her head.

"Did he ask to be your lover?"

Why did Marie Claire think that would cause such depression? "No."

"Did he ask you back to his apartment?"

"No." It was more of a groan, one resonating from the bottom of her heart.

"Did he kiss you?"

"No."

"Lainey, what happened?"

"I tried to break his heart, but I think I broke mine instead."

****

Early Monday morning Lainey awoke with a faint tickle in her throat. For breakfast, she skipped her usual chocolate and hurried to work.

In their department meeting, Yves ignored her when she raised her hand for a suggestion. The rest of the supervisors glanced from her to him, then back again.

At the end of the discussion, Yves finally called on her, avoiding eye contact completely, directing his gaze over her head or around the room, signifying her input was of little importance.

As the meeting broke up, Luc leaned to Gui and said in a whisper-shout, "I think *le chef* and his *petite-amie* are having a fight."

Yves shot him a terrible glance with his dark eyes shadowed by his fierce and contracted brow and stalked out of the room.

Once more, Luc smiled an I-told-you-so smile.

Back at her desk, Lainey opened her laptop, readying for her assignment. But with a dry throat, she needed some water. On her way to the cantina, she met Yves and Luc conversing together, heading toward her down the hall. Her heart beat heavy. *Fake smile, Lainey.*

As they passed, Yves spoke first. "Mademoiselle Peterson." He gave her a tight nod and formal greeting.

"Monsieur Claremont." She nodded.

Luc's face was pinched. They continued in their conversation without stopping to say anything more.

In the cantina, she poured water from the tap and drank, soothing her scratchy throat with the glacier water. At her desk, she retrieved the last bar of chocolate in her drawer, nibbling and typing to cope with this horrible day.

By noon, she had a drippy nose. Allergies, no doubt. Leaf mold was common in autumn.

With several trips to the women's restroom, she wiped her strawberry-red nose, and tucked a few extra pieces of tissue into her pocket.

On the way back to her seat, she passed Yves again. "Having trouble concentrating on the task at hand, Mademoiselle Peterson?"

"No, Monsieur Claremont."

He then continued into another room.

Before she left for home, her head ached, and her nose was so drippy there wasn't a dry tissue anywhere near her. Slumping up the hill to her apartment, she wrapped her coat tight around her.

At home, she curled up in bed with a roll of toilet paper with the subtle texture of sandpaper. When Marie Claire came home, she peeked in her room. "You okay?"

"Sick."

All evening, she slept without eating anything for dinner but a bit of medicinal chocolate, the only thing within reachable distance from her bed. She needed all those antioxidants and flavanols, the vitamins A, D and K. The smoothness tickled her throat, and she began to cough.

And cough.

And cough.

All night she coughed, wishing for a twenty-four-hour pharmacy and some meds. She slept between fits of coughing and weird dreams of Yves and Hiroko fighting giant bugs in a dress shop.

By morning, she shook, coughed, and wheezed as if she were an eighty-year-old lung cancer patient. Her throat was dry, as if she'd swallowed the whole Sonoran Desert complete with scratchy cacti.

Marie Claire came in with a bottle of *syrop*. She spooned Lainey some and poured her some water, telling her to lie down and sleep. She'd check in at lunch. "Don't worry," she cooed. "I'll let them know you're sick."

Marie Claire's words faded as she slipped into a comatose state. At noon, Marie Claire returned, poured Lainey a glass of water, feeding her more *syrop*.

In the afternoon, Lainey dreamed Yves came to see her and dragged her out of bed to work, though in her dream he shackled her to the desk, preventing her from going to the bathroom.

When she awoke, she had a boulder in her bladder. With effort, she sat up, then swung her legs over the bed, her body like a beached whale. She shuffled to the restroom.

At dusk, Marie Claire entered. More *syrop*.

Lainey fell into a restless sleep.

By morning she was better, though her nose was still drippy and stuffy at the same time, which defied laws of science. Her throat stung from post-nasal drip, but she had no headache or fever.

Once up, she glanced around the room, squinting in the late sunlight of Wednesday morning. Down the street the recycling vehicle dumped millions of bottles from weekend binge drinking into the back compactor, shattering the silence. The sound harrowed her peace.

In her PJs, she padded into the kitchen, hoping to

find something to augment her chocolate diet of the last few days. As she passed the hall, she noticed her box from Nadine missing, the one with her dress in it. She shuffled back to her room to see if Marie Claire had cleaned and put it there. Not there either.

Instantly, she knew where it was. Unthinkingly, Marie Clare put it out to recycle. Nadine's bridesmaid dress was sitting out on the curb and the truck was coming.

With glacial speed, she slid on sweats and slipped on flip flops and notwithstanding not having showered in two days, she ran—or slumped—downstairs to save her dress.

Just as she opened the door to the lobby, two men threw her box on the back of the truck.

"No!" She shouted in a hoarse voice sounding faintly louder than the squeak of a mouse, and certainly not louder than the roar of the compactor.

One of the men squeezed the lever, crushing it to pieces.

"No!" she cried again, faint as the first. But it was too late, her box and the dress were now in a crumpled, tangled mess.

One of the men, noticing her, smiled and waved with a gloved hand, picking up cardboard from the sidewalk before hopping in the truck.

Lainey watched it continue down the street, unaware of anything else around her. Until she heard her name.

"Lainey, what are you doing?"

No.

Her head slumped, and she peeked at her reflection in the lobby doors. Her hair was modern art sculpture.

She hadn't showered in days. She wore her least attractive sweats, which gathered too tight around the ankles and fell too loose around the thigh.

She paused, hoping to disappear, but Yves Claremont, as fresh as a loaf of bread, strode up to her. His detail-seeking eyes glossed over her sweats and her matted hair. "You are sick. You should be in bed."

"I was just going for a morning stroll," she managed from her froggy throat before coughing. Her body ached, her throat hurt. Her nose was a dribbling mess.

He wrapped his arm around her shoulders, guiding her through the lobby doors. His cologne wafted up in pleasant drafts. If she smelled him, he must have been able to smell her, too.

"I came to see why you were not at work. I called but your phone is off."

"The battery is dead, I'm sure." She hadn't been out of bed for two days. Even inside the lobby, her teeth chattered, and she clasped herself around her elbows, before pressing the elevator button.

The elevator opened, and he held it. "I came to tell you about your new assignment I promised you. Since I will be occupied preparing our contract with Atatakai International to close on our new product line, I will not have the time to dedicate to your instruction."

Barely blinking, Lainey stared at the vinyl squares on the floor of the lobby.

He continued, still holding the elevator doors. "When you feel well enough to work, report to Luc for further instructions."

She nodded, wiping her nose with the cuff of her sweatshirt, not even staring at him with her itchy eyes.

"Luc wanted to set you up with a VPN so you can work from home until you are feeling better."

A lady noisily stamped down the stairs and glared at them. And the elevator.

Yves removed his hand from the elevator, allowing it to close and go at someone else's beck and call. He faced Lainey, his eyes urgent, almost pleading. "Luc will be able to help you in ways my schedule will not allow. Reporting production needs for the opening of the Pacific Asian market, detailing plans for growth, factories in Japan will take all my time. This is really the best way for you to get the most of your intern experience. I cannot be your proper mentor." Yves' eyebrows peaked, resembling less the impatient and important M. Claremont and more like a school boy. "Luc is quite capable. Likely to become department chair when I am..." Yves stopped short, perhaps realizing the tender subject of his promotion. Clearing his throat, he continued, more serious and direct—typical M. Claremont. "I hope you are pleased with your new assignment. For the remainder of your internship here in Pet Care, report to him for further instruction. I leave you in his competent hands. And Luc can decide on your recommendation to Chocolate."

This was an opportunity to retract what she said at the restaurant, to beg for forgiveness, but she couldn't. His promotion was too important to him. Once, she thought she only needed chocolate to be happy. Now, she needed him to be happy first.

He waited for her to say something, anything.

"Thank you for bearing with me," she said in her politest, most formal French.

He opened his mouth as if to say something, but

instead, spun on his heel and opened the lobby doors and stepped out to the street.

Chapter Thirteen

Lainey awoke to the phone ringing. How long had she been asleep? An hour maybe? It was ten o'clock.

"Lainey?"

"Mom, why are you calling so late?"

"Everything is packed and we're taking off. It will be a while before we have Internet or a phone line so the best way to reach us is by mail or you can call our real estate agent out there. I emailed you her number. Aren't you excited?"

"Mom, this goes without saying: I think you guys are nuts."

"You can come and visit us before you start your career hunt after the holidays. Our new place has five bedrooms. And a beach view, just out the veranda. Don't bring any sweaters, just your Arizona clothes."

"Yeah, it's pretty cold here. I might take you up on the Costa Rica visit." She'd given up on the idea of Luc giving her a recommendation to Chocolate. "I just have a few more weeks here, Mom."

"Have you and Aaron made up, yet?"

"No. We're not going to."

They hung up, but her mother's question lingered in the cold air. Without any hope of a chocolate internship, or a relationship with Yves, Lainey dialed Aaron.

"Wow, you're calling me," he said.

"How's work going?"

"Fine, the four-wheelers are selling well. So, what did you call me for?"

She sighed. "There's this gala dinner at the end of November with promotions and speeches and stuff. It's kind of formal. I even bought a dress already. It's cute with bits of—"

"Lainey, you're babbling."

"Right." She breathed. "I was wondering if you'd be willing to fly over and be my date."

There was a pause. A long one. Lainey was unsure what it meant. Maybe he was thinking. Maybe he didn't hear. Or watching football. Cardinals.

She continued. "I'd pay for you. Your ticket, I mean. I'd pay for you to fly out and your hotel and tux rental—everything, so you don't have to worry." She couldn't believe how desperate she sounded.

"Tempting. I don't know, Lainey. November is a busy time here, gearing up for the holidays. Employees take vacation, I have to fill in the gaps."

Her resolve hardened. She had to have a date. "You owe me," she said through gritted teeth. "After what happened at the going away party."

He sighed. "I'll see what I can do."

He didn't sound too hopeful.

****

Lainey waited for Luc outside his smallish office, not wanting to talk to him. She braced herself against his cold manner and opened the door.

Luc was speaking with someone, though it was difficult for her to discern who through the crack in the door. She caught Yves' name.

"Public humiliation?" asked another man. "Utterly

destroy his career and reputation?"

"I told you not to talk about it at work." Luc's voice.

"Nothing's going to happen."

"I'm just saying if we get caught, it will cost your job as well. You're in it just as thick as I am."

"Is it too much?"

"He has to be totally ruined. I'll send an email with more details."

Lainey's heart lunged. She backed slowly away, barely letting the door slide shut, making the slightest tick sound when it closed. She winced. They hushed. They heard her. Footsteps approached the door.

Lainey had to think of something. With one hand on the doorknob, and the other on her cell phone, she lifted it to her ear, just as the door swung open. "Right, I only ordered three of them." She glanced up to Luc staring at her, and Gui, behind him, texting on his phone. She smiled, her heart pounding with the charade. "Of course, of course. Thank you. *Allez-bye*." She hung up and faced Luc. She hoped his hawk-like eyes didn't see her hands trembling when she returned her phone to her pocket.

"I'm here to report." She forced her lips upwards.

Luc blinked, his eyes black pinpoints under a large forehead. Lainey bet he was wondering if she heard anything. She hoped her smile took him off guard.

She feigned relaxation, even humor. "Didn't Yves tell you I'm your problem now?"

"Sometimes I don't understand your French."

"Sometimes I don't understand *your* French."

His body melted from rigid tension to tentative calm. He swept back his slicked hair. Fidgeting with a purple paisley tie hanging from his blue and white striped collar, he glanced nervously behind him to Gui. The man needed some fashion sense. But this was not the greatest beef she had with him. "Right now is not a good time. I'll let you know when I'm free." Luc slammed the door in her face.

Backing from the door, she heard unrecognizable French penetrating the wood door.

****

Lainey didn't know how legal it was. Or if it was even possible. If she got caught, it was all over. In a booth near her apartment, she called Nadine.

"Hey, Lainey, you're on speaker phone. I'm washing dishes, and Martin's here, but he's on his computer so we're basically alone."

"Great, I need to talk to Martin."

A pot dropped. "Really? You can't convince him to change the wedding date just for you, Lainey."

"Har, har, Nadine. It's something for work."

"I'll get him." Rustling sounded in the background. Perhaps Nadine was rousing him from his screen.

Lainey and Martin had never spoken on the phone, and she was sure he was shocked. Or amused. Or annoyed.

"Okay, Lainey," Nadine said. "Martin is listening."

"Hey, Martin. How easy would it be to hack into an internal email system?"

"How easy for me? Or for a theoretical person."

"Either."

"Where?"

"Uh, Alpine Foods."

"In Switzerland?"

"Yeah."

"Hm, you couldn't give me something easy? The US Embassy perhaps. The Swiss have security as their middle name. Just out of curiosity, why?"

"It's for a good cause. I just want to sort of spy on a co-worker. I have some reasonable suspicions they might be plotting something."

"You're asking me to risk going to federal prison to spy on a co-worker."

"I think he might be sabotaging someone?"

"On your boss/boyfriend?"

"Geez, you guys, he's not my boyfriend. He's dating Hiroko, all right? Got it? No more! And no spying on him, either."

"No spying on Mr. Hotty Boss. Got it." The insinuation in his voice was rich. She blushed. Martin continued, "Breaking in to Alpine Foods will be almost impossible. Firewalls, encryptions, credentials, password protections, not to mention just the physical distance. If I were there, working on a computer, there might be a chance, but the odds of success are astronomical."

He wasn't going for it. Lainey would have to think of something else.

"Therefore, I accept."

"Really?"

"Should be fun."

"You'd jeopardize your future life, get slapped with a possible felony to spy on some people for me at work?"

"It's a challenge."

"Yeah, but they can lock you away. You'd never work for your Silicon start-up, become some prison rat's boy-toy—"

"Lainey, I said I'd do it. You don't have to remind me what's at stake here. So, who's the guy you need hacked?"

"His name is Luc Pessereaux. No, it's not my boss. I mean he is now, since M. Claremont sloughed me off to him."

Nadine giggled again in the background.

"Hm, if only I had a VPN or some local access," Martin said. "I can hack around your corporate firewalls if I have to, but it would speed things up with VPN access."

"What's a VPN?"

"It's a tunnel from the outside network into your internal network."

"When I was sick, they gave me the password to access from home?"

"Bingo."

****

When Lainey returned to work, her desk was gone. Luc moved her into her own cubicle. Lainey suspected M. Claremont situated her in the hall on purpose to humble her after begging for an internship.

When she opened her laptop, Luc emailed her first assignments for the day:

Deliver a bag of dog food to a lady who forgot her bag at the pet give-away project

Take flyers down to the copy shop for printing

Mail a package

Meet with the chef at the Grande Hôtel De Vevey, Alexandre Dobrinsky, to pick up the printed menu for the gala banquet.

What was this list? Lainey was now an errand girl? In a quick phone call, she set an appointment to meet with the chef at the hotel, a real hotel this time, where the gala would be.

Before she left for errands, she stopped by Luc's office to gather information and packages. "Can I just take any old bag of food for this lady?" she asked Luc who was reading the newspaper at his desk in a small room slightly larger than a broom closet. "And do you have her address?"

Without glancing up from *Le Temps du Temps*, he flipped the page. "You have to retrieve a specially prepared bag from Yves. He wrote a note apologizing for the oversight." He searched his desk for a scrap of paper. "Here."

Lainey read it. Annette Pettit. Her address and the directions to her house were scrawled below the name. Taking a deep breath to calm her heart, she proceeded to Yves' office.

His door was open, but he was out. Lainey breathed with relief. A package of dog food sat on his desk with an embossed notecard taped across a dog with a gleaming coat and a smiling owner. Wow, a hand-written note. Paper this pretty must come from the *papeterie*, the only place still selling stationary. She opened the note and read it.

Madame Pettit,

Thank you for your phone call. We apologize for our oversight. Please let us reward you with this extra-large bag of Premium Puppy Meal. As I stated in our conversation, you cannot do better than the fresh and nutritious ingredients found in our product. Happy eating,

(Signed) Yves Claremont

Even reading his name warmed her face. She

snatched the bag with a crumpling sound and tucked it under her arm. First stop, copy shop. She caught the bus to *centre-ville*.

At the copy shop, she waited in a trailing line. She juggled the dog food, the package, and papers.

In the US, she didn't have to carry things everywhere because she had a car. Her arms ached from carrying a few kilos of pet food. She set it on the floor and kicked it forward as the line progressed. At the window, the worker took forever to process her order. No wonder the line was so long. When finished there, she marched up the block to the post office.

At the great glass doors, she yanked on the handles. They didn't budge. She checked the hours. Closed from noon until two. She checked her watch. A few minutes before one. Her appointment with the chef at the Hôtel De Vevey was at three, and Madam Pettit's township was beyond the Hôtel De Vevey. She didn't have time to make it there and back to the Hôtel by three.

Her stomach growled. The rest of the town closed for lunch. She might as well find something to eat, hit the post office when it opened, then the Hôtel and Madam Pettit's. On the way to a *boulangerie*, she passed a *pâtisserie*. A waft of chocolate poured from the open doorway. Shopkeepers did it on purpose. It should be illegal. Lainey had to stop.

Inside windowed cases were the most beautiful cakes and pastries—confection for the eyes as well as the tongue. A chocolate *tarte* filled with raspberries caught her eye, then a chocolate cake with an overlay of golden filigree icing wrapped around chocolate flowers. Another case had a cake dusted with colored sugar in a stenciled design, tarts filled with colorful fruit held in place with a glossy gel shining under the lights. Cakes piped, coated, painted. Then the chocolates truffles, hand painted with delicate flowers and leaves in autumn crimson, yellow, and orange lined the last vitrine.

Who needed lunch? Eat dessert first. She lugged the bag of Premium Puppy Meal all around creation today, after all. It was practically a multi-hour arm workout, and she needed those extra calories.

She bought a couple of chocolates to eat immediately, stuffing one in her mouth, and bagged a few to eat after lunch. And a few to share with Alexandre, too. He sacrificed his time to meet with her.

She stopped by a *boulangerie* to grab a sandwich on fresh bread and ate it on a park bench, observing the pedestrians pass by on one of the last days of sunshine before the winter-grays. When the church bells rang two, she returned to the post office and posted the package. At half-past two, she caught the bus for her appointment with Alexandre, glad she could relax on the bus instead of asking people questions while worrying about M. Claremont's penetrating scowl.

At her stop, she jumped down and climbed the giant stone steps to the hotel. The hotel. *The* hotel. Memories of their photo shoot tumbled through her mind. But she quickly dismissed them.

The five story Tudor-style building brought fashion to old-fashioned. Before anything else, she asked the reception desk to hold her Premium Puppy Meal. No way she was hauling dog food to a meeting with a chef.

She met Alexandre Dobrinsky in the sparkling foyer of the Grande Hôtel de Vevey. His traditional toque and chef's whites contrasted with the other black- or gray-suited men crossing the highly polished cut-marble floor. In greeting, he touched his massive chest, covering a thick gold cross hanging from an even thicker twisted chain around his neck.

After giving Lainey two *bises*, he offered her a seat. There was a reason these guys studied hospitality; his gentlemanliness made her feel special. She gave him the chocolates after he sat.

His thighs pressed through the delicate arms of the Queen Anne's chair, like bread dough caught in a tight fist. "Thank you." He inspected the mark on the outside of the chocolate bag, eyeing her with approval. "A well-chosen gift."

Before giving her the menus, he insisted on probing deeper into personal stuff. At first, his Polish-accented French was difficult to understand as he related to her his religion—deeply Catholic—expounded his heritage—yes, Lainey did know former Pope John Paul II came from Poland—dramatized his parents' immigration to Switzerland when he was nine, complete with gesticulation and facial expression, and unfolded his career beginning at the L'Académie Culinaire until present, the chef of the Grand Hôtel de Vevey. The gold cross swung as he poured out his monologue, without hesitation, without reservation. He just served up his whole history for her to ingest, as if he was presenting the feast of his soul begging for Lainey to partake.

She liked him.

"And you, Mademoiselle Peterson—"

"Lainey."

"Yes, Lainey, what have you come to intern at Alpine Foods for?" He said Alpine Foods with a bit of a sneer.

"You dislike Alpine Foods, I take it."

"Does man search his whole life for mass-produced art? No! Neither should he eat food produced for the masses." He leaned forward in his chair, his eyes bright, his gold cross clanking on his double-breasted buttons. "You see, Lainey, God knows man requires food. He commanded him in the Garden. 'Of every tree you may freely eat,' he says. Except, of course, the forbidden fruit. He," Alexandre pressed his hands together and glanced heavenward, "knows the importance of daily nourishment, of feeding the body as well as the soul. This commandment is my personal mission. We are to eat, and we are to eat well. Fresh, close to the earth, as natural as the Garden, clean and simple as fruit itself. Lainey, if you do not believe this philosophy, you do not belong in the food business. Food is the one pleasure sanctified by God to be enjoyed at least three times a day. Or, if you are blessed, a whole day in the kitchen, partaking of God's greatest creations." He stopped himself. "Ah, but you see I am passionate about my work. I am sorry to bore you."

"Not at all."

"Surely, you have something you are passionate about?"

Lainey's heart lifted. For the first time since she had come to Switzerland, someone asked her what her purpose was, what she was passionate about. She didn't need a second invitation.

"Chocolate."

"Chocolate!" He leaned back and clapped his hands. "I knew, when we met, we were kindred spirits. Tell me more."

"All my life I've studied chocolate and the people

who made it happen: François-Louis Callier, Daniel Peter, Rodolphe Lindt. I know about tempering chocolate, about baking with chocolate, molding chocolate. I've personally sampled hundreds of brands of chocolates, kept notes, done my own research on the best time of day to eat chocolate. I've studied cooking, baking and melting differences in milks, darks, and although they are not my favorite, whites."

"Oh, wonderful!" His chest expanded like bread rising, his excitement building. He absorbed everything she said.

"And my whole life, I've wanted to work for Alpine Foods in their chocolate department, spreading my joy of chocolate."

She glanced at him, knowing he would understand her mission, her passion. She searched for it on his face.

But Alexandre was punched down, like over-proofed bread dough. He glared at her with a shriveled brow.

"What?" she asked.

He shook his head.

"What?" she asked again.

"You do not want to work for Alpine Foods."

"I don't?"

"No, Lainey. With the kind of passion you have about chocolate, you cannot work for a company who cares so little about chocolate. You cannot work for a company who has a whole department dedicated to deciding how to wrap a bar. You cannot work for a company which lobbies the government to allow them to use vegetable fat in place of cocoa butter. *Tsk, tsk, tsk.* A woman with your passion, your experience, your knowledge, needs a boutique shop, an artisan shop, to dedicate your life to making the best chocolate you can for people who truly enjoy chocolate. Do not waste your time on a mass-produced bar for children and candy lovers."

At first his advice wounded her, offending her to her ganache-chocolate core. "My whole life I've wanted to work for Alpine Foods. They are the largest suppliers of chocolate in the world. Who has more of an impact?"

"It is the small people, not the great ones, who make the biggest difference in the world. You remind me of Gregorio Benito, one of the great names in Alpine Foods Chocolate."

Her ears burned hearing his name. While preparing for the internship, she studied M. Benito. He commanded the chocolate department for twenty years, just before Mme Grocher, modernizing production at Alpine Foods, created greater output efficiencies, even changed the logo imprint on the bar. But he was probably best known for his introduction of the Alpine Foods Exclusive Dark, one of their premium dark chocolates with 90% cocoa. He retired from chocolate to pursue politics.

Alexandre must have noticed the light of recognition in her eyes. "You know him? Switzerland is such a small country. He, too, wanted to use the mass machine to spread the joy of chocolate to the world. In his ideals, he commenced as a purist, but now, now he is in the forefront campaigning for cheaper chocolate."

"But—" she rushed to defend herself, but he held up his hand to cut her off.

"Ah, you think you will be different. That you can stand up to the conglomerate."

"Yes, actually, that was what I was going to say."

"Sadly, Lainey, even as the department head, you do not have very much power to control the machine of a conglomerate. If they say cut, you cut. If they say more, you give more. If they say vegetable oil," he sniffed at this, "you say, yes. In the end, when you produce for the masses you have to sacrifice quality, passion, control."

At his words, Lainey bowed her head in contrite contemplation. Would she be better off working in a boutique shop? Walking away from Alpine Foods? Giving up her childhood dreams? The thought pained her.

"I see I have hurt your feelings, Mademoiselle Peterson. I am sorry. Maybe you will be the one to make a difference. Who is Alexandre Dobrinsky to say? I am a nobody. A nobody who humbly does God's work. And maybe this is God's work for you. Who am I to deter you? Now you are sad. To cheer you up, I will give you a tour of my kitchen. We eat together, then I'll give you the menu."

They stood. She followed him through halls, passed service elevators and stairwells and some of the less glamorous parts of the hotel until they reached twin doors. Alexandre paused reverently, whispering before parting the doors, "This is where I pay my sacraments to God."

Through the worn doors, Alexandre stepped into his kitchen, a shrine where he offered up his talents in consecration. Here she met the priesthood of food, Alexandre, the high priest.

At first, she was overwhelmed with smells and the commotion of underlings, the aroma of their efforts. He introduced his subordinates, who wrapped, dunked, drizzled, and stuffed in every corner of the stainless steel and white tile kitchen, barely noticing the heretic.

Then he spied a man in a corner, shaking spices onto a chicken breast. Alexandre yelled, first in Polish then in French.

The *rôtisseur* immediately cowered, set the dish on the butcher block and, complying with Alexandre's instructions, scooped up the herbs from the bowl and rubbed the seasonings into the meat. Alexandre, once the chicken had been saved, resumed his discourse as they stood next to a large, oven-like appliance with whole, rotating chickens inside. Heat and roasting scents better than Thanksgiving radiated from it.

"As you see, God has given man many gifts. Those gifts inspire man to create inventions to glorify God through food. You see, Mademoiselle Peterson," he said over the clank and clamor of the pots and their wielders. "God gave us fire for man to cook. And man invented the rotisserie. And God gave us cocoa beans for pleasure. And man invented the chocolate bar."

Lainey nodded. "God invented electricity so we can have the microwave."

He stopped short, his hand over his gold cross. "No, Lainey Peterson. God does not glory in the microwave. Man invented the microwave, and man forever ruined food. Look around you." He splayed his arms as the bustling, steaming room carried on around him. A *potager* chef and an *entremetier* in white jackets poured liquids from one pot into another, chopped vegetables with precision. Flame burst in a corner where a *saucier* shook a frying pan. "Do you see one microwave? No." Wagging finger. "Nor will you ever.

Using quick methods is man's cheapening of food, making it accessible in one minute." With an exaggerated grimace, he mimed opening and closing a door and pushing buttons. "Wrrrrrrrr. Ding!" He opened the door again, retrieved the food, and held it out to her. "Your preservatives and trans fat are ready." His hands dropped. "No, Mademoiselle Peterson, the microwave is not one of God's inventions."

Ugh, she was so tossing out the microwave when she returned home!

****

Enveloped in Alexandre's final embrace, she breathed in his briny kitchen smell and sweat. He pecked her cheek. "It has been a joy to find someone who is equally excited about food."

"Thank you for letting me be a part of this experience. You've given me so much to think about." She placed her hand on her full stomach. "And much to eat. You fed my mind and my soul."

He grabbed both of her hands in his, and gave her the *bise* as if they were old friends. "Thank you. Only one with passion can feed you." With a sigh, Alexandre returned to his kitchen.

This conversation, no, this whole meeting had left such an impression on her. Changed her. She must think about this more. What did she really want? Did she even know what she wanted? She thought she did.

Before leaving, Lainey stopped by the desk to retrieve her package. She stepped down the stairs of the hotel to wait for the bus.

Only one more stop until she could at last part ways with the bag of Premium Puppy Meal. She hoped Madame Pettit's puppy enjoyed the food taxing her arms all afternoon. She checked the posted schedule, then her Swiss timepiece. She had ten minutes to wait.

The now overcast sky gave a supernatural glow to the valley. Across the street, breaking the skyline, was some kind of park. If it had been warmer, there might had been picnics on the grass and volleyball in the sand pit. The lake, only a few yards away, rippled in the wind. The shining water enticed Lainey to draw closer.

Nearer the water, on the rocks lining the bank, was a familiar woodsy smell of dampness, of too many overcast days, of rain, of rotting leaves, and moss. The wind blustered, blowing her hair in a rush all around, nearly stealing her breath. The wind was exhilarating against her, as if it could pick her up and carry her to the lake.

But she glanced at her watch. The bus should be coming soon. To ensure she had the right route, she found the directions to Madam Pettit's house. She did not want any mishaps.

As she returned to the bus stop, the wind ripped through her, rustling her clothes, blowing her back, tugging at the directions in her hand. She crumpled it more securely in her fist. The wind picked up, violently rushing against her. And then, in a blink, her paper was torn from her grasp.

It spun high, high up into the air caught in a whirlwind. Then it settled on the sand, scuttling crab-like on the beach. Lainey stepped toward it. It fluttered away. She took a few more steps. But it blew more, tugged by an invisible string.

Frantically, she chased it, but it was always a few paces ahead of her. Finally, it halted in the rocks by the edge of the water, taunting her. She lunged for it. The wind blew again. *Pift*, it landed in the lake.

Posted near the edge of the lake was a sign saying, *Interdit,* and a picture of a blue swimming figure marked out with a circle. No swimming.

She hesitated at the shore, debating entry. The paper floating out of reach. She checked her watch. If she returned to the office for another copy, she wouldn't have time to catch the last bus out to Madam Pettit's.

She envisioned Luc's contempt at her predicament but called him anyway. No answer. And his mailbox was full so she couldn't leave a message. Time was short now. The bus would be here any minute. She needed to catch the paper.

The wind carried it on the waves, farther into the lake.

She set down the bag of dog food, removed her shoes, and rolled her slacks to mid-calf. She removed her watch and phone and dropped them into her shoes, then stepped tentatively onto the silty bottom. Lainey imagined the feel of stepping in a pan of freshly made brownies, mud squeezing between her toes. It was not swimming. Just one step.

The paper was almost within reach. Another gust. Another step, and water tickled her calves.

She stopped and rolled her slacks up to her knees. Another step. She must get the paper. She couldn't face Luc if she failed.

She waded faster, chasing the paper, her wake pushing it farther from her. It was as if all nature wanted this paper away from her.

Water splashed up to her mid-calves. She ran. Each step was harder as the mud trapped her feet. The lake churned around her, the color of weak milk chocolate.

The paper was just inches from her. Up to her knees, she was about to lunge for it, when someone yelled behind her in French.

"*Mademoiselle, mademoiselle*."

She stopped, sinking into the mud. A *gendarme* stood at the edge of the lake. Clad in black, he motioned for her to come to shore. She wanted to yell at him how important it was to have the paper. The words of frustration and longing in French stalled on the end of her tongue. And yelling at police in a foreign country was never wise.

Over her shoulder she watched as her directions, her passport to humiliation-free return to the office, her freedom from her Premium Puppy Meal shackles floated out to France. Just out of reach.

He motioned again. Bowing her head, she nodded to show she understood. She attempted to step, but the mud trapped her foot, like a wooly mammoth in the La Brea Tar Pits. Losing her balance, she faltered, water splashing on her shirt, white turning brown. She lurched forward then backward, still unable to catch her balance, her arms windmilling to stay upright. The shore, then the sky, all cloudy and gray, flashed before her eyes. Then *ploosh!* She sat butt first into the water.

Cold, wet. Water entered her mouth. Ewwww. Shivering, muddy, she gasped to catch her breath, gaping like a hungry carp. Sputtering, coughing water, she attempted to stand, but her feet remained locked in mud. Waves splashed her when she pushed her hands into the lakebed for stabilization. On her feet, she fell again. Forward, this time. Her hands hit the water first, then her chest, finally her head. Hair streaming with water, completely soaked, she managed to stand upright and untrap her feet. Wiping water from her face, she marched with as much dignity as she could muster toward the shore. Behind her cascading hair, she peeked at the *gendarme*. Was he laughing? Videoing? Applauding her impromptu Swan Lake performance? None of those things. He stood there, stone-faced.

Wow. Marie Clare was right. The Swiss really did not have a sense of humor.

The officer generously waited for her to reach shore before giving her a ticket for swimming in the lake. When she explained she was *not* swimming but *wading* in the lake and failing to retrieve a piece of paper, he gave her another ticket. For littering. Her bus drove by as he filled out the second ticket.

Wet, discouraged, cold, and no bus. The bag of dog food grew heavier by the minute. She pocketed the ticket. At least her shoes were dry. She trudged up to the bus stop. Thirty minutes now until the next bus. What was she to do?

And then, she spotted it. A chorus of angels sang hallelujah as she stumbled toward her salvation. A blue Swisscom booth. She ducked inside and set everything down, using both hands on the keyboard to search for Madame Pettit. She ignored the water dripping from her clothes onto the clean floor of the booth.

She typed in her name. There were three Annette Pettits in the valley. She read each address, matching them with what she remembered of the address on the paper. She found the right address. No directions, but at least she knew which bus to catch, and she had an address. She typed it into her phone. No more paper. She hauled the dog food back to the bus stop, freezing as the wind whipped around, mocking her as it dried her clothes.

By the time the bus arrived, she felt as if she were in one of those horror movies where the characters step into the deep freezer and find a frozen corpse. She would be the corpse.

She stumbled up the stairs of the bus, fumbling with stiff hands to pay the driver. His expression was either disgust or pity, but Lainey didn't care. She collapsed on a bus seat, the bag of Premium Puppy Meal next to her to keep her company.

When she finally arrived at Madame Pettit's address, it was well past dark. Realizing how disarrayed she must appear and how late it was, she was unsure if she should disturb the occupants. It might not leave the best impression on Alpine Foods.

But she couldn't leave a bag of dog food on the doorstep. And she was not about to lug it back to headquarters. Not after everything she went through. So she rang the bell.

The door cracked open, and an old lady peered out. She was a bit crusty at first, but softened when Lainey handed her the bag, and after she read the note. "You're here late, young lady. Business calls should have stopped hours ago."

Lainey nodded and mumbled she ran into a few difficulties along the way.

"So I see. Hold on a minute." She disappeared inside, taking the dog food package with her. When she reappeared, she handed Lainey a scarf. "Take this, at least. You'll catch your death out there!"

Gratefully, Lainey accepted the scarf and wrapped it around to warm her neck. And her heart.

Back at headquarters she hoped Luc had left for the

day, but his office was open, and he was waiting for Lainey.

"Can't you do anything right?" he asked, slamming down hard copies of some graphs. In his outburst, a strand flipped up from Luc's slicked-back, shellacked hair. His nose, although fairly small, became ginormous when his nostrils flared. "Annette called hours ago and said she still hadn't received her bag of dog food. Where have you been? And what happened to your clothes?"

Lainey leapt to the defensive. "I delivered the dog food. But I ran into some difficulties, so it took longer than I expected. I tried calling you, but you didn't answer, and your voicemail was full. What was I supposed to do?"

Luc sighed a huge aggravated sigh. "This assignment was so simple, even you should have been able to do it without problems," he said. Then, under his breath, "*Imbécile*."

It sounded too similar to the English word for her to mistake his meaning. She glared at him. She would be delighted to find some nasty dirt on Luc.

To punish her, he made her email Yves and tell him about delivering the dog food late. Yves was in Japan. Lainey explained the situation, asking him what he wanted her to do.

"Don't worry about it, Lainey," came his emailed reply. "I will apologize to Madame Pettit for your tardiness."

Lainey had never failed before.

****

At eight that night, the phone rang. Lainey answered it. She assumed it was for her. Marie Claire had been leaving it in Lainey's room since nobody called for Marie Claire on this phone.

It was Aaron.

"What do you want?" It came out more terse than she intended. It had been a long day, complete with a dunk in the lake. She had returned home, taken a shower, and cuddled up with an Alpine Foods Special Dark.

"Whoa, who put a scorpion in your pants?"

"I'm sorry. I've been going crazy here. Luc has me working some crazy tasks."

"Luc?"

"My boss."

"The one with the Maserati?"

"No, a different one. Yves dumped me off on him."

"Yves?" He grunted. "The one with the Maserati. When did you start calling him Yves?"

"Everybody does. I was the only one calling him M. Claremont. Anyway, it's no big deal."

"You sound stressed, Lainey."

"I'm just busy."

"No, I've heard your 'busy-stressed.' You're worried about something else."

"Everything I do is wrong."

"You're just being too hard on yourself."

She paused, struck by his tone.

"I'm sorry, Lainey, I shouldn't have snapped at you. This isn't how I wanted this to go."

She didn't know what to say. So she bit off more of her Special Dark.

"I've cleared my schedule so I can go the gala."

"You did?" Finally, a piece of good news.

"Why do you sound so surprised?"

"I'm happy."

"You're still buying the ticket, right?"

"Right." The bottom of her heart sank, as if it wasn't going to happen. It made for lousy conversation so they both hung up after generic parting words. Lainey bet he, too, dreaded seeing her again and discussing the incident.

With the chocolate bar still hanging from her mouth, she glanced at her profile in the mirror, fluffing her tummy, then sucked it in. She wanted to look her best for…Not for Aaron. No, she wanted to look her best for the gala.

She knocked on Marie Claire's door. "Can I borrow your scale?" She inclined her head to the bathroom.

Lainey found the scale and stepped on it. Seventy kilos. Minus the 100g of chocolate, of course. Wasn't a kilo half a pound? That didn't make sense. She couldn't weigh thirty-five pounds. How much was seventy kilos? She ran to get a conversion chart and calculator.

"Two point two times," she murmured as she typed her weight into the calculator. "Equals…"

Nooooooooooooooooo!

She could not weigh so much. Impossible.

She'd know if she'd gained so much weight. Her clothes would be too tight. However, she hadn't been wearing her jeans, just her baggier, wider slacks.

From underneath her bed she slid out her suitcase and held out her jeans. Out came one leg from the sweat pants, then the other.

On went the jeans.

Around her thigh, butt, and waist was so tight. She sat on the bed.

"Maybe the humidity and lack of drying in the

dryer made them tight," she said aloud, mostly to the calculator, which must have been wrong.

She did several squats to loosen them. Still no luck. She'd gained nearly twenty pounds. Twenty pounds. How? She walked to the market every day. To buy more chocolate, a voice inside her whispered. No, she was not blaming this on the chocolate. She walked to work, too. Where she sat around most of the day, the voice said again. Eating chocolate while she worked.

Arg!

Her dress for the gala? Did it even fit?

She slid on the dress. Nope. An inch of zipper at the top refused to zip up. Maybe if she wore her hair down.

This was ridiculous.

New goals: Get up and jog every day for the next few weeks. And maybe lay off the chocolate.

She rehung the dress in her closet when her work phone rang. "Martin? How did you call my Swiss cell? It only works with European numbers."

"I got a Swiss VOIP number and then called you."

"Have you found anything?"

"Some interesting things. Took me a few days to hack into their system. Then a few more days to sort through endlessly boring emails about dog food. But I did come across something interesting. I took the opportunity to do some research on your boyfriend."

"Who?" She blushed, knowing exactly who he meant.

"A Monsieur Yves Claremont." Only his accent was terrible.

"Oh?"

"I don't think Yves is dating Hiroko."

"What makes you think so?"

"I'm just perusing their correspondence. There's no 'Hey, Honey, how was your day, Love?' "

"He's a Swiss man and not prone to affectionate name calling."

"They don't set up dates and stuff."

"He has a phone, Martin. Not every guy uses the Internet to woo women."

Martin had a snarky laugh. "Funny, Lainey. Just trust the Guy Instinct. The way he addresses her, the way he only talks business. He's not into her, not like that."

Her heart beat hard through her lungs. "You don't know Yves Claremont. He always talks business." She shouldn't hope. It didn't matter anyway. They could never be together.

"They are going to some gala, though, together. You know, right?"

Her heart dropped.

"He says some complimentary things about you, though, Lainey."

"What does he say?"

"I don't know if I should tell you. I did this experiment to help you save his job, not so I can play Lonely Hearts."

"Don't be a jerk, Martin."

"Ah, no name-calling. *Tsk, tsk*, that's not how you get what you want."

"All right, Martin, what do you want?"

"I'm a simple man. I only want your first-born child if this goes anywhere."

"Martin!"

"Joke. Geeze, Lainey, where's your sense of

humor? I'll settle for your second born."

"Martin…"

"Still too much? Fine, fine. Bring me back a ton of milk chocolate. I run on sugar, so anything sweet. With caramel."

"Done!"

"My, how anxious you are to hear about what your boyfriend tells his mother about you."

"His mother? How can he email her? I can't email outside the LAN."

"Easy, he has higher security clearance. Let's see. I copied the exact phrase here. 'The new intern, Elaine Peterson works hard, but often below her potential.'"

"Hardly complimentary."

"Yes, but the fact he's telling his mother about it is a compliment. What guy tells his mom about a new intern, let alone she's a hard worker?"

"What was the date on the email?"

"Oct. 9."

"Yeah. We sort of had a falling out later on so disregard anything before then."

"A falling out?"

"A fight, okay. Unpleasant exchanges, insults batted around like tennis balls."

"I can search a specific date so see what he wrote about it. Want to hear it?"

"I don't know."

"Yes, you do."

"Uh," she said. But she was dying to know. She told him the date.

He clicked at his keyboard again. "Nada."

Hm, weird.

"How about the day after your fight?

"What does he write?"

"Yes, day after your tiff, he wrote his mom to thank her very politely for letting him stay the night at her house and tells her after enlisting the aid of the waiters, he searched through the vineyards the next morning and found his keys. Lainey, what happened? Did you throw his keys?"

She sighed into the phone. "No, it's a long story."

"Anything else?"

"No, thank you."

"At any rate, he doesn't mention you anywhere else."

"At all?"

"Not by name. In fact," he clicked again. "Your name, not Lainey, not Elaine not Peterson, none of those appear in any emails other than the first one to his mom."

"This was supposed to be about Luc and his secret plans."

"I haven't gotten there yet."

But her heart had been ripped from her chest. "That's all I wanted to know."

"I'll keep reading. I've got nothing better to do—no finals, no projects, no work, no wedding dinners, and rehearsals."

"Thanks, Martin. I know you're a busy guy."

"It'd be so much easier if it weren't all in French. Except for your boyfriend. His are in German, Italian, Japanese, English, French. How many languages does he speak?"

"I really don't know."

Chapter Fourteen

The last few days had been torture for Yves. His focus had been disturbed. At his ten o'clock meeting with the Vice Presidents, his thoughts wandered, wondering how Lainey was doing. How had their relationship changed?

At first, he thought her a rather clumsy American. Or did he? Tapping his phone, he remembered seeing her for the first time, when she fainted on the floor. Did pity stir him or something more? Her intellect had always impressed him. How she endured him chiding her, pushing her. And she bore it patiently. At first, he thought he was a mentor, nothing more. His care for her was limited to only as an intern.

Frédérick asked him a question. Yves had to ask him to repeat it. "Yes, correct," he replied, then sank back into his thoughts.

Even during their street contacting, he could have chosen a different partner for her, but he wanted to be with her, was intrigued by her. But even when she let him read her journal, he still kept his feelings separate. No, it wasn't until he took her to Anïse's that he realized his true feelings for her. A moment. One moment when he knew he would give everything to her. And it scared him.

Without her, nothing had meaning. He needed her near him, craved her close. But having her near was torture, insatiable desire, seeing the curve of her neck and not being able to kiss it. He was powerless against her. And no way to right it.

And so he threw himself into the merger deal, securing his promotion, the only way he knew to deal with wanting but not having. All his energy focused on work, on securing the deal.

If only there were some way around the rule, to relieve his suffering. He imagined them living together, a happy, complete life, coming to work in different vehicles, so no one would suspect. But no, someone would find out. Someone always finds out, and he wasn't willing to risk her career on his selfish desire.

The meeting ended. He shook his head to clear her from his mind. There were no notes on his paper.

After the meeting, Marie Claire cornered him in the hall; her blue shirt with silver spangles nearly violated dress code. "You know Lainey invited her boyfriend to the gala."

"Why do you think I would be interested?"

She cocked her hip and studied him. "I am not blind, Yves Claremont."

This was exactly why he couldn't ever let his feelings show for Lainey. Even intuition was a strong accuser. "Thank you for your concern." He paced with a folder in his hand, trying to focus on the graphs displayed there.

Her boyfriend was coming here. He slapped the folder against his hand, pacing in front of the cantina.

"Everything okay, Yves?" Marie Claire asked.

He couldn't have asked Lainey anyway. With the timing of the merger, inviting Hiroko, his chief liaison with Atatakai International, was the perfect opportunity to review the last details before departing together to Japan for the signing.

But he would've been happier even if she'd just gone by herself. "What kind of man is her boyfriend?"

"I don't know, but she is paying for him to come out here."

A moocher, eh? She deserves better than a moocher.

He found Lainey in an actual cubicle on the fourth floor. "So, you have a date to the gala," he asked directly. He refused to make eye contact, but pretended to be interested in the statistics in his open folder, attempting to act casual. The tendons in his neck twitched.

"Yes," she replied

"Your boyfriend flying out?"

"I like to keep my personal life just that, M. Claremont…personal."

Slapping the folder shut, he finally made eye contact. "Grab your jacket. Come with me," he said, turning down the hall, folder still in hand. Yves would show her what she was missing in her life. What she desired but she could not have. He motioned to Lainey to follow him to his office. Yves set the folder on Sabine's desk with instructions to refile it.

Sabine's golfball-sized eyes followed Yves.

In his office, he slid on his coat, flipping up the collar, then wrapped his scarf around him, and released his gloves from his pocket. Through the maze of halls to the elevator, he remained silent.

"Where are we going?" Lainey asked when they stood side by side in the elevator.

"I need your ever-ready opinion." His eyes focused

forward, his usual scowl on his brow. Focus and control. He controlled his breathing.

The engine hummed as he zoomed eastward along the lake on the main road toward La Tour De Peiltz. Lainey sat in silence for the ten-minute drive until he stopped in the middle of the street with his blinker on. After a gut-wrenching U-turn, at 100 Grand Rue in Montreux, he parked on the sidewalk in front of a jewelers.

His seatbelt clinked against the interior as he flipped it back into its case, jumping from the car. Once outside the car, he tugged Lainey inside the jewelers.

The shopkeepers recognized Yves and approached, obsequious and polite, with white gloves poking from the sleeves of their stiff jackets.

Yves paced through the store, amid the glass cases filled with precious gems, pointing at the displays of diamonds, pearls, emeralds, rubies, designating his choices. What would Lainey desire most? "We are searching for something particular for my date."

The first shopkeeper, the elderly man, Henri, eyed Lainey. Yves selected three necklaces from the vitrine, the light glinting off the metals and stones. The younger one, Richard, removed them one at a time.

The first necklace was a twenty-inch white gold chain embedded with ruby pomegranate seeds dripping off a silvery thread. Lainey's lips parted at their beauty.

Yves grabbed it as if it were a dog collar he wanted his pet to try on.

The shopkeepers bowed and smiled.

He opened the clasp and motioned for her to try it on.

Lainey swept up her liquid honey hair when he

bent forward to clasp it around her neck. The smell of her heat intoxicated him. He stood back as Henri placed an oval vanity mirror in her direction.

"*Magnifique*, *mademoiselle*," said the older salesman.

Lainey examined herself in the mirror. Entranced, she caressed the smooth metal, traced the stones. Even on her plain shirt, there was no denying the pure beauty of the liquid design.

Yves imagined her in a fitted dress, the rubies dripping off her skin. He shook the image from her mind. "What do you think?" Yves asked, staring right at her, not even acknowledging the necklace. "Would it please the date of a future Vice President of the second largest food company in the world?"

She lowered her eyes and then her head. With fire she lifted her gaze to him and replied with spunk and gusto, "Yes, I dare say she would love it."

"Let's try on another." He hadn't found the right one. The one she desired most.

Next he placed a lariat strand of creamy pearls with an antiqued silver clasp and a cluster of deep purple gem berries around her neck and stood back. Her eyes never left the lustrous cultured pearls dripping down the valley of her chest.

"This becomes *mademoiselle* very much. This piece also comes with coordinating ring and bracelet." Richard slipped the two other pieces toward Yves, who shooed them away.

Yves intently observed Lainey.

She slid a finger along a few perfect eight-millimeter spheres as she stared at her reflection. They almost had an interior glow. Each a shiny ball of satin.

Yearning burned in her eyes. This was it. He sensed it. "What do you think, Lainey?"

At his question, she dropped her eyes. "Equally fine."

"Another." He had to be sure. Yves dared not touch her. Next he grasped a diamond necklace.

"This is a beautiful piece for a beautiful woman." Henri swept a bead of sweat off his forehead. "Total carat weight, twenty."

Yves leaned to attach the dripping diamonds around Lainey's neck. A huge pear shaped-diamond hung in the middle, with several smaller ones radiating outward.

Lainey didn't even glance up to the mirror.

"How about this one, Lainey?"

Her dark gaze rose to him, fierce, but she maintained control of her voice. "It's hard to tell which is best without knowing the style of her dress."

Seeing her distress, he nearly collapsed, begged her forgiveness, and showered her with the jewelry. But he remained in control. He forced a smile. "*Bon.* You are right." He addressed Henri. "We'll take all three, and she can choose later which is best."

Henri stared at Yves as if he'd produced a pearl of his own. Above the cashier hung a printed sign saying *All Sales Are Final*.

"*Volontier*." Richard recovered first.

"*Mademoiselle* is fortunate." Henri flashed Lainey a nervous half smile.

"What?" Yves faced him, annoyed this whole episode had backfired, stirring more feelings in him than in Lainey. "Mademoiselle Peterson only came to model the jewelry."

The man bowed and whispered, "*Pardon*," and continued the checkout procedure.

Lainey leaned forward, glaring.

Yves slid the necklace off her neck. He handed it to Henri whose brow bubbled with sweat as he totaled the bill, filling out the records proving someone purchased the items. Both salesmen signed the card. The register blinked the total.

Yves handed over his bank card and asked them to be delivered to his apartment.

Lainey left the store before him with a twang of a bell. "You can feed a third world country on what you just spent on jewelry," she said when he arrived on the sidewalk next to her.

Ah, so he did provoke some emotions in her. "Or I can please the woman I love. Which is better?" He beeped the alarm on his car and opened the door for her.

"That's reckless consumerism!"

"Would you feel better if it was spent on you?"

"I'm not jealous if that's what you mean." She answered too quickly. "It's ridiculous to spend so much money on something easily lost or that could accidentally slip down the toilet."

"She's not going to flush them down the toilet."

"I'm saying, they're just things."

"But you admired those pearls." He indulged in a glance in her direction as they fastened their seatbelts. She didn't disagree, and he knew he hit his mark. He smiled inwardly. "Would it appease you if I had my own foundation to feed the poor in Somalia?"

"Do you?"

He laughed. "Would it appease you?"

"Maybe." She crossed her arms across her chest.

"Then don't worry about it, Lainey. You are awfully concerned about other people's money. It's a very bad habit."

Lainey smoldered on the leather seats, and he had never desired her more.

****

The wind whipped under the veranda covering the quays the Friday before the gala. Lainey stamped her foot impatiently waiting for Marie Claire to return from a business meeting in Fribourg.

Cold. Snowy. Lainey hated ice and snow.

Gurgling from her stomach reminded her she was hungry.

A light shone in the darkness. A vending machine. Someone was a genius to install a choco-bar vending machine on the end of the platform. She squinted to view the wrappers. They didn't sell gum and chips in there. No. It was all chocolate.

They had the Seasonal Alpine milk and white chocolate bar. The saliva glands moistened her mouth. Oh, she just needed a nibble. Maybe she should start carrying more chocolate with her. Who knew when she'd be stranded at a depot waiting for her roommate in the cold? Wouldn't want to starve to death. She pinched her change purse open, counting the silver coins in her hand. Just short, by twenty *centimes*.

A train arrived with a shuddering roar. Passengers flooded the quay.

She poured the coins into her purse and snapped it closed. Lainey didn't need the chocolate. She'd refilled her depleted stash. She had forty plaques of chocolate in her room, right? And she had been trying to shed the extra weight. She returned to the front of the quay and waited patiently for Marie Claire. The wind blew through her. She buttoned her coat and tucked in her scarf.

The mass of commuters left the platform. A few stragglers waited for the next train.

The light from the vending machine beckoned her.

Lainey faced away. A huge billboard across from her advertised the specialty bar. Those advertisers.

Maybe there were some coins at the bottom of her bag.

Rummaging around in her bag, rustling through chocolate wrappers, receipts, and bus tickets, train tickets, business cards littering the bottom of her bag, she headed toward the vending machine. The train rumbled to the quay.

She held up her bag, lowering her head farther down, trying to see the bottom. If she missed her chance to buy this vended chocolate, then she'd have to make a trek to the store in the wet and cold to buy this specialty bar. The quay burst with people, boarding and alighting the train, ebbing and flowing like the tide.

With a few glances up from her bag, Lainey dodged the crowd. For the most part, she avoided hitting people, glancing up now and then to say pardon when she clipped a shoulder or hit a bag. In the farthest reaches of a zippered pocket, a coin sparkled.

A twenty *centimes*. It had to be. She almost had her fingers on it—

Smack!

Stepping back, Lainey realized someone hit her. Her shoulder throbbed from the collision. She glanced down at the offender on the cement.

"*Pardon, pardon*." Lainey dropped the coin in her

bag, offering her hand to help the dainty woman off the quay.

Through her sheet of black satin hair, a pair of almond eyes from the East glanced up at her. And she was not dressed like a student. A designer watch wrapped around her slight wrist. Her black fur swing jacket and layered skirt smelled of money. Or a lot of debt.

No wonder she was so off-kilter. Huge carrier bags hung all over her arms.

Unable to just leave her kneeling on the ground over some scattered packages, Lainey helped her gather up her bags.

The woman opened the box that broke her fall. Inside was a collection of sea shell-shaped china. In her layered pink skirt, she knelt over the box, assessing the damage to her purchase. With a careful hand, she examined one of the sea shell-shaped dishes. One had a small hairline crack through the undulating edges.

Lainey asked her if everything was okay in French.

The woman didn't glance up, but shook her head. "*Je ne parle pas français*," she said, with a terrible accent.

"English?" Lainey asked in English.

She glanced up with large grateful eyes. "Yes." She flashed a wide smile filled with teeth. "Sorry."

"Is everything okay?" she asked again in English.

"Sorry. Everything is fine." The woman tucked the broken dish back inside the box. "Sorry. I was not watching where I was going." Still gathering her bags, she blushed from all the stares from the other commuters. Not overt stares of course, but sly, out-of-the-corner-of-the-eye stares.

Lainey held open the bag for her to slip the box in. At such closeness, Lainey delighted in the woman's expensive perfume emanating off her silky-textured skin. How Lainey envied her poise. And style. Pure elegance. Even in her haste.

"It was me," Lainey said, suddenly feeling clumsy.

"No, it was my fault."

Maybe it was her fault. It was easy to topple in such high heels.

"Sorry. I have to go." She arranged her bags across her delicate forearms, flashed a grateful good-bye smile, and quickly crossed the quay barely sliding in the doors of the train as they closed behind her.

Footsteps approached behind Lainey, and someone tapped her shoulder.

Marie Claire stood in the wind. "What were you saying to Hiroko?"

"Who?"

"Yves' girlfriend. You were just talking to her."

Lainey's stomach roiled as if she'd eaten cheap chocolate.

Hiroko was gorgeous. And shopping in Switzerland. She wished Hiroko wasn't so pretty or well-styled or rich. Or nice.

Maybe she wasn't rich. Maybe Yves bought her all those expensive things.

She swallowed bile raising from her stomach. She had never needed chocolate more.

Chocolate. She needed to stop by Albertos. She remembered the distracting coin at the bottom of her bag. She retrieved the coin. Ten *centimes*. A ten *centimes* coin? Still ten *centimes* short of buying a chocolate bar.

****

The afternoon of the gala, Lainey stopped at an Internet café to check if Aaron's plane was on time. But first she checked her mail. There was an email from Martin:

From: <Martin Whetten> Trekkigeek@email.com

To: <Elaine Peterson> chocolatesrus@email.com

Subject: Interesting read

Laines—

I copy and pasted some emails from his mom. They're easiest to read since they are in English so I read those the most. Some of them are even funny.

"No, not Yves Claremont," she said aloud, scaring a Chinese student sitting next to her. "He's not funny."

He keeps mentioning a siren or 'la sirene' is how he writes it, but I really have no idea what he's talking about. When I translate it, it means siren. Have any idea what it means?

"A siren, as in a fire alarm?"

The Chinese student gave Lainey sideways glances and scooted her chair farther away from her.

It doesn't make sense to me. I'll search Luc's emails next. Anyway, peace out!—M.

Lainey was dying to read the attachments, but she had to pick up Aaron from the airport. But there was an email from Aaron. Dread bubbled in her heart. He was supposed to be landing…

****

"Oh no!" Lainey entered the door after a few hours of moping. Where was Marie Claire? She stepped out of her room in the blue feather duster dress.

"What's wrong, Lainey?"

"He can't come."

"Who?"

"Something came up last minute. He's not coming."

"Aaron?"

Lainey gulped. "One of his employees became ill. He had to cover for him." Did he ruin the gala for her on purpose? Or was this legit? Either way, Lainey paced back and forth, pushing hair out of her face.

"What am I going to do? Everybody else will have a date." More specifically, Yves Claremont would have a date. "And I'll be the idiot American intern who is not only stupid but dateless. I can't do it. I'll just stay home, watch a movie, order pizza."

"Ridiculous."

She was right. There was no Internet in their apartment, and pizza delivery guys drove mo-peds. Highly dangerous. She refused to risk some guy's life to deliver a pizza.

"I'll call Jean. One of his friends can take you."

"Pity date," Lainey said in English.

"You always say the oddest things, Lainey Peterson." She spoke fast French on the phone. "There, Jean has a friend who would love to come."

A friend of Jean's who was free on a Saturday night and didn't have a date/girlfriend of his own. Should she be nervous?

****

Lainey unhooked her gown from the closet. For some reason, it still didn't fit. She tugged and she pulled. She swore at it for good measure, but no luck. The zipper still didn't zip all the way up. She stomped into her room and threw herself onto her bed. Smothering her face with a pillow, she heard a bit of a rip from inside her dress.

"You can't eat a big lunch and a big dinner, Lainey." Marie Claire stood at her door. "That's not how we eat here. Americans eat in such excess."

It was true. She ate too much. Too much, too much, too much. Except chocolate. She could never eat enough chocolate. Maybe she should've just eaten the chocolate and nothing else.

She uncovered her face. Marie Claire held a mirror and lined her lashes with blue eyeliner, matching her darker blue eyes, as if her irises were leaking onto her lids.

Lainey was envious. Marie Claire was model gorgeous. She was rail thin, had longish legs and flawless skin. She covered her face again.

"Lainey, you have to hurry and get dressed. Drinks and *apéritifs* begin at six."

She raised her head from the bed. "How 'bout I just stay home?"

"Lainey."

"I don't fit in my dress. It's too late to buy another one."

"Why are you freaking out?"

"I just feel so stupid."

"Why?"

"I just feel wrong all over."

"It's because you like Yves."

"What? No, I don't."

"Yes, you do."

"No, I don't."

"Yes."

"No!"

"Lainey, stop lying to yourself."

She held her breath. Truth shattered the dam behind her eyes. Tears leaked from her lids. Her nose burned red hot. Her lip quivered. She sneezed. "I do want him. I crave his attention. I desire his gaze to linger on me just a tad longer than necessary. I want him to want me. But he's made it quite obvious he doesn't want me.

"I've tried to persuade myself not to want him to protect myself from the hurting reality. I have to hold on to the lie a bit longer. Just one more night. If I can just make it through the night, seeing him with his girlfriend, believing I do not care about him, then maybe I can bear it."

"Oh, Lainey! This changes everything."

"What hurts the most is the hope he must care something for me. But he doesn't. And it hurts like a gunshot wound. What am I going to do?" Her heart burst, and with it came fresh tears.

"Confess your love. Tell him how you feel. You have two weeks left at Alpine Foods. What have you to lose?"

"My internship, my career, everything I've ever wanted. And worse. He wants his promotion. What if I confess and he says he wants his promotion more than he wants me?"

She continued. "He won't, Lainey. I know he wants you."

Lainey shook her head. "You don't know."

"Oh, yes I do. I have eyes to see things you do not."

Lainey wrung a tissue, hoping it was true.

"You make him nervous. I've never seen him listen to anyone else's advice as he listens to yours. He asks you questions. There must be something keeping him from telling you."

"What about Hiroko?" The tissue fell in rolled bits. "Are they still or were they ever dating?"

Marie Claire sat next to her, soothing her hair. "Does it matter? You go and you show Yves how desirable you are. You go and have fun, smile, and you make Yves want to drop everything else faster than imitation chocolate. Find some way to be alone, then tell him how you feel. Then, make him want you."

"In this dress?" She nudged the red disaster crumpled around her, tulle itching her in awkward places, satin stretching impossibly far around her waist, straining the seams.

Marie Claire slipped out of her room and returned in seconds with a sleek black gown. There was not much to it. There was more fabric to her bath towel.

"Aren't you glad I bought two dresses?" she asked, holding it up.

"It's strapless."

"So?"

Lainey hesitated. "I can't wear strapless."

"Just try it on. *Tsk, tsk, tsk*. It's not the dress. It's what the dress conceals which appeals. Besides, if he found you attractive in those horrible American clothes, he will like you in this. Now, hurry and get ready."

Lainey sat in her room by herself, holding the sleeveless dress on her lap. She had never worn a sleeveless dress before. Would people ask about her scars? What would she say?

After she squeezed into it, Lainey admired herself sideways in the mirror. The same pink scars had been with her since her childhood. They rippled across her shoulders in plain sight.

Her hands trembled as she dispersed blush on her cheeks. In her mirror, she gave herself a pep talk, readying herself emotionally for the night. She blew out her breath. As if.

"You can do this. You are more important to him than his promotion. You love him more than chocolate. It will all be okay."

Lainey planned to lure the man she passionately loved away from his gorgeous girlfriend and confess her undying love. She had a blind date, was wearing less than a slip. This was going to end in disaster.

She called Martin while doing her hair. Something about Luc's secretiveness continued to disturb her. "Hey, Martin, you busy?" she asked when he answered.

"Lainey, I don't know if you remember, but uh, today is kind of a special day," he said. "The one day in my life I wear a tux."

"Did you find anything out about Luc?"

"Oh, yeah. Not yet. But since I'm bored at this pre-wedding party, I can run a search on his emails. Keywords?"

"You have your laptop at your wedding party? Never mind, you don't have to answer that. Check his mail for anything with Yves' name in it."

"Over three thousand emails came up. This is going to take some parsing."

"I just know there is something there. How about cutting it to communication between him and Gui?"

"Anything else? I have a few minutes to kill."

"No. You're a peach, Martin. I hope you and Nadine will be happy together."

"She always sighs and says, 'If only Lainey could find someone as perfect as you are, Martin.'"

"Impossible. Doesn't exist."

"I dunno. I'm kinda liking this Yves-guy. He seems pretty all right. Luc is a schmuck though. Is now a safe time to be on your VPN?"

"Sure. Everyone will be at the gala. No one will be using the network."

Chapter Fifteen

When Lainey finally met Jean, he gave her an obvious up-down and didn't even stare at her scars. Marie Claire slapped him. "She's not for you, Jean. She's for Yves Claremont."

Jean's eyebrows shot into his dark bangs. "Lucky guy."

"Oh, stop." Lainey blushed.

At the car, Marie Claire introduced Lainey to Jacquot in the backseat. She crawled next to him, careful not to expose him to either her cleavage or too much thigh lest he get the wrong idea about her purpose for him tonight. He greeted her with a *bise*.

Lainey grazed his unshaven cheek.

He went in for a second, but Lainey had already backed into her seat.

Oh yeah. Two in France. One in Switzerland.

In the passing lights, she examined her date. He might be more attractive if he had fewer tattoos, especially if he eliminated the most prominent one on his neck, a gorilla with some overly pronounced male parts, stretching up to his ear. He'd be slightly more attractive if he had hair. Well, he had plenty on his chops, just none on his head. And maybe more teeth. Or even clean teeth. Or white ones, or at least not wedged with long-unflossed goodies. What kind of people did Marie Claire hang out with on the weekends?

During their ride from the apartment to the Grande Hôtel de Vevey, Lainey only caught half of what he said. He spoke in slang too quickly and jumped topics like most people jumped rope. She caught bits about how he avoided his two years mandatory military service by feigning a broken leg. Then he rattled on about his last girlfriend. It didn't end well, but Lainey wasn't sure what he called her. Was he even speaking French?

Luckily, he didn't ask her any questions, and the stories he told needed no reply. Mostly, Lainey contemplated what the night would hold. He rocked side to side in the backseat, not in time to the music. ADHD? He flicked his fingers together before scratching his arms and legs. He sweat in his tuxedo, smelling of sour mayonnaise left in the sun too long. His salacious glances in her direction caused Lainey to retreat to the farthest corner of the car.

At the Grand Hôtel, Jean handed the keys to the valet, telling him to be careful not to scratch the paint or get mud on his floor mats. Lainey raised her eyebrows. The car had probably spent fifteen years carting Jean and his friends to *discotheques* and showed its age.

As she slipped from the car, a blast of wind nearly separated her hair from the bobby pins. Definitely testing their tensile strength. Icy peaks rippled on the lake as the wind blew through the valley bringing dark, bottom-heavy clouds. There was a threat of snow.

Cold wind whipped through her hair, freezing the gold hanging in her ears. Despite her wool peacoat, her teeth chattered like a wind-up toy. Her coat clashed horribly with her formal. She envied Marie Claire's sleek wrap gracefully covering her shoulders. Even in the chill, she was elegant and unaffected by the weather. They gathered inside in the small cloak room.

When she removed her coat, Jacquot exhaled in a whistle.

"Lainey," he said as if seeing her for the first time, and arguably, this was the first time anybody had seen some of this skin. No one seemed to care about the scars. "You look amazing."

Marie Claire, in her glittering heels, tugged Jean who straggled behind, ogling Lainey. "Keep your eyes to yourself."

Marie Claire was not jealous, was she?

"Do we have to go in?" Jacquot raised a pierced eyebrow. "I say we find ourselves a room here and see what happens, see where the next step takes us."

Eeeeeeeeeewwwwwwww! Lainey retched inside. "The next step is down this hall."

Undeterred, he hooked her arm, escorting her to the hall. They entered the antechamber to the dining room. Several heavily curtained floor-to-ceiling windows faced the lake, lining one whole wall. A crowd of people murmured in background noise.

Jacquot parked himself at the wet bar, flirting with a cute blonde in a gold sequined dress who understood him. Lifting a glass from a uniformed waiter, Lainey scanned the crowd for Yves. Was he late? Not Yves. Something important kept him. At the far end of the room, a gilt Louis XIV clock struck six o'clock.

"It's snowing!" Someone pointed to the tall windows facing the choppy lake and cloud-hidden mountains. People gathered at the window, watching the large flakes float down from the overcast sky. Glancing at Jacquot, Lainey set down her flute on a sideboard. He was still entertaining the blonde. She darted as quickly as her high heeled shoes and tight short skirt would allow down the hall to the cloak room for her coat, then she bolted for a side door.

Growing up in the desert, she'd never really seen snowflakes before. The closest thing they had was the pebbly snow in the mountains north of Phoenix.

This side of the building faced away from the busy entrance where gala attendees arrived. It was quiet and peaceful.

A blast of cold air greeted her as she stepped down the stairs and into the silent garden. Every bush had a white cap. Snow overcame the boundaries of her heels, surprising her feet with icy chill. Only a few lights blinked in the night along the street, and the snow obliterated the mountains, wrapping everything in silent white.

The flakes fell into her hair and transformed into tiny diamonds as they landed on her coat. With her face upturned into the sky, she felt she was in a 3D movie as the snowflakes fell toward her.

The door closed behind her. Someone paused at the top of the stairs.

Yves, in a long overcoat, made another set of footprints beside hers on the snow-covered stairs.

Lainey's heart pounded, realizing this could be the private moment she'd been hoping for, if she didn't chicken out. "I've never seen fresh snow before," she said when he reached the bottom step. The low-lying clouds hid most of the mountains, giving the impression of a flat plane instead of a valley. "It's beautiful."

"Yes."

They stood in silence, listening to the snow landing

softly on drifts and the occasional car passing through the slushy roads. She pretended not to notice him staring at her. How was she going to bring it up? She couldn't just blurt out, "Hey, Yves, you're everything I've ever wanted in a guy, can we give it a go?"

Yves cleared his throat. "I followed you out here to tell you something in private."

Lainey's heart lunged in her chest. A confession of love?

He kicked snow from his shoes. "Several somethings, actually."

Her whole body shook. She faced him. His figure was backlit by the bright lights of the hotel, making it difficult to discern his expression.

"First, this has been my most trying year at Alpine Foods." He breathed a sigh of relief. "But I wanted you to know I secured the promotion. I was told unofficially before I came tonight. They'll be announcing it at dinner. I commence my new post after the holidays at the beginning of the new year. Tomorrow, I am heading to Japan for the signing, so I'm afraid I won't be seeing you again before you leave." He paused. "As expected, Luc will be taking my place as department chair."

With much effort, she swallowed. He chose his promotion over her. "Congratulations. You've worked very hard. You deserve it. You will be happy." A few flakes fell on her lashes. She blinked them away.

He brushed off the compliment. "You are, of course, welcome to stay with Pet Care for the remaining two weeks."

She nodded. He meant it as happy news, but the realization gutted her. This was goodbye. "Thank you," she said. "You have been more than kind and patient with me."

If she was going to say something, she needed to say it now. But she didn't have a chance.

"I have something for you." From his overcoat, he produced a black velvet box with a gold ribbon tied around it. "A thank you and parting gift."

"Thank you? For what?"

He stepped closer. Now she could see his smile. "For being you, Lainey." He untied the ribbon and opened the box.

"The pearls," Lainey whispered with awe. Even in the half light, they were as luminous as a ring of glossy moons. For a heart-stopping moment, she wanted them. But accepting them too eagerly would incriminate her. She swallowed. Besides, wearing expensive jewelry when her date might have a prison record was not the brightest of ideas. "I can't." She pushed them away, as if she'd had one too many chocolate bars.

"Please." He thrusted them out again, catching her eyes and smiling. "Just for tonight then."

Yeah, right. If she wore them for a night, she'd grow attached to them. What girl wouldn't? But she conceded.

"I'll help you put them on." With a quick movement he tugged the long line of pearls from the case, snapping it shut with the other before depositing it in his pocket of his coat. Lainey removed a simple chain from around her neck, holding it in her hand.

He swung the strand around her neck and secured the clasp, letting one finger slide down the milky pearls, retracting only when reaching dangerously too far south.

"Thank you," she whispered.

"In Switzerland, we show gratitude with a kiss."

His eyes flashed seriousness, but Lainey didn't think he meant *that* sort of kiss. The *bise*. Slowly, she leaned forward, barely grazing his cheek, planting a kiss in the air near his high-boned cheeks. *One in Switzerland. Two in France.* Sadly, they were not in France. One peck didn't show nearly enough gratitude.

She held her cheek to his for a few fractions of a second, feeling his warmth, smelling his scent, infusing every ounce of thankfulness into one gesture.

He returned a faint kiss on her cheek before she stepped away, her body flashing with heat.

Now! Her mind screamed. *Tell him now*. But she hesitated. She was too afraid to ruin the moment. Her body trembled all over. Swallowing, her voice disappeared. Her heart beat too hard. She stepped forward, braving the wind and her thundering heart.

But the door opened behind him.

Luc stood at the open door. "There you are, Yves. M. le President is searching for you."

Yves' attention was drawn away. Her time expired, the opportunity melted as quickly as a snowflake on skin.

Yves stepped back, pointing the way with his hand. "Shall we go in? There is someone I want you to meet inside."

Who, Hiroko?

"Madame Grocher. The Chocolate supervisor. You have borne Pet Care well. She says she has a position open and is interested in my recommendation."

"You're really going to recommend me after all?" Working for Alpine Foods as an employee would definitely keep her from ever having a relationship with

Yves. She worked so hard for this. Her heart sank.

"Lainey." He paused, searching for words. His shoulders sagged. He exhaled loudly. Then his expression changed. Straightening himself, he flashed a smile and offered his arm. "Shall we go in?"

Once inside the cloakroom, Yves shook off his overcoat to reveal his regal, desirable, movie staresque tuxedo. Even with his back to her, the cut of the tux accentuated his slim and fit figure. Diamond ice crystals shone in his black hair. He ruffled it free of snow. Glancing up, he caught her staring at him. His gaze brushed her dress before their gazes locked.

Lainey flushed.

A half smile of approval, which was so difficult to obtain from Yves, but meant even more when he gave it crossed his face. They held each other's gaze longer than required. His expression boosted her confidence. He didn't examine her flaws, the scars on her shoulders. He stared straight into her soul, read her secrets, and communed with her mind.

In a few short months, she had grown to respect Yves Claremont more than any other man she had ever known. He gave her confidence to wear the sleeveless dress. Respect swelled as a balloon in her heart, then grew into admiration, then burned into…Maybe she should tell him now.

But his gaze lifted over her head. The overpowering scent of a familiar designer perfume bit her nose. Another woman's perfume.

Hiroko, a figure of red licorice in her designer bias-cut dress, had rounded the corner and held out her hand to him. Around her neck dripped the pomegranate rubies. He smiled warmly at her, wrapping her gloved arm around his own. Her sheet of silky black hair parted from her face, and Hiroko smiled at Lainey.

Red was definitely her color.

Yves introduced them in English. "This is the intern from America, Elaine Peterson. Mademoiselle Peterson, Hiroko Takeda of Atatakai International."

Under Hiroko's smile, Lainey's confidence faded, shriveled, died in her throat. Hiroko shook Lainey's hand and responded in English. "A pleasure to formally meet you. I've heard a lot about you."

Lainey couldn't say the same. Swiss men didn't talk about their love lives with interns. Of course, he would tell his sweetheart about the ditz at work. They probably spend their evenings chortling about the stupid things she did.

Hiroko complimented Lainey's dress and pearls but not with jealousy or sarcasm.

Lainey had gone with Yves to buy Hiroko's necklace. Perhaps it was normal for interns to buy jewelry for their bosses' girlfriends.

"Thank you." Lainey refused to meet Yves' eyes. Wishing to disappear, she stuck a thumb over her shoulder. "I'd better rejoin my date."

They bowed slightly before parting.

"What was I thinking?" she asked herself, tearing down the sumptuous corridors to the cocktail room to finish her drink. She pressed the back of her hand against her forehead. "I cannot love a man who loves someone else."

Opening the door to the crowded conference room, she slid next to her date who didn't notice the extra bit of jewelry. He greeted her with too much enthusiasm, born from a soaking in alcohol. She smiled at him, slipping an uneasy hand over the pearls.

Unless he didn't love her.

She needed to observe.

He'd never given her reason to suspect he didn't love Hiroko. The door opened once more. Hiroko and Yves entered the room, engaged in conversation, smiling at one another. She beamed at him, admiration shining in her eyes. He placed a supportive hand on the small of her back, guiding her around the room.

The memory of his hand on Lainey's back flashed through her mind. A green vine of jealousy sprung in her.

Not likely. Lainey was a fool.

Yves retrieved a glass from a tray and handed it to Hiroko. Taking one himself, he pressed it to his lips for a quick sip. The two joined another couple where Yves introduced Hiroko. They smiled with too-white teeth, and Hiroko bowed. The two worked their way through the crowd, whispering, smiling. Even an occasional laugh. She made him laugh.

Mince!

Only a French swear word would do.

He introduced her to other couples as they circled the room. Now he scanned the crowd with a heightened consciousness, as if he were aware Lainey was watching him. But he never made direct eye contact with her.

Turn and look at me.

But he continued on, sometimes turning, glancing over her head to search the crowd for acquaintances, avoiding her stare.

Fine.

Lainey fixed her attention on her date, her date

who was using a toothpick on his teeth. Before dinner. Maybe it was not rude in Switzerland, but it grossed Lainey out. With all the acting skills she could muster, she beamed her eyes on him, adoring everything he said or did. She hoped it wouldn't backfire.

Jacquot ogled Lainey when she laughed too loud at his passing jokes.

When she stepped back for a breather after such forced laughing, and to find her Yves-bearings, she bumped into someone.

"*Pardon*," the bump-ee said.

She swirled. "Pardon."

Yves towered over her. While she was so involved in fake laughing, he and Hiroko had circumnavigated the room and had, when she lost track of them, wound up behind her.

"Mademoiselle Peterson, you haven't introduced me to your boyfriend," he said in English, nodding toward Jacquot. A smug light shone in his eyes.

Boyfriend? Oh, no! Yves thought the bald, heavily chopped, mayonnaise-sweating man was her boyfriend.

Before Lainey replied, an elderly lady in a shockingly purple, sequined dress approached Yves. "Yves, *mon coeur*!" She grabbed him and gave him a lipsticked *bise* on his cheek. Yeah, she had been drinking too much. It was weird to see the uptight Swiss let loose under the influence of alcohol. But Yves never lost his cool.

"Madame Grocher," he said.

Lainey couldn't understand Madame's slurred reply in French but she smiled anyway, wanting to make a good first impression.

Mme Grocher leaned toward Yves, her whole body

wavering as if it was blown up by an air mattress blower, balancing on shaky stilettos.

"Yes, this is the intern I was telling you about," he said in French, pointing to Lainey.

Mme Grocher swung her head around, then pitched her body toward Lainey.

What is she saying in such garbled French? Lainey continued smiling and nodding. She hoped she displayed the correct reaction.

Mme Grocher gave Lainey an extremely wet *bise* and not without commotion. Out of the corner of her eye, Jacquot roused, aware someone was kissing his date.

"Come to my office, and we'll talk." She patted Lainey's arm before hobbling off.

Lainey barely caught the last phrase and gave Yves an appreciative grin.

"Now, please introduce me to your boyfriend."

And her grin fell.

"Actually," she began, swallowing hard. She searched the room for a viable exit.

At the far end, a man entered in a white short-waisted coat and announced, "Dinner is served."

En masse, couples funneled toward the door. In the shifting crowd, Lainey grabbed Jacquot by the elbow, pulling him toward the doorway, losing Yves and Hiroko in the throng.

Relieved they were lost, she found Marie Claire.

"Did you tell him yet?" she asked.

"No, I didn't have time."

"I have an idea. During one of the long boring speeches, you slip out to the hall, and I will send Yves out to you."

"No, don't. I'm chickening out. I can't do it."

"If you don't tell him, then I will." She gave Lainey an evil eye before stepping through the doorway. Inside, they separated.

Banks of tables lined the length of the high-ceilinged room. Diners peeled off to find their seats among the long, clothed tables.

Crystal chandeliers reflected off the great mirrored walls. As the room filled with people, their reflections tripled the appearance of people. Lainey found their place cards on a table in the back near a side door. She snatched Aaron's name card and tucked it in her purse.

But it was unnecessary; her date was oblivious. He was too busy admiring the abundance of silverware and gawking at the waiters in white suits pouring wine into one of three bottomless glasses. Jacquot slumped in his chair, drinking the wine.

Yves entered, sliding out a chair for Hiroko, then seated himself next to her.

Lainey faced away from him, focusing instead on the speaker who, standing at the podium positioned on the table, welcomed them and introduced the itinerary. An embossed white card on their plates also spelled out the menu for the night.

19:00 *Salade Verte avec Sauce Vinaigrette*
19:15 *Soupe à l'Oignon Grantinée*
19:30 *Poisson en Papillote*
20:30 *Steak au Poivre*
21:00 *Crème Brûlée et café*
Awards and presentations

Lainey remembered the courses Alexandre Dobrinsky shared with her. Her stomach growled as she read the menu. As if on cue, men and women in white uniforms entered from the double doors to serve the meal. The homeliest salad with the most tasty dressing, bread as soft and sweet as a marshmallow.

Her date ate as if he had not had a decent meal for days, food spraying from his mouth as he talked, gulped and drank, constantly holding up his wine glass for the steward to fill. Just as the first speaker stood, Lainey's cell phone chimed. Anybody who could call her should be in this room. As she picked up her purse from the floor, she glanced to Marie Claire to see if she was calling her to remind her to leave, but she was sitting in rapt conversation with Jean.

She glanced at her phone. Martin. "Excuse me for a minute."

Jacquot was in the middle of a bite. He nodded. At least he was enjoying himself. She slipped out the door and answered the phone.

"Martin, why are you calling?" She checked her watch. "You should be getting married right now." They wanted to get married Friday but the preacher was out of town for Thanksgiving.

"I had to call you. I found something you need to read, ASAP."

"Does Nadine know you are on the phone?"

"I pasted two documents in SecurePasteBin."

"You better not be keeping her waiting."

"She's fine. Lainey, geez, will you listen to me? A document modified last night."

Another event distracted her. Down the hall, Yves stepped from the dining room. Great, did Marie Claire urge him to follow her when Lainey left? She did not need this right now.

"Something he shouldn't have been able to

modify," Martin continued.

She caught Yves' eye. Her hands grew clammy and her heart trembled.

He headed her way.

Someone opened another door. M. le President. He detained Yves. They conversed in whispers.

Yves' expression changed to a frown. He bowed his head and stuffed his hands in his trouser pockets. He glanced up at her, met her gaze for a fleeting second, then glanced away.

"By Luc." Martin's words brought her back to the conversation.

"Luc? What is it?"

"It was in Japanese."

"You didn't read it?"

"Lainey, I'm in a tux in a church five seconds before I get married. I didn't have time. But I think it's a contract. There's something else."

"Uh-oh, I gotta go." M. le President and Yves charged toward her.

"Lainey, wait. The last time I tried to get on the VPN, I couldn't get on." A pit formed in her stomach. "Maybe your time expired or your account was—"

Lainey hung up. Yves and M. le President arrived.

Chapter Sixteen

Lainey had never seen Yves this way. His eyes burned dark and terrible, wild almost, with anger. Agitation ran all through him, as if all the energy of a pacing tiger had been encapsulated in his body. Even more angry than at Restaurant Terrasse, where he was more in control.

"Step this way, mademoiselle," M. le President said. The man only had two settings, abrasive and more abrasive in speech. This was of the more abrasive variety.

Dazed, she followed them into a small room. Inside, M. le President actually acquired one more setting on his decibel scale: ear-splitting, rocket-expulsion yelling.

And it was directed at Lainey, so loud and so fast, she couldn't understand. Spittle sprayed her face in his tirade.

What caught the attention of the CEO? At least in French, it was easier to distance herself. Yelling pierced so much more in English. In French, it was surreal, like watching TV. Finally, he stopped to breathe.

Ears and face beating red-hot, she glanced to Yves hoping for a translation, an explanation, anything.

"Corporate espionage," Yves said at last in English, his lips tight, his eyes darting from her eyes to the door.

Her heart sank. Her, a spy? Steal corporate secrets?

“Lainey, either you or someone else hacked your VPN and has been spying on the inner workings of Alpine Foods.”

The heat must have been on full blast. And the gravity. She struggled to move. Her stomach fell to her feet. “Blair in IT found some log entries detailing your VPN account accessing unauthorized files.”

She was mute, guilt plastered over her burning face. Martin. How did they find out? He said he would be careful, not leave a trace. But it was not corporate espionage, he was just reading email to see if Luc conspired against Yves. Of course, she couldn’t confess everything.

“I’m not spying for another company,” she whispered feebly at last. “I promise you, Yves, I’m not spying. It might have been hacked by someone else—”

“Don’t you see?” Yves said tightly in English, inches from her face.

She would have preferred M. le President’s bombastic yelling instead of Yves’ controlled anger. His face was set, his jaw tight, flexing with his breaths, his dark eyes fierce, and burning right into hers.

She withered under his stare, stemming the tears rising in her eyes. Hard to believe she almost confessed her love to him and dreamed of staring into his eyes only a few minutes before. Now she wanted nothing more than to avert her eyes. She trembled beyond control. Misting eyes distorted her view. And she sneezed.

“It doesn’t matter. Whether you purposefully or carelessly allowed someone access to your VPN account to compromise our system, it is the same.”

“There is no forgiveness for this,” M. le President

yelled. "You are terminated. You must leave at once."

Lainey was riveted to the floor, staring at him in disbelief.

"Did you hear?" Yves asked. "You're done, Lainey. It's over. Pack your belongings tomorrow morning and leave."

Chest heaving, she slid her fingers up around the pearls, before she even knew what she was doing. "I'm sure you wanted these back." She unclasped them, letting them pool into her palm before handing them to Yves. Sobs choked her throat.

Yves held them, then backed away, retreating to the door, his eyes full of hurt, betrayal, distrust.

M. le President opened the door for Yves who, without glancing back, slipped through it. "You are lucky, mademoiselle," M. le President said, holding the door, speaking slowly for her to understand. "As you are an intern, we are not reporting this to the authorities or pressing charges if you go quietly, quickly and without incident. We will not tell anyone about this. However, do not try to beg for clemency. I will not rescind this order. If I even so much as see you again, I will make sure you never work in the food industry again."

The door slammed behind him.

Lainey sank to the floor.

He thought she was a spy.

****

Lainey was not a spy, was she? Yves broke through the double doors of the hotel, without his coat. Everything he thought about her had to be reexamined. He handed his claim ticket to the valet. Slush pooled around his dress shoes, but he didn't care. He paced on the front step. Maybe she was sent to ruin him.

He slipped his hand into his pocket and brushed against something cold. The pearls. He closed his eyes. Her expression when she removed the pearls contrasted so completely with when she had received them. Horror compared to delight.

His car hummed into view. Yves handled the valet a few bills and slipped behind the wheel. Without hesitating, he forced the car into gear. By now the roads were cleared and almost dry. Shifting into high gear, he headed out of town. He didn't care where he went, as long as he went fast.

His mind raced, full of her. He didn't believe she was a spy. Careless, yes. Silly, maybe. But a spy? But if she were, and this was some grand design to ruin him…Perhaps he had been giving her too little credit. Perhaps she was sent to ruin him, as she joked. And everything he wanted hung in the balance.

His engine roared as he entered the freeway. Because of the weather it was practically empty.

The phone rang. His audio voice broke his concentration. "A phone call from Marie Claire Remonter." Her name flashed on his dashboard. From his steering wheel, he silenced the call.

Mostly he was mad at himself for not seeing her for who and what she truly was. He had been duped by her large brown eyes and soft, amber-colored hair. Her infectious smile came easily and often. He loved how she smelled of vanilla. His jacket carried her scent after the Restaurant Terrace. He draped it over his shoulders when he slept at his mother's and smelled her all night long. Pure torture.

He shook his head, staring out onto the illuminated

road, focusing solely on what those beams held. He had planned to confess his love for her after the gala. Now the thought pinched his head. With all his frustration, he forced the metal all the way to the floor. Street lamps and exits were a blur. He didn't dare look at the speedometer.

To drive, to feel the power of his engine respond to his anger, liberated him. He wanted to drive and not think.

Lights flashed in the rearview mirrors.

****

It was dark. For a second, Lainey didn't even realize her eyes were open. She must've fallen asleep on the floor. The timer had flipped off the automatic lights. Her eyes ached, and her parched throat wanted water. Her head throbbed when she sat up. For now, she sat in the dark, relishing not having to see anything, think about anything.

What time was it? Slowly, she crawled to the edge of the room and leaned against a stack of chairs. With the light seeping under the door she checked her watch. A few minutes after nine o'clock.

Dinner was over, they were probably in the middle of speeches, awards, and promotions. Strange no one wondered where she was. At least her date didn't notice. He was no doubt enjoying his never-ending wine glass and wouldn't even remember he came with someone.

And Yves. What was he doing? Sitting with Hiroko, forgetting all about an uncomfortable scene with a spying intern. She'd soon be an unpleasant memory. Someone who almost cost him his promotion. A mistake. A regret.

She reached up to scratch at a tickle on her cheek. Wetness. Tears. She closed her eyes to block out the situation before her but his eyes burned with anger behind her lids.

Gone, everything gone. Everything she hoped for, wished for, worked all her life for, gone. Didn't she think of the consequences when she asked Martin to spy on Luc?

Maybe it was just her. A failure. Failure in work, life, love. Love.

She squeezed her eyes closed, holding her breath against her grated heart. Yves hated her, thought she threatened the company. Her nose was clogged, hot, and burning. She refused to face anyone out there. She cried off all her makeup.

Her phone buzzed. Martin? She picked up the phone. No. Marie Claire.

"Lainey, where are you?"

She wiped her running nose on the hem of her skirt. "In a storage room, I think."

"What are you doing there?"

"Long story."

"Did you talk to Yves? Did you tell him how you feel?"

A sob pulsed in her chest, about to burst out in tears. She struggled to control her voice. It hurt holding it in, but she didn't want Marie Claire to know she had been crying. "No."

"I thought maybe you two were together."

"He was with M. le President."

"M. le President just announced his promotion, but Yves isn't here to accept it. No one can contact him on his cell phone, either."

"Maybe he and Hiroko decided the party was lame and rented a room."

"She's here, too, Lainey, as baffled as everyone else. And his car is not here. I just checked with the valet. He is gone, Lainey. Where did he go?"

"I don't know where he is." Harping on his mysterious disappearance didn't help the hurt.

"Yves never runs off. He's always where he's supposed to be. Why would he miss out on the announcement? I hope he isn't flaking out over the merger. Some men just can't handle the stress, go crazy, you know. I wouldn't guess it of Yves. Still, the Board of Directors might not approve of this action. It makes him too much of a wild card."

Each time she mentioned him, another dagger twisted in Lainey's heart.

"As long as he shows up for the merger deal," she continued. "I guess they'll be okay."

"Why would the Board of Directors care?" These crazy Swiss executives, caring about such minutia, whether someone was there to pick up an award or whether he decided to skip out on it. Did it really matter?

"Because now as a VP, in a few years he'll be in contention for being appointed Chair. Really, Lainey, don't you know how business works?"

A bubble popped over her head. Ah-ha. She understood. He wasn't interested in just becoming the youngest VP; he really was ambitious. He had his eye on loftier things. The room whirled.

"I don't feel well. I need to go home."

"Oh, my poor dear! Listen, I'm coming to get you, and we'll go home. Where are you?"

She stood, opened the door, and blinked in the hall light when Marie Claire, hanging up her phone, charged for her.

"Oh, Lainey!"

Lainey wrapped her arms around Marie Claire and sobbed into her neck, leaving an awful black smear.

"Never wear non-waterproof mascara, Lainey! You look awful!"

****

Dull sun illuminated the parquet floor where Marie Claire and Lainey knelt over her suitcase, folding clothes and packing souvenirs. Every outfit evoked painful memories, a flash of M. Claremont examining her outfit for his approval. How she craved his eyes to shine with admiration. Craved. She'd never see him again. A granite roller had flattened her heart. She didn't sleep a wink the night before.

"Even if it's just a misunderstanding, there's nothing I can do," Marie Clare said, after Lainey explained she'd been terminated over her compromised VPN. Marie Claire didn't need to know all the details why or how. What's done was done. The secret would go with her to the grave, or at least to the airport. Did the US extradite to Switzerland?

"M. le President has the ultimate say. If he says go, you are finished. If he had said stay, then no one could get rid of you. It is politics and business. He's right. You are lucky they choose not to prosecute. Fifteen years in prison, Lainey. Promise me truthfully you are not involved in espionage."

"I'm not. I promise."

"I believe you. But in business, you cannot even be careless."

Business. Lainey sneered. Maybe Alexandre Dobrinsky was right. Maybe Alpine Foods didn't deserve Lainey's passion. Maybe she should find a small shop and try a more personal approach. Right now, she needed time to heal.

"All packed?" Marie Claire sat back on her heels.

"Yes, I'll run down to the Internet café and buy the earliest ticket out of here."

"I have to escort you to headquarters, no? After you clean out your desk, you can use my computer. I have Internet access at work."

Of course, she would. How else would she access all the information needed to hire and fire people?

Hauling her luggage across the black granite foyer of the Alpine Foods corporate headquarters, located on the bank of Lake Geneva, Lainey came full circle. Yes, the grass was no longer green, but covered in snow. The sky a dull grey instead of indigo. The lake choppy instead of calm. She arrived here full of dreams and expectations. Now those hopes were dashed, ruined.

She would always remember this place. How it smelled of rotted apricots and lavender cleaner.

Marie Claire slid her card through the security reader. Lainey paused where she first met Yves Claremont, where he asked Sabine to serve her lunch, where Marie Claire first suggested he take her in his department. Had it really been four months?

Threading through the corridors, Lainey overheard tidbits of conversation from two women pausing at a door frame.

"The biggest fine for a speeding ticket."

She followed Marie Claire into the doors and into the elevator. A man in the elevator told another, "He was going over 160 kilometers an hour!"

When she and Lainey stepped out of the elevator to the second floor, a long hall stretched before them, hung with oil-painted portraits, mostly men, in thick gilded frames. The brass nameplates wedged in the wood were so tarnished it was difficult to read when she passed by. Charles S. Bonhomme 1866-1879, Daniel F. Diddier 1879-1883, Muller, Gernoud, Nier, Theriot. After reading each nameplate, she glanced up to see who might be the bearer of the name Jean-François Pernot. A man with Albert Einstein hair in a turn-of-the-century suit and cravat holding a pipe.

Near the end, her eyes arrested on a shinier nameplate. Bernard Y. Claremont 2005-2010. Lainey's heart leapt, quivering like a phone on vibrate, as she scrambled to park her luggage, resisting the urge to search M. Claremont's, *the* M. Claremont's eyes, albeit in a portrait. She had to know if he resembled Yves. Heart pounding, she raised her eyes.

So this was the man who raised Yves Claremont. Yves must get his dark hair from his mother. And his brow was definitely the same. And his eyes, the same intensity, but softer. A kindlier expression than some of the other CEOs parked alongside him. She'd seen the same expression before, in her dad's eyes.

Her dad was not a great businessman. He didn't hire the most skilled laborers, rather adopting those who needed work. What was the expression? Compassion. And M. Claremont's lips, his lips were almost curved into a smile, but not quite as if savoring something sweet in his mind, a joke perhaps or funny memory.

What kind of a dad was he? What did he teach

Yves? She failed to imagine them playing football on their grass. Was he always too busy on business trips, too busy running a world-leading company?

"Are you coming?" Marie Claire asked. She'd already rounded the corner, then returned. "Oh, I see. M. Claremont."

"Were you here when he was the CEO?"

"For a few years."

"What was he like?"

"Intimidating. Compassionate. He held fast to the old ways, hiring people who've worked inside the company rather than foreign-trained businessmen, qualified in theory only." She leaned closer and studied his portrait for a brief second. "I believe he truly loved Alpine Foods and its workers. Wanted to see it succeed."

"What happened? I mean, why did he leave?"

"Alpine Foods hit some hard times. Board called for five hundred layoffs one summer. M. Claremont wouldn't do it. Asked for more time to consider other options. Huge back and forth battle. The Board won. M. Claremont quit. Died of a heart attack shortly after. Too much stress."

With a shrug, she continued down the hall. At the end of the hall, on the intersecting wall, hung a portrait of the current governing body of Alpine Foods. Seeing the current CEO, even in portrait, made Lainey shiver. Around him hung several smaller photographs, less than three-foot by two-foot portraits, of the vice presidents. Yves' picture wasn't up there yet.

They continued down the hall, passing more employees, working overtime because of the merger signing. Marie Clare unlocked her office, strode to the desk and awoke her computer. Eyeing a fish tank with bubbling fish, Lainey sat when the screen blinked to life. She clicked the icon. Out of habit, she opened her email first. Fifty unread messages?

Oh, Martin. He sent a ton of emails. She clicked on one.

Yikes!

He had copied and pasted Yves' emails. She should delete the evidence out of her inbox. She glanced up to Marie Claire, but she was focused on files in a drawer. Lainey's finger itched on the mouse. She should save them until she arrived home. There was no immediacy now. The arrow hovered over the sign-out button.

Wait, Martin's phone call. After everything with Yves and M. le President, she had forgotten about it.

Instead of closing out of her email client, she opened it, peeking again to Marie Claire perusing some folders. Then she remembered the hurt in Yves' eyes last night. And the fierceness.

She closed it.

But a tug in her heart said something was wrong. An instinct, a gut-feeling. Yves needed her to watch his back.

She opened it.

But he didn't care about her, she told herself. Doing this would get her into trouble.

She closed it.

Marie Claire opened the door, saying she'd be back in a minute.

Lainey should buy her ticket and get out of here. Breathing deeply, she opened up a new tab to the airline. Clicked Book a Flight. She typed in Geneva in the From field.

To field? She paused. Where was she going? Her parents were in Costa Rica. She wouldn't be able to get a job there. She refused to stay with Nadine and Martin. Too awkward. Where else was there?

Home. It killed her to go home unsuccessful.

She typed Phoenix into the To field. At least she could search for a job in her stomping grounds.

Her eyes flitted to the check mark to the side. One way? it asked, jumping out at her, and a big old red question mark over a box. She stared at it.

One way. Never coming back.

One way. It sounded so final.

One way. She'd never see Yves again.

An ache deeper than any pain weighed in her heart as the curser hovered over the box. She breathed. Bye-bye dreams. Her finger lifted to click the box when her phone rang. Yves? Calling to apologize, to beg her to stay?

Nope, it was Martin. She answered it.

"Does your wife know you're on the phone with another woman on your honeymoon?"

"Har, har, she's sitting right here. Geez, we're not having romping sex every minute of our honeymoon."

"Thanks, Martin. Now that's stained in my brain. How was the wedding?"

"Great. Lots of alcohol."

"Nice."

"Did you ever figure out what happened with the VPN?"

"Yes. Busted."

"Uh-oh."

"But I don't want to talk about it."

He sucked in his breath. "What's the damage?"

"They found some log files on my VPN snooping around some corporate settings. They won't press charges—"

"Did you say log files?"

"Yeah, they said log files showed someone violating corporate files." She wanted to remind him he wasn't very sly.

"Impossible. I was rooted and went behind me and deleted all my files. I told you I would get in and out without a trace. Hm…Amateur."

"Wait, you think someone else has compromised my box?"

"I'm saying only someone who doesn't know what he's doing or heh, maybe he—or she, let's not be sexist—does know what he's doing—and he's framing you."

"Someone's using my box to access Alpine Foods and letting me take the blame. I am getting sent home for this. I can't even stay the rest of the two weeks of my internship."

"I think I'd be finding out who this is."

"How?"

"My guess leans toward the usual suspects."

"Gui and Luc?" It was a statement more than a question.

"Bingo. Hey, I have some good news for you."

A breath escaped her lungs. "That would be really great right now."

"I figured out what the *sy-reen-nay* is. Sorry, I just butchered the pronunciation. You on the 'Net? Open up the email to his mom from November tenth."

Placing her phone in the crook of her neck, she searched through the emails for the one written

November tenth. "You're seriously doing this stuff on your honeymoon? Martin, you're crazy."

"Hey, it's for my wife's best friend. If she knows you're happy, then she's happy and if she's happy then I'm happy."

"So you're self-serving." Found it. Click.

"Yup."

"Okay, what is it?" She waited for the email to load.

"*Who* is it."

"Okay, *who* is it? It's a person?"

"Read it: '*La Sy-ree-ney*,' or however you say it—"

"*La Sirene*."

"Yeah, yeah. I took Spanish."

Her eyes ran over a phrase. "'I invited La Sirene to Anïse's house.'" She blinked, reread the sentence, a plume of understanding tickled her brain. Trembling, she nearly dropped the phone with the realization. "Oh my gosh, it's me. I'm the siren."

"You? You're the siren? There are tons of hilarious stories about you then. You stayed up all night translating French into Italian?"

Lainey ignored him. Her eyes were transfixed on the email. All the details were there. Their dinner with Anïse and Christophe, their chat in the driveway after dinner. She read until, "It might have been a mistake to take her to my cousin's." A small flame burned in her chest. What did he mean?

"Are you there, Lainey?"

She nodded, but he couldn't hear her head rattle. "Yes."

"No way. There are so many goofs, I never thought it would be you. Not our Ms. Perfect Lainey.

Unbelievable. So, why does he call you a siren?"

"Probably because I'm always alarming him. I don't know." It wasn't good news. "Is it a compliment or an insult? From a guy's perspective."

"I think it's kinda cute he has a pet name for you."

"But it's not a pet name, it's derogatory."

"Whatever, keep reading."

Through the glass walls, Marie Claire's shadow loomed. "Crap, I can't. I have to go."

"Wait a minute, Lainey, let me do one thing." Clicking of keys crackled in the phone. "Sixty-eight times."

Marie Claire paused at the door, talking to someone down the hall, her hand on the knob. "What? What are you talking about?"

"La Sirene is mentioned sixty-eight times in his email. You're frequent news, Lainey. At least in M. Claremont's email."

"Yeah, but he might be telling her about how much I screw up. It's not indicative of anything."

He mumbled into the phone. "Numbers you need: how many times you're mentioned total; how many times you're mentioned in emails to his mother. Then the enrichment by hypergeometric distribution has a p-value of ten to the minus sixteenth.

"It means out of 207,969 emails he's sent. Wait, he's only sent 1,709 since you've been there. Let's use that calculation. So sixty-eight out of 1,709. He mentions you at a frequency rate of one out of every fifteen point eight six emails. More specifically, it probably means he mentions you more often in his emails to his mom than he mentions pet food to companies in Germany."

Lainey struggled to absorb all this.

"And let's run it through my linguistic program and see how many are positive and how many are negative."

She only half listened as Marie Claire came in. With heart racing, she clicked out of her email account. Shaking, she glanced up at her and smiled, Martin still mumbling on the phone.

"Martin, I speak two languages, and 'geek' is not one of them," she whispered in English. "What does it mean?"

"It means, my numerically-challenged friend, your boyfriend has the hots for you."

Chapter Seventeen

He liked her? Then Yves' face flashed in Lainey's mind, hurt contorted in distrust. "Perhaps before last night," Lainey said into the phone in English.

Marie Claire had returned and caught her babbling in English. "*Pardon?*"

"*Rien.*" Lainey switched to French, to speak to Marie Claire. "I'm just on the phone arranging my flight home. Hey, Marie Claire? What does La Sirene mean?"

Martin spoke. "Uh, hello Lainey! I don't speak French. Oh, got it. Someone else is in the room, too. Shall I go?"

"No, just hold on," Lainey said in English to Martin

"*Une Sirene*?" Marie Claire translated it into English. "Mermaid."

Martin again. "I'm only catching half of this conversation, Lainey."

"Or," Marie Claire continued in French, "it can also mean temptress."

"What?" Lainey's head jerked around to face her.

"You know," she said in halting English. "A lady who is sexually tempting to you."

"Whoa, Lainey, I understood those words. You hear me? He totally thinks you're hot!"

Almost in a trance, she slid the phone from her ear.

"For reals?"

Yves nicknamed her a sexually tempting woman. Images flashed in her mind as she conjured her exchanges with him, assembling them into context, reframing the meaning of every interaction. Dinner on the lake, Anïse's house, even being chosen as his streeting partner.

"Why do you want to know?" Marie Claire leaned forward.

Lainey held the phone up to her ear to say goodbye to Martin. Kissing sounded in the phone. Nadine was utilizing her super powers to get him off the phone. Martin's voice came in spurts. "Lainey, as much"—*smooch*—"as I enjoy listening"—*kiss, kiss*—"to half a conversation in French, I've got to go. Did you ever look at the Japanese document? I bet it will give us some clues."

The changed document. She completely forgot.

She needed to confirm her suspicions, even at the risk of M. le President's threat of blacklisting if she did not go quietly. "Opening it right now."

"I ran a diff"—*kiss, kiss*—"between the two documents and you may want to"—*smooch*—"focus on lines 278.8 and 289.9 where Luc made changes." One really long smooch. "And this is where I sign off."

"Thanks." She set the phone down and used both hands now.

Marie Claire asked her something, but Lainey focused on the email. She copied and pasted the document in the STS reader. Japanese to English. Bingo.

It was the contract between Atatakai International and Alpine Foods. Luc shouldn't have been messing with this. Lainey searched for the lines Martin mentioned. Most of it was outrageous legalese. But Luc had altered the terms of the agreement. In favor of Alpine Foods.

"Did you get your flight?" Marie Claire glanced over Lainey's shoulder and read the contract. "What is this?"

"Uh." Lainey burned with guilt.

"Lainey, what do you have?" She scrutinized the text. "The contract? What is going on?" Confusion grew into certainty. She grabbed her desk phone. "I'm calling security."

"No, wait!" With two hands, Lainey yanked the cord from the wall. Marie Claire unhitched her cell phone from her hip. But, utilizing a judo move, Lainey grabbed it and chucked it in the fish tank.

Marie Claire's eyes grew wild in disbelief. She stalked for the door. Jumping over the desk, Lainey beat her there, wedging herself between her and the door. "Wait. Listen to me. It's not what you think." With a scuffle, Lainey managed to close the door. "Will you hear me out?"

"Corporate espionage."

"No. Someone else hacked my VPN."

Marie Claire paused long enough to listen.

Lainey related her suspicions of Luc and Gui and the whole conversation she heard.

"Then how did you get this contract?"

"I came across this document," Lainey said keeping it vague. "I didn't even know what it was until I opened it just now. There are two lines where Luc modified the document Friday night."

There was still suspicion in her eyes. "He doesn't

have access."

"Someone must've given him access. And now the terms are changed. And nobody knows. If they sign this, Yves will be ruined. Help me save Yves. Please."

Her expression softened.

"Call Yves and tell him not to sign the contract without running another redline."

Marie Claire jabbed a thumb at the desk. "My phone is in the fish tank, remember?"

"You can use mine."

With a hint of a scowl, she dialed his number.

"Voice mail. Either he is not accepting phone calls from you, or he is still in flight. I'm not sure which it is."

Lainey paced. "I'll print out both documents and you can take it to M. le President, tell him to stop the signing. Gui and Luc are attempting to sabotage Yves. He'll trust you."

"You don't know what you are asking of me."

"You would save Yves's reputation. And in turn, the company's reputation."

"If I go to him with information I do not have access to, then what will M. le President do? It will only end one way, termination. And if I do not turn you in, then it will still end my career. Perhaps he would be more understanding if you explain to him yourself."

"But I can't go to him. He already threatened blacklisting if I talk to him again. Please."

Marie Claire bit her lip until it blanched. "Sorry, Lainey, I cannot help you."

Lainey stepped back, crestfallen.

"But I will not stop you either. I will just pretend I did not hear or see anything. You are on your own."

"Not even for Yves."

"It's business. In these precarious times, I cannot risk my job. Even for him."

"Not even for Alpine Foods?"

"If they continue with the signing, Alpine Foods may be hurt but I can still work, but if you interrupt the signing, it looks bad on our side. I recommend against it, but if you have to save Yves, then you do what you feel you have to do."

"All right." Lainey circled the desk and hit the print button.

"The printer is in the tech room."

Lainey already opened the door. "Sorry about the phone. Both of them."

"I'll tell them to get me a new one. It was old anyway. Go!"

The printer was already spitting out pages, hot and smelling of toxic emissions, when Lainey arrived. She retrieved each sheet as it emerged from the printer. Her eyes glossed over each line. She whirled when she heard footfalls.

"You still here?" Luc stared at her with a simpering stare.

She stepped in front of the tray where the papers landed face up. Wait. How did he know she was fired?

"Yes," she said, struggling to remain calm. Her teeth chattered with nerves, her mind raced to make sense of his precognition. Did Yves tell him? M. le President? Betrayal colored her face. "Just wrapping up some unfinished business."

His phone chimed the jingle from the Alpine Foods dog food commercial. Nice. With a touch of a button, he ignored the phone call, his sleazy stare focusing on

Lainey.

"Did you hear about Yves' speeding ticket? *Tsk, tsk.* What upset him so much to get such an expensive ticket?"

"What are you talking about?" Lainey asked, genuinely interested.

"Yves went for a ride last night. In his expensive car, it's easy to forget the speed limit, but here in Switzerland we have rules. One of the laws requires you to pay a fine, based on income. He paid dearly for his joy ride. What made him drive so fast? Was he so elated to be Vice President he skipped his own announcement? Or was it something else? Something upsetting, perhaps?" Despite the faux concern in his voice, his eyes were lit with glee.

She didn't want to discuss what upset Yves right now and thought of a change of subject. "So, are you excited to be the new Pet Care chair?"

Taken off guard, he stared at her, wildly, as if she were crazy.

Come on. She silently willed the printer to hurry as it continued to spit out pages. If he caught her, it would be all over.

"What are you printing out, there?"

She gulped. She'd never been convincing at lying on the spot.

"My flight itinerary." Several more pages slid out of the printer. He was not stupid. An itinerary wasn't ten pages long. She needed something better. "And addresses of boutiques where I can have my legs waxed before going home. Know of any good places?"

She hoped it would keep him from asking anymore questions.

After a pause of contemplation, he returned his focus on her. “Danielle’s. Thirty-one Vigne in Crosier.”

Shocked he would know of a place, Lainey nodded, drawing paper from the machine. She didn’t even want to know why he knew of a good waxing boutique.

Suddenly he leaned closer, tugging her papers. “Let me see. Perhaps I can recommend something closer?”

Lainey held them to her chest. “No, it’s not important. I just wanted to, you know, look my best when I return home.”

He snorted at her. It was obvious he didn’t think much of her looks.

Lainey wanted to retaliate, to respond in kind, but thankfully the printer paused. In a flurry, she snatched the remaining page, thanked him, and headed down the hall away from the printer.

Shuffling through the pages she counted them…Seven, eight, nine. She counted nine. There should have been ten. Pausing in the hall, she counted them again, her heart burning, her breath quickening. She licked her fingers and separated them again searching for the lost page. It was not there.

From the end of the hall, she glanced back to the printer.

Luc shuffled through his pages, reading them briefly. At the end of the stack, he read, his brow knitted in confusion. Then he lifted his widened eyes to Lainey.

“Come back here.”

But she had already broken into a run. Doors passed by her in her rush down the hall. She lunged to the right and opened a door to an empty cubicle room.

Sinking to the left, she dropped to her hands and

knees and followed the breezeway to the other set of double doors. The door opened behind her. She froze. She ducked into a cubicle and folded herself under a desk and listened.

"Lainey, I know you're in here."

Her breath caught in her chest. She was afraid to exhale.

"Lainey, this all may seem unjust to you. But you don't understand how to play the game." The carpet softened his slow but urgent footsteps. "Yves has his father's name to promote him. I have nothing, no money, no connections. It's not fair to be in competition with someone whose family already has a reputation for excellence. This exercise is just to even the score a bit. Other companies have contacted me, begging me to use my resources to help them, but I resisted. Until you came along. You were the perfect scapegoat."

She held her breath as he stepped just behind the felt-lined wall where she hid under a desk. His voice neared. "What were you going to do, Lainey? Run and show him the contract? It will only make you look more suspicious, confirming you used the VPN to spy. Oh, yes, I know what's going on. I would not be a very good spy if I didn't." His black Italian shoes halted next to her.

Her heart was a bass drum, beating in her ears.

"Can you believe it? There are companies willing to pay big bucks for corporate secrets. Think you're going to run to the police with my admission? Even if you tell them, who are they going to believe? An intern with a compromised VPN or a trusted and valued Alpine Foods employee?" Laughing, he moved now away from her in impatient steps.

Lainey swallowed. He had a good point.

"You should've heard how angry Yves was when he found out his trollop was the corporate spy."

Her heart burned at Yves' name.

"That's why he got into his fancy car and drove away last night. See how you've managed to capture his heart. Now I can get rid of you both. My plan worked better than I thought." Near the door, he raised his voice. "Listen. I don't have all day to play games with you, Lainey. So, I'll tell you what. You come forth with the contract right now, and I will use my influence to get you a softer punishment. However, you will not get out of this building with the contract. I am composing an email telling everyone you have sensitive corporate information and you must not leave the building. Compose." He paused. "To? All Alpine Foods employees. What will you decide? You have five seconds, and then I hit send."

Five seconds. She glanced at her watch. One fifteen. Should she just give him the contract, let him win?

No, she didn't need to show it to M. le President. He didn't trust her, she needed to take it to Yves and those working for Atatakai International in Japan. They would listen. With them she had the greatest chance of being believed. Their meeting was early tomorrow. Even if she took the blame, at least Yves will be spared humiliation and backlash from Atatakai International.

So should she risk everything for Yves? Even if he believed her a spy? But shouldn't bringing this to his attention convince him she was not out to ruin the company? Could she live with saving Yves yet have him despise her the rest of his life? Her heart ached. But she refused to let Luc win. How dare he impose this upon her, frame her, and then make her choose between Yves and her own career.

He mocked a sigh. "Oh, Lainey. My, you are stubborn."

Hearing him made her angry. Yves was in Japan with the Japanese representatives, unaware of what was going to happen. Yves who, despite what Luc said, had triumphed on more than his own name. Yves was one of those rare people who respected others even if they didn't agree with him. Her heart swelled. She wanted nothing more than to ensure his success.

"Time's up, Lainey. Such a shame. You're were a great hop-and-go-fetch-it. But now, you'll have no choice but to get caught. I'm sending the email. Now everyone in Alpine Foods will be looking for a spy and an altered contract. You'll never get out to warn him. I hope you'll enjoy prison. *Adieu*, Lainey."

With a clank of the door, Luc left. She leaned back against the felt of the cubby wall and closed her eyes. If Luc sent an email now, then leaving before anyone read the email was her only chance. The sooner the better.

When her heart calmed to the slow pace of a drumroll, she crawled out of her hiding spot and opened the double doors. Glancing both ways down the hall to make sure it was clear, she found the stairs and thundered one flight down to the granite foyer.

As she opened the door, she peeked to size up her chances for escape. The security guard was not at his usual desk. Oddly, he was in a huddle of ten or so people in the middle of the foyer, near the reception desk.

While he was distracted, she might get out of the

building. Letting the door fall softly closed, she sprinted about twenty feet from the crowd. She hid behind a huge box the size of a New York apartment with the word “Alpie” printed on it. She bided her time, waiting for the perfect time to dash for the door.

Just when she prepared to run, the crowd parted, exposing the distraction. A huge tawny and white St. Bernard shook its head, its collar rattling.

Lainey froze.

She’d never seen a dog so huge. It was at least twice her weight. The dog released a resounding bark, shaking her ribs.

She slid down again beside the box, heart pounding, nausea rising. She swallowed to keep it down. Fear strangled every other emotion.

“Hush, Alpie,” someone said over their laughs.

Gathering her strength, she peeked around the corner again to judge her distance, about another twenty feet or so, to the door.

“A true descendant of the great Barry, this one is,” said one of the men in a strong Vaud accent and rough outdoor work clothes.

She needed to run now. But her limbs refused to respond. Now, now!

Too late. The guard left the crowd, bored with the scene. If he had read his email, there was no way to sneak by him. Her eyes returned to the gathered people.

“Barry?” asked some lady.

The Vaudois tried his best to restrain the dog as he sniffed a giant potted plant. “A St. Bernard who rescued more than forty people in his lifetime in the Alpine Mountains. One boy got lost on a ledge high up in the mountains. Barry persuaded the boy to climb on his back and brought him back to safety, he did." The Vaudois man crouched to pat the beast on its head.

The crowd dispersed, and her chance with it. She squinted her eyes.

The Vaudois continued. "Claremont is giving him as a gift to the president of Atatakai International. I just thought I'd bring him up front, to show him off a bit to you good folks before taking him over."

Of course Yves would give Atatakai International their national dog, though Lainey wasn't sure they were going to appreciate this big "gift." Sometimes bigger was not always better. Someday, she would have to explain this to Yves.

The man continued talking as one by one, the employees left. Lainey barely listened, scanning the foyer for a way out of the building. She kept glancing to the kennel. The dog was going to see Yves. She needed to talk to Yves. She had to go with the dog.

No. Noooooooo waaaaaaaaaay.

There had to be another way out. Walk casually out? Maybe the guard hadn't read the email yet. Of course, maybe he wouldn't recognize her from the first day. Was fainting in the foyer memorable? There was no way to know unless she passed by him.

But if she got caught, it would be a free ride to the police station, and they wouldn't be as accommodating as when she forgot her permit.

She studied the security guard. He was reading a paperback, didn't seem particularly alert. Her eyes trained on him, she crouched, ready to stand and walk. Before she arose, his phone rang. He listened, nodded and hung up. With a distinct slap, he closed his book. His eyes swept the foyer.

Great. She sat back on her heels.

She leaned against the kennel, out of sight. This was the only way.

Did it have to be with a giant dog? What if it got car sick? Or barked the whole time? Or worse, what if it bit her? Lainey shuddered. Not again. What if it had to go? She would drown in his Amazon river.

As if on cue, a sound similar to a shower nozzle interrupted her thoughts. She peeked to see the dog, leg cocked, releasing a foaming river onto the man's sturdy boots. A reflective lake formed on the granite. On the bright side, at least it wouldn't have to go again for a while.

The effect was immediate. People dashed around grabbing tissues, then paper towels, yelling to clean it up. The stench was amazing.

The secretary, in his starched purple shirt, grabbed a small garbage can, presumably for the used paper towels. On his way to the puddle, he slipped on some stray wetness, landing on his elbow and butt, trash flying everywhere.

Lainey knew how hard the granite was.

The attention switched from the puddle to the secretary, his shirt a darker purple where he slipped in the liquid. Seeing him grab his elbow in pain, Lainey pitied him, but recognized her chance.

In the commotion, she gathered her breath and courage to seize the opportunity. While everyone fussed over the man, no one paid the slightest attention to a girl unhinging the gate and pausing at the entrance to the kennel.

She smelled dog.

For a split second, she couldn't do it. She paused,

smelling the scent of memories. Her legs and arms froze. They wouldn't listen to her. Then she thought of Yves. Courage poured through her, giving her strength.

Trembling, she climbed in. It was dark. The ventilation holes offered little light and little ventilation. Her heart throbbed and her stomach lurched when she smelled dog sweat. Claustrophobia gripped her throat.

She was about to back out and give herself to the police when the Vaudois and the dog approached, with claws clicking on the granite. The man's rough fingers unhinged the grate.

At first Alpie growled and wouldn't go in. The dog was going to give her away. But the Vaudois ducked the giant dog's head into the door, forcing Alpie in.

After smelling dog breath, her mind flashed back to the terrible day. She stuffed her fist in her mouth, gnawing at her knuckle to keep from screaming.

Brushing her with a wet nose, the dog sniffed her as she backed to the farthest point possible. With its face inches from her, it let out a bark, leaving her temporarily deaf. Its breath was warm on her face as it leaned closer.

It was. Going. To. Bite. Her. Head. Off!

Its mouth opened exposing sharp teeth and a pink tongue.

Chapter Eighteen

She didn't die.

Chapter Nineteen

A wet, pink tongue lolled out of the enormous mouth of the St. Bernard. No, no, no!

Ew! Wet doggy slobber pasted all over her lips.

Only for Yves Claremont would she do this.

Its giant paws nearly trampled her as it filled the kennel, suffocating her with hair and heat. Turning, it settled on its forelegs, its head near the front gate. Then the kennel began to move.

"He seems heavier," someone said.

"Maybe you're getting weaker," the Vaudois said. "Dead weight is always heavier, and the shot will keep Alpie knocked out for thirteen or fourteen hours."

They entered an elevator. Lainey listened to the conversation.

The St. Bernard was going on an express flight to London, then from London to Tokyo.

Thankfully she'd grabbed her purse with her passport. But she'd have to get out at the airport to buy a ticket somehow.

She started having second thoughts. What if they didn't have any tickets for an immediate flight?

On the helicopter ride, she debated internally about when to buy a ticket, in Geneva or London. If she was stopped for any reason, she would jeopardize her ability to get to Yves. Getting to him was the most important thing right now.

And with the St. Bernard asleep, how bad could it be?

From the helicopter, they hauled the huge kennel to a conveyer belt, lifting them into steerage. Once in the confined space reserved for pets, wine, and breakables, Lainey was grateful for ventilation holes even if it did nothing to relieve the smell of the dog's breath.

Next to Alpie's furry face, Lainey cuddled into his chest, rising and falling heavily with each loud breath. Did dogs snore?

Inside the steerage portion of the vessel, there was only minimal heat. Thankfully, Alpie's tawny and white coat kept her warm. After they closed the door, she peeked out the holes. In the dim light, she made out other crates and boxes and a few other pet carriers.

Above her, passengers loaded. She imagined First Class passengers filling their wide seats drinking wine from glass glasses and eating butter cookies while the rest loaded like cattle. They waited and waited.

Finally, they left the gate. If flying was uncomfortable in cramped seats, this was horrible. There was no communication from the captain, no warnings of turbulence, no beverage service, or even a meal. Or a seat belt. Finally, the thrust of the throttle and the roar of the engines roused her as they raced to the edge of Geneva's runway.

The whole ride was short and bumpy and loud. Other animals whined and barked. A bird screeched the whole time. Her ears were going crazy, and she was envious of Alpie's drug-induced coma.

In London, they waited. Lainey managed to find somewhere to relieve herself and ate some emergency chocolate stashed in her bag. She snatched a bottled water from a shrink-wrapped cube.

They sat and waited. And while she waited a thought came to her. The vet said the shot only lasted fourteen hours. They had already passed four of those hours. They still had ten more to go.

What would happen if Alpie woke up?

****

Her first experience of Japan was a horrible one. Somewhere over the North polar region, Alpie awoke, a few hours early. Perhaps the vet underestimated Alpie's size in considering his dosage or maybe it was because of delays but whatever the reason, Lainey was in trouble.

At first the dog acted groggy, but then, due to the air pressure or maybe the medication itself, whatever the reason, Alpie decided to throw up.

The sound of a giant St. Bernard heaving whatever was left in his stomach was a memory Lainey would never forget. A cow giving birth, or perhaps a musk ox in heat? There were no words to describe the heaving and the groans coming from the pitiful creature. If it hadn't stunk so bad, Lainey would've pitied the dog. But chunks of dog vomit in her hair was not something to be easily to be forgiven.

Then of course there was the issue of bowel problems. She witnessed a rush of water not unlike the Gocta Falls in Peru. But it was one thing to see it. Quite another to feel it.

She was drenched, head to toe in burning, reeking liquid.

Nothing, nothing would feel better than clean air and a shower. But she waited until the door unlatched.

The first Japanese steerage loader opened the door

and exclaimed something in Japanese.

Lainey imagined this: "Holy cow, what stinks?"

The second Japanese man, gawking at the trail of liquid said this: "It's the giant Swiss dog who's wet everywhere."

Suppressing her gag reflex, Lainey pressed herself down, near the dog vomit so they wouldn't see her. They stood at the foot of the kennel admiring the breadth and depth of the river flowing from the kennel. The dog, sick or exhausted, kept silent and still, thankfully.

They yanked the kennel free from the cabin, allowing a small bit of wet salty air into the ventilation holes as they loaded them on the conveyer belt downward toward a truck.

Noises, completely foreign to Lainey, reached her ears. Cars. People. She didn't dare to peek out of the truck to see Tokyo in all its glory from the peephole of a sick dog's kennel.

With a bit of water from its bowl, Lainey washed some vomit from her hair. The dog lifted his eyebrows, wondering what she was doing. So she washed a bit from his fur, as well.

At a building, they stopped. They were outside in some park, near a group of people speaking excitedly in Japanese.

Lainey's head throbbed, and she still stank. "Thanks, Alpie, for keeping me warm."

Alpie, still sick, rolled silently to the side of the kennel. She inched Alpie away from the latch, sticking two fingers outside the bars to release it. Then she saw him.

M. le President.

He was sitting next to a gray-haired Japanese man in a dark suit.

If he saw Lainey…He had threatened to blacklist her. And he was the type of man who meant what he said. So she had a choice. Her career or Yves'.

"What should I do, Alpie?"

With her fingers still on the latch, she paused. Alpie, done up-chucking, was sedate, his breath tickling the hairs on her arm. He looked so pitiable, Lainey felt sorry for him. With a tear in her eye, she stroked his head. The motion calmed her, gave her the strength to continue. She thought it would be easier to give up her dream of making a difference with chocolate, forever. Was she prepared to sacrifice over a decade of preparation, of passion, of just plain hard work? If she stepped out of the kennel, it was all gone.

Through the grate, she spied Yves. Even with the dark circles under his eyes he still looked very much in control and in charge. Her decision would be easier if she knew for sure he still wanted her. If she convinced him she was not a spy…

Would he listen? She'd have to try. "Here I go, Alpie. Wish me luck." Before she unlatched the grate, a man approached.

They wanted the dog. The young Japanese man bent over the latch and freed the door.

It was now or never. With a push and a leap, she was out! She immediately drew attention from the crowd gathered to witness the merger deal. The noise around her resembled the sound of a flock of geese.

Lainey relished being able to stand. She almost missed the shock on everyone's face. And their hands covering their mouths and noses.

She looked awful. And smelled even worse.

Lainey ignored all the flashes and clicks of the men and women of the press hoping to have a cover story to report. A few phones poked above the crowd of people gathered to witness, capturing this moment on video. Great. Someday she would see this on YouTube, all the chunks hanging from her hair, digitized in HD glory.

With the contract in one hand and combing through her clumped hair with the other, she strode toward a table. To Yves.

M. le President broke the awed silence. “Get her out of here.”

Two men in green business suits stepped from behind the table. The elderly Japanese men had bewildered expressions, knocking heads together whispering in Japanese.

“Wait,” she said, holding out the papers like a restraining order. “There’s an error in the contract.”

Men grabbed both her arms, tearing her from the meeting.

“Let go!” she shouted. Even if they didn’t understand English, they understood body language. She shook them free, stepping closer to the table. The seated Japanese men leaned away from her in their chairs, their eyes bulging in shock. Or disgust.

The men in business suits tugged her away again, the whole area erupted into chaos.

“Yves,” she yelled over her shoulder. “It’s a frame up. Lines 278.8 through 289.9, where they discuss terms, are changed. Let me go!”

Dropping all her weight to the floor, she extracted her arms from their grip, scrambling back to the table on her hands and knees. She must have resembled a lunatic, but she didn't care. "Luc wants to get rid of you. See?" She spread the papers on the table, pointing to the lines.

Yves stared, stunned.

The rest happened in slow motion: the CEO of Atatakai International held his hand to the men extracting her. They freed her. Pinching the pages, the Japanese CEO scrutinized both versions. Several men in conservative ties near him at the table flipped through the contract. The CEO of the Atatakai International called someone, probably their lawyer, over to examine the terms.

Fast motion: M. le President stamped his fist on the table. "Yves, get rid of her now."

Revived, Yves jumped from his chair, grabbing her soggy arm, half dragging, half pushing her toward the gate. "What the hell are you doing?" he asked in a harsh whisper, the anger flashing in his eyes. "Are you purposefully ruining this venture?"

"No." His fierceness made her tremble. The grip around her arm hurt.

"Then what are you doing here?"

Her voice froze. She thought he'd be grateful she warned them of the discrepancy. Tears tingled at the corner of her eyes. She sneezed. "I overheard…Luc and Gui…He used the VPN to change the contract. Confessed to me…Luc is the spy, he's the one who hacked my VPN." Her sobs interrupted her. She spoke in crazy, incoherent sentences.

Yves shook his head. "How can I trust you?"

"I came in a dog kennel, for crying out loud! You know what that means. Yves—"

Her words silenced him into contemplation. Before

he spoke, M. le President joined them.

"Yves, I cannot believe this outrageous behavior from one of your subordinates. This is the last straw. Our reputation is ruined. They are reexamining the contract." Pointing a heavy finger at Lainey, he glared. "I told you if you ever approached me again, you would never work in the food industry again. This is it." He faced Yves.

But Yves stared, his hand still affixed to her arm. "Wait, he told you he'd blacklist you if he saw you again?"

She nodded. The reporters pressed near, catching every word of the story. She wished everyone would disappear so she could talk to Yves.

"Get rid of her." Sweat formed on M. le President's receding brow. "Now."

"Give me a minute to talk to her." Yves stared him straight in the eye, challenging him. "I just want to clarify some things."

M. le President's face purpled. "She sneaked in here under contrived circumstances, covered in who knows what, carrying illegally obtained evidence, attempting to stop a venture deal. What do you need to ask her?"

"She's brought up some claims against another employee, which should be investigated."

"Of course, she's going to accuse someone else. She'd do anything to save her skin now."

Yves faced him. "I think we should hear her out."

M. le President glanced from Lainey to Yves. A smirk played on his lips. "Oh, I see what's going on. You've let this girl get under your skin. She's played you for a patsy. And you fell for it. And now she's going to ruin us all. Would you defend her at the risk of your career?"

Yves recoiled. "My career?"

"Yves," she pleaded.

But he was deep in thought.

Behind him, the Japanese businessmen grew restless. M. le President growled with impatience. His voice lowered to a deep rumble, stepping close and in Yves' face. "Yves, get rid of her now, or it's your career on the line."

Yves reeled back as if he'd been slapped, his eyes wild in shock. "You can't be serious."

"Of course I am. I respect you and your father so I'm giving you the choice. This girl or your career, Yves. What's it going to be?"

She willed him to choose her. His eyes rolled with conflict.

Yves was supposed to stand up to M. le President. He was supposed to defend Lainey. He was supposed to rush to her and say his career was not worth it.

"Yves, you know me. *You know me*." The acid smell of the chunks in her hair sickened her. "I would never use you."

"Yves, if you don't get rid of her, I will." Bits of spittle flew from his reddened face. He puffed, his eyes boring into Yves.

Yves hesitated.

And that was all she needed to know.

A bubble burst inside her opening a hole, imploding her whole life. He didn't love her. Not more than his job. His eyes were transfixed on a spot just above her shoulder, as if he were frozen in time.

She caught her heart before it plummeted to the

basement of her guts, and held it there and squeezed it to harden it.

“Don’t bother,” she said, retreating to the nearest exit. “I’m leaving.”

Flashes sparked as reporters vied for the best photo of the crazy girl leaving the scene. From the archway, she surveyed her wreckage, Yves standing on the bow of a sinking ship, his mouth slightly agape.

Outside the gate, a tide of thronging commuters swept her along the sidewalk. She coursed with the crowded flow, aimlessly at first, her mind blocking out the scenes, the sting in her heart deadening her to all other pain. A gust of wind laced with chill reminded her how stupid she was to come unprepared, to not even have a jacket or cash. One problem confounded another. How was she going to get home?

Triangles of sunshine stretched into the ravines of the buildings. At an intersection, Lainey glanced in every direction, searching for street signs, guessing the direction to the train station.

He loved his job more than her. Perhaps he always loved his job more than her. Why did she think he cared for her?

Tears stung her eyes, mimicking the grueling pain in her heart. She sneezed. Someone nearby stepped away. In the glass of a building window, she shut her eyes away from her horrible reflection.

She refused to feel sorry for herself. She had to keep going. Without realizing it, she had been holding her breath to block out the pain. She let it go slowly.

At the intersection, she stared at the signs a few seconds, her mind still wandering. When she focused, the unreadable signs in Japanese characters, even with the romanized letters, confused her.

"Train station?" she asked someone in English, hoping someone was bilingual or at least knew some English. Surely, the international citizens of Tokyo knew some English. But she stank, and her hair was matted with dog vomit, so she understood all the harsh glares and side steps.

"Train station?" she said to another one, who flashed a hand to brush her off.

Too cold to continue outside, she entered a glass building, to search for a bathroom to wash up, her fingers as numb as her heart. She needed more than a sink. She needed a shower. And a bathroom.

Inside the stalls were bidets, but with unreadable buttons. Too drained to even care, she pushed one mildly, hoping for a flush, but instead it sprayed a stream of water in her face. She planned on washing it anyway.

At the sink, she scared away an older lady with deep red lipstick when she stuck her head under the sink to wash her hair, not caring what anyone thought. She lathered with hand soap. The acid still smelled through, but at least the chunks were gone. She dried her hair under a hand dryer so she wouldn't drip. Her clothes still stank. She shrugged it off.

Warmer and cleaner, smelling of Japanese soap and with damp hair, she emerged from the bathroom ready to find a way home.

At the reception desk of the business building, she asked again. "Train station?"

The receptionist nodded to a street, giving Lainey directions in handwaves and Japanese.

She followed the directions to the train station and

deciphered the noise, the ticket counters, the destinations, and even the times and quays. People bustled all around, bumping into her while she stood and stared. She stood in line to buy a ticket, tightly packed in.

When it was her turn, the lady behind stood too close. Her breath tickled Lainey's neck.

"English?" She asked through the plastic barrier. Or maybe it was glass.

The young Japanese man smiled and said, "Yes."

Lainey nearly cried from relief. "I need a ticket to the airport."

"On which train? At what time?"

"Which one is the fastest?"

"Shinkansen."

"I'll take it."

He told her the amount.

She held out her Swiss bank card. He shook his head.

"Visa, Mastercard?" Her cards were at her apartment.

She shook her head. She searched for cash to exchange. Not enough for the Shinkansen.

"There is a cheaper regional train," he said, returning her rejected credit card. He quoted the price, but her wallet didn't hold enough cash.

She bit her lip, begging the tears not to come. It hurt her face to keep it in. She shook her head and dropped from the cashier, wondering what to do next.

Chapter Twenty

At a shoeshine place, she sat, burying her head in her hands, which still smelled slightly of dog vomit, and cried. Pain throbbed from her chest.

Lainey needed a good cry. She could only lie to herself and keep her pain at bay for so long before it crushed her from the inside out. Yves' rejection, the horror on his face when she jumped out, his hesitation all roiled inside her, erupting in heaving sobs.

People stared, their footsteps slowing as they approached before hurrying by the uncomfortable scene. Lainey didn't care. Her face burned hot and sweaty. Yves ripped her heart out of her sore chest, causing real physical pain. It reminded her of when her wisdom teeth were surgically removed yet the throbbing pain remained in the sunken gums. Her chest was a giant pit where her heart used to be. Everything ached.

Then reality settled upon her. She couldn't get home, couldn't work, and couldn't stay anywhere. She had no one to call. Her parents were in Costa Rica. Nadine was on her honeymoon. She had no money. Even Marie Claire's phone was in the fish tank.

At the sound of footsteps approaching, Lainey wondered if the authorities would fine her for sitting here.

"Lainey?"

Her breath caught in her throat.

Yves stood over her. She blinked in disbelief. His eyebrows knitted together, but he was not angry. “Lainey, we are in a lot of trouble.”

Her heart leaped. “You came all the way to tell me this?” Her voice sounded froggy.

“I just don’t know how I can afford to pay all your fines when I don’t have a job.”

“What?”

“I quit.”

He must have been teasing. But no, he was as serious as if he had said she needed to take a bath. “I left Alpine Foods. M. le President said he was going to blacklist you from the food industry, and I told him if he did, I’d quit. When he didn’t back down, I walked.” His eyes focused on Lainey, gauging her reaction.

Lainey’s mouth dropped. “Thank you!” And she babbled a bit more while he lifted her to her feet, feeling as light as a chocolate pastry. Floating on air!

“Thank *you*.” He lowered his head, staring into her eyes.

His phone buzzed.

“*Moshi, moshi*.” He spoke Japanese. Then continued, “Yes, oh I see. Yes, oh, he does, does he? Thank you, Hiroko, I’ll be awaiting his phone call.”

Lainey’s heart dropped. Oh, yes, his girlfriend. “What’s going on?”

He clipped his cell phone back on his belt. “You’ve saved the day. There was indeed an unauthorized contract modification. Now, tell me all. How did you come to find out about the contract, and how did you get inside Alpie’s cage? I’ll have to admit you made quite a spectacle of yourself.” Then he glanced her up and down as if seeing her for the first time. "But first, let us get you to a hotel and get cleaned up."

With his cell phone, he arranged a ride—in a limo! A heroine's reward.

Once in the car, he slid across the leather seats, still keeping a careful distance. "So, tell me all about everything. Tell me about the contract."

She explained how she overheard Luc and how she printed a copy of the contract and sneaked out in the kennel. She left out the VPN hacking source. Hopefully, he wouldn't seek too many details.

"You are one brave girl."

"But you still ended up losing your job."

"No, I quit."

"But I wanted to prevent your ruination." Everything she worked so hard for, ruined.

"Well," he said, checking his phone. "It just so happens word travels fast in the food industry."

"What?"

"Now I have some things to tell you. First, you were right about the contract. When the Atatakai International lawyers reexamined the contract, they found evidence of tampering after the redline. But because Alpine Foods was the one to bring it to their attention, they considered it more honorable and went through with the merger, figuring there was still more to gain if the whole thing went through without a hitch. They printed off more copies of the contract, untampered copies, and the merger went through. Luc was fired, by the way, two minutes after the verdict of the Japanese lawyers."

"But you only had my word as evidence."

"It wasn't just your word. We knew you wouldn't

do it. Or I knew. Not when you came out of the kennel. I knew what that meant to you. It proved your sincerity. Apparently, Luc spread the false accusations to the newspapers and hacked your VPN. He admitted culpability and went without a fuss."

"What a relief."

"Now, I come to my news."

"But…"

He held out his hand. "There is a choice. M. le President is begging for me to come back to Alpine Foods. Or," he eyed Lainey carefully, "I also got a call from the CEO of Swiss Food Company asking me if I want to work for them. As Vice President of Chocolate."

Lainey sat back, surprised, a hand over her mouth. Then she removed it hurriedly because of the smell. "Which one are you going to take?" she asked.

His fingers cased the sides of his phone, and he avoided eye contact. "It all depends on you."

"Me?" Her heart leapt into her throat. She didn't know why his decision to work one place or the other depended on her. But before she asked, they arrived at an imposing hotel.

Inside the lobby, he paid for a room. Once in the room, without waiting for anything else, she ran for the washroom and flipped on the shower.

"I'll be right back," he called.

Sweet and exotic fragrances replaced the acidic stench of vomit. Lathered, soaped, rinsed, lathered, soaped, rinsed, repeated. Repeated. Repeated. Repeated.

Lainey, now warmed and cleaned, needed to stretch out and sleep. She inspected her clothing. She'd never wear these again. Ever. She threw them in the sink and poured shampoo on them, hoping to neutralize the smell. She tied on a fluffy monogramed robe and flopped on the bed.

She must've fallen asleep for the next thing she knew, Yves knocked on the door and then entered, a department store bag clutched in his hand. So, he had a key, too. Interesting.

"Hiroko assures me these will do the trick."

He set the bag with Japanese writing on the bed. After digging through layers of tissue, Lainey finally extracted a cute outfit. A gray layered skirt with a white blouse. She examined the tag. She didn't know how much a yen was, but there were a lot of zeros.

"Did Hiroko pick these out?" How considerate of his girlfriend to be so attentive. She wished Hiroko wasn't so compassionate.

He texted with one hand and waved to Lainey with the other. "Yes. Go change."

She crumpled the bag to her chest and headed into the bathroom. Of course, nothing fit. Did she think Lainey a twig? The shirt halted at her shoulders. The skirt didn't even come over her hips.

Leaving the bag on the floor, she opened the bathroom door, clutching her bathrobe at her throat, not even bothering to tie it up as it hung loosely around her shoulders. She approached the bed. "Nothing fits," she announced, dejected.

Lying on the bed, his eyes lingered over her, his lips in a half smile. He'd shed his jacket and tie, unbuttoned the top button, his sleeves rolled to three-quarter. Her knees weakened, and her heart galloped.

He nodded, sitting up on the edge of the bed. "Ah,

then Hiroko was right. They did the trick." In one slow movement, he wrapped his arm around her waist and drew her to him.

Her confusion overwhelmed her. She had to know. She blurted out, "What about Hiroko?"

"Hiroko?" He tilted his head back, stunned.

"Aren't you two dating?"

"An assumption Marie Claire made. I only courted her company, never her. I've only wanted you. You have no idea how badly I wanted…you." His gaze bored into hers with intensity, stealing her breath.

Every inch of her body ached for him. Her heart expanded like a vat of warm ganache. Her clenched fists loosened at the top of her robe. "Me, too."

"In that case…" He drew her down on the bed, his lips hot and fiery on her. His breath stole hers between each embrace. The smell of his skin was intoxicating.

Lainey kissed him hungrily, months of pent up passion and desire overwhelming her senses. She opened to him, wanting him, her skin pricked with needles.

He broke while Lainey continued to kiss his neck. "I've wanted to kiss you for so long." He sighed. He was not satisfied.

Neither was Lainey.

"I just want to be close and hold you." His whispered breath warmed her ear. He slid his hand across her shoulders under her robe. Her body tingled, wanting him closer. "You have no idea how pained I was not to have you." He kissed a bare shoulder. "The restraint I exercised when I just wanted to take you and make you mine."

"Why didn't you?"

He drew back, observing her, his thumb tracing her cheek. "You were so angry at the Terrace."

"Marie Claire said it would jeopardize your career if we started seeing each other."

Yves furrowed his brow. "And Luc threatened me or I would've come after you. I thought it was my heart alone I was risking."

"You were so harsh to me after Restaurant Terrasse," she said.

He kissed her forehead, the tip of her chin, across her cheekbone, any exposed skin. She relished every touch. "Only to keep myself from you, Lainey. I was more harsh to myself than to you. I wanted you, desired you more than I have ever desired anyone or anything."

His eyes searched hers, reflecting her longing. He sensed her questions, but enveloped her mouth in the sweetest kiss. Smiling, she found the back of his neck, gently guiding him toward her.

All this pent-up desire, all the love and respect in her heart surged through her body. Every part of her wanted him, to give full expression to her desire. Finally, she found something she wanted more than chocolate, something she craved more than cocoa. Something that beckoned to her yet satisfied her more than chocolate cake covered in dark chocolate ganache frosting with a side of chocolate ice cream.

And she was not sharing with anyone.

****

"So how many bad things have happened so far?" he asked.

"Hm?" she asked between kisses, nuzzled against his neck, kissing his jaw. "I've stopped counting."

"Good girl." He leaned in to kiss again, a long and

passionate kiss.

And all Lainey's worries melted away.

****

After a night's sleep and rest, Yves and Lainey ate a late breakfast out on the patio overlooking the city. Lainey couldn't keep her eyes off Yves. A relaxed Yves, with an Oxford shirt unbuttoned at the neck.

"No croissants," he muttered. Earlier he found regular bread, which the Japanese call *pan,* and fruit.

He bit into his buttered bread. When he had finished chewing, he said, "While you were sleeping, I found out what we need to do to get you home." He jabbed his butter knife at her in mock scolding. "The Japanese officials are not very happy you sneaked into their country. When I explained the whole story, they were more lenient and charged only a ten million yen fine."

She held a glass of orange juice midair before her lips. "Who's going to pay the fine?"

"Alpine Foods, out of gratitude for saving the day. So, you never said. Are we going to Swiss Food?"

"We?"

"I assume you want a job, too, in chocolate?"

Feeling empowered and unstoppable, she posed her own question. "What if I wanted to open up my own confectionary?"

One eyebrow arched. "In competition with me? I relish a challenge."

She smiled wide, biting her bottom lip. "But where should I open it?"

Yves glared at her.

She mused to herself, mocking him. "Not Pennsylvania, they've already got Hershey. Not San

Francisco, Ghirardelli's is there. Maybe the Mid-West somewhere," she ended airily, enjoying watching him squirm.

Yves was horrified. He didn't appreciate her tease. "Switzerland, of course," he said. "It is the only option."

"You think I should live in Switzerland?" she asked with a coy smile.

His bread forgotten on his plate, he stood, enfolding her in his arms, placing a gentle kiss on her cheek. "Where else could you make the second-best chocolate?"

"Second best?" As if she'd only be second-rate.

"After mine of course." He smiled, his eyes flashing. He kissed her again on her lips, warm and fresh. "You'd have to stay forever."

"Forever?" She slid back to give him a sideways glance. "As long as I have a house."

He grinned, his eyebrows raising in defiance. "You'll have to marry a Swiss man."

"Oh, I'm planning on it."

His eyes flitted to her lips. He leaned in, gracing her lips with his. "Perfect," he said. Then his warm and tender lips found hers.

Author's Note

I have always loved Switzerland. When I was nine years old, I was obsessed with the country. I knew they had four national languages—German, French, Italian, and Romansh—and I studied the country for a grade-school project complete with a homemade native costume (thanks, Mom) and crêpe suzette (Mom again), and I studied French in high school with a hope to someday travel there. By some stroke of luck, or by the grace of God, I was able to live there as a missionary for nine months in my early twenties, an assignment I didn't choose but gladly accepted.

Living in a foreign country, even one as nice, as beautiful, and as polite as Switzerland, can be a challenge, at least it was for me. Learning French was difficult. Much like Lainey, I made many mistakes while trying to understand the culture and customs of the people, and this experience was a defining moment in my life. While I loved Switzerland as a child, I grew to love the Swiss people while living among them.

Living in Switzerland changed me in more ways than one. Unlike Lainey, I had to grow to love chocolate while I was there. I never liked chocolate before tasting Swiss chocolate, and it is, in my opinion, among the best. For this book, I did hours of research learning about (and eating) chocolate and, sadly, only about two percent of what I learned made it into the manuscript.

I hope, too, that you will grow to love Switzerland and their people while reading this book. While at fictitious Alpine Foods, Lainey has many experiences similar to my own, and I hope through her eyes you can see what I saw and learn what I learned, and come to appreciate and love their culture as well. The places are real, the culture is real, but the situations and people are fiction. This book is a tribute to a country and a people who have my heart.

~*~

Easy Chocolate Mousse
for 6 people

Ingredients:

4 eggs, separated
80 g. Sugar (3/4 c.)
175 g. (6 oz) of chocolate (milk or dark)
30 g. Butter (2 Tbls.)

Directions:

Beat egg whites and sugar together with a mixer until soft peaks form. Melt butter and chocolate in a double boiler until just melted. Add egg yolks one by one, stirring with a wooden spoon. Remove from heat, and allow to cool. Fold in egg whites.

~

*Although this recipe doesn't require whipping cream like the recipe Lainey discovered, this is a recipe I brought home from Switzerland. It's really easy. You can be adventurous, and try it with white chocolate or add different flavorings.

A word about the author...

Amey Zeigler received her B.A. in Communication from University of Arizona. While attending university, she put her studies on hold to live in France and Switzerland for a year and a half.

She now lives with her husband and three children near Austin, Texas.

Follow her on Twitter or sign up for her newsletter at:

http://ameyzeigler.com

Thank you for purchasing
this publication of The Wild Rose Press, Inc.

For questions or more information
contact us at
info@thewildrosepress.com.

The Wild Rose Press, Inc.
www.thewildrosepress.com

To visit with authors of
The Wild Rose Press, Inc.
join our yahoo loop at
http://groups.yahoo.com/group/thewildrosepress/